C000253797

GAELEN FOLEY

Duke of Scandal

MOONLIGHT SQUARE, BOOK 1

Also By Gaelen Foley

Ascension Trilogy
The Pirate Prince
Princess
Prince Charming

Knight Miscellany
The Duke
Lord of Fire
Lord of Ice
Lady of Desire
Devil Takes a Bride
One Night of Sin
His Wicked Kiss

The Spice Trilogy
Her Only Desire
Her Secret Fantasy
Her Every Pleasure

The Inferno Club
My Wicked Marquess
My Dangerous Duke
My Irresistible Earl
My Ruthless Prince
My Scandalous Viscount
My Notorious Gentleman
Secrets of a Scoundrel

Age of Heroes
Paladin's Prize

Moonlight Square
One Moonlit Night

Gryphon Chronicles
(Writing as E.G. Foley)
The Lost Heir
Jake & the Giant
The Dark Portal
The Gingerbread Wars
Rise of Allies

50 States of Fear
(Writing as E.G. Foley)
The Haunted Plantation
(Alabama)
Leader of the Pack
(Colorado)
Bringing Home Bigfoot
(Arkansas)
Dork and the Deathray
(Alaska)

Anthologies
Royal Weddings
Royal Bridesmaids

Credits and Copyright

Table of Contents

About the Author

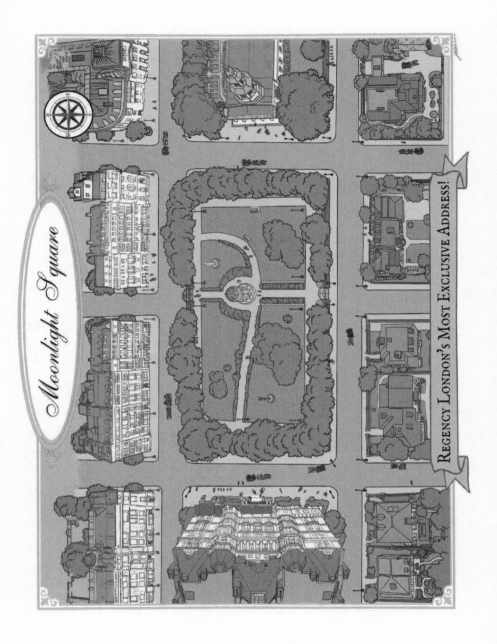

Moonlight Square

Regency London's Most Exclusive Address!

CHAPTER 1

The Accidental Heiress

"*A*re you sure this is really all right, dear?" Mrs. Brown asked with a fret as the ladies' town coach rolled along.

Miss Felicity Carvel pondered the question, but then could only sigh. *Honestly, I'm not sure of anything where that rogue is concerned,* she thought.

"Perhaps you should have sent another letter," her chaperone suggested.

"He's ignored the two I've already written," Felicity answered with a shrug. Indeed, she suspected that her letters were, even now, sitting in a large basket of neglected correspondence on the duke's desk.

Naughty Netherford was too busy having fun.

Felicity shook her head. "If the matter were not so urgent, I should not have minded waiting, but under the circumstances... Well, don't worry, Mrs. Brown. We shan't be long," she assured the older lady. "And besides, we've taken every measure to ensure propriety." *As much as can be had when dealing with a rakehell of the first order.*

"Hmm, yes, well, I suppose it *is* early yet," her chaperone conceded. "With any luck, we may escape his neighbors' notice. These fashionable folk usually lie abed till noon. Keeping such late hours is not healthy," she added with a disapproving frown.

"No." Felicity leaned toward the carriage window, peering out at the aristocratic neighborhood into which their coach now turned. "This place certainly is impressive."

"You've been to Moonlight Square before."

"Only at night, for balls and such, actually. Never in the daytime."

"Ah," said Mrs. Brown.

At night, Moonlight Square had seemed to her to brood beneath the stars in elegant, lordly excess, like some dark, decadent poet. Even now, the glistening spring morning full of sunshine and birdsong could not quite dispel the eerie cast of melancholy reflecting off all the smooth Portland stone facades. Perhaps its sinister history as a hanging ground explained the pall that still hung over the place despite its current terraced perfection, all classical, columned porticoes and lacy wrought iron balconies.

In antique maps of London the area was labeled Hell's Watch, but a decade ago, the Prince Regent's own architect, Mr. Beau Nash, had built the magnificent garden square right overtop of the old, macabre memories of public executions and doomed rogues hanging in man-cages.

Nowadays the *ton* called this place Olympus on account of all the peers who had moved in. With a duke on every blasted corner, it might as well have been the home of the gods. And yet it did seem to attract a certain type of resident…

The wild, dark lords of Moonlight Square definitely made up their own dangerous breed. They fit right in with the haunted atmosphere that still lingered in this place, as though they were drawn to it. Each an island of gloom and brooding isolation unto himself, they drifted through Society like great, ominous thunderheads, crackling with the tension of pent-up lightning and liable to rage into a storm at any moment.

No wonder *he* had moved here.

At that moment, Felicity's driver slowed the clip-clopping horses to a halt before the giant corner mansion of the Duke of Netherford.

Right on cue, she felt her foolish heart begin to pound. She leaned toward the window, letting her gaze travel slowly upward over the five-storied splendor of his London mansion. She shook her head to herself.

Lud, sometimes it was hard to believe that the scandalous seducer who dwelled in such pomp was the same wiry rascal of a boy who had gone traipsing through the countryside with her and her elder brother, Peter, growing up. Or rather, the boys had gone traipsing. She, four years younger and a mere *girl*—as though it were a disease—had been tolerated only so long as she could keep up.

What happened to us all? she wondered. *We used to be so close. We used to have such fun.*

Wistfulness filled her for the happy childhood that had faded like a dream. She had known such freedom then, and *he* had once been innocent.

But that was long ago.

Ah, well. It was obvious what had happened: they had all three grown up. Life had taken its toll on each of them in various ways, and now here they were. Her brother and Jason were still as thick as thieves, but Felicity had long since been left out of the equation.

Of course, she had brought it on herself through her own youthful folly, throwing herself at her brother's best friend that humiliating day eight years ago.

She closed her eyes with a faint wince at the memory.

Jason's gentle rebuff still hurt a bit to this day, truth be told. Thankfully, however, she was long over her painfully intense infatuation with the heir to the Netherford dukedom, who had grown up on the neighboring estate.

She supposed any girl might have fallen for him back then. He was funny and kind and took an interest in what she had to say; he was reliable and good-hearted, for all his teasing, merry roguery. It had been a concoction her young heart could not withstand. Unable to bear her secret adoration of him any longer, at the ripe old age of fifteen, she had finally confessed her devotion to the older boy.

The then nineteen-year-old Jason had been, in a word, horrified.

Felicity shook her head, cringing. Now twenty-three, she could not imagine what degree of everyday familiarity between them could have possibly made her imagine it was anything other than scandalous to plop herself down on his lap, drape her arms around his neck, and flirt with him the way she had, with a big, naïve, beaming smile.

He had gone quite ashen, and too late, she had realized he was aghast at the position in which she had put him. Instead of declaring his undying love in return, as she had somehow foolishly expected, he had set her aside, stood up stiffly, and walked out the door.

Later that evening, before she had even recovered from her shame, Peter had marched into her chamber and yelled at her for making a fool of herself, risking her reputation, and bothering his friend.

Things between her and Jason had never been the same after that.

She was lucky Peter had decided not to tell Mama, but he only kept it to himself because their mother was still fragile from losing Father the winter before to a fever. Peter, now man of the house, had said it would probably "kill" their mother to hear that her daughter had behaved in such a fashion.

Ever since that day, Felicity had been very careful to comport herself with the utmost prim-and-proper rectitude at all times. No matter how bored she grew with her existence sometimes. No matter how much she might resent it.

Ah, but back then, in her tearful innocence, she had told her brother she had honestly thought her beloved Jason *liked* bold girls. Based on some rather scandalous conversations she'd overheard between the two rowdy young bucks, it was an understandable mistake. And she had *so* wanted Jason to love her as she loved him—for himself—who he was, not for his dukedom or his wealth or anything like that. Such things were meaningless to a lovesick girl of fifteen.

But alas, her moment of brash forwardness had ruined everything between them. Jason had all but forgotten she existed, particularly after he had ascended to the title, taking the place of his horrid cold fish of a father.

Felicity could only pray that perhaps by now he had forgotten the whole embarrassing debacle. Likely he had, given the sea of women these days who regularly threw themselves at the hard, polished libertine he'd become.

Still, that was no excuse for him to ignore both of her frantic letters. It wasn't as though she expected such an *important* personage as the Duke of Netherford to give her a personal response. She was quite content to deal with His Grace's secretary.

All she wanted was one simple piece of information: whether or not he was able to get a message to her brother for her.

It was urgent, and since Jason could apparently not be bothered to answer his mail, she had come in person to get the details she needed from someone, anyone, on the duke's staff.

As her coachman walked back from the driver's box to hand the ladies down, and her footman ran her card up to the front door, Mrs. Brown tapped Felicity on the shoulder. "My dear?"

About to get out of the vehicle, she glanced back at the matron. "Yes, ma'am?"

"What will you do if we see the duke?" Mrs. Brown asked, worry in her dark eyes.

Words quite failed Felicity at the question.

Hope the earth opens up and swallows me? But she dared not reveal any sign of her misgivings to her chaperone, who was even more prim and proper than she was.

"That isn't going to happen," she finally clipped out, forcing a confident smile. *He's probably sleeping it off in a brothel somewhere across Town right now, anyway.*

With that, Felicity stepped down, smoothed her ebony skirts, gripped the handle of the black reticule draped over her arm, and walked to the rogue's front door with her head held high.

Her plump chaperone and skinny maid, Dorcas, who'd been riding on top of the coach, both hurried after her for moral support, and together, the three of them presented a bastion of respectability at the Duke of Scandal's door.

His butler had already answered and taken her card from the footman.

"Miss Carvel?" the butler greeted her in astonishment. The sweet-faced old man had lit up when he had read her card, obviously recognizing her by her brother's last name.

Peter did tend to have that effect on people—bold, swashbuckling charmer that he was, and a decorated war hero, too.

"Goodness me! Miss Carvel, do please come in, come in!" The butler beamed, opening the door wider for them. "Ladies," he added, nodding kindly at her two attendants as they walked between the sculpted topiaries flanking the elegant entrance.

Mounting the few front stairs, the three women filed into the duke's opulent entrance hall.

The butler was still staring at Felicity, rather marveling, as though she were a wonder of the world.

Odd.

"I am Woodcombe, Miss Carvel. How may I be of service?" he asked gravely as he shut the door behind them.

Felicity faltered as butterflies crashed about in her stomach. She suddenly felt just a bit idiotic standing there. Despite her outward composure, she could not *believe* she was standing in Jason's house. Her heart pounded with ridiculous excitement. She tried not to gawk while she glanced around at everything.

Was this a mistake? What on earth would he think when he learned from his servants that she had popped by? Would he fancy, in his vanity, that she had come around mooning over him again?

Worse…would he be right?

All things considered, she despised herself for the illicit thrill she felt at this small glimpse into her former idol's current life. His home was certainly beautiful...

The butler raised his bushy white eyebrows, waiting for her to state her business there.

Felicity cleared her throat, pulse thumping. "Yes, thank you, Woodcombe. You know my brother, I believe? Major Peter Carvel."

"Oh, yes, indeed, miss! We are all great admirers of the major round here. He is a very brave man, if one may say so. We are all most eager to see what discoveries he might bring back from his grand expedition—especially His Grace."

"Hmm, yes, quite. That is the reason I am here, actually. I have written two letters to His Grace over the past sennight. Perhaps you noticed them?"

"Why, yes, miss. I put them on the master's desk personally."

"Did you? Oh! Well, thank you very much. I must say, I am relieved to hear it. I was beginning to think they hadn't arrived." Thank goodness at least somebody here had a brain—and was sober. "Um, I don't know if anyone's had a chance to read them yet," she ventured ever so politely, "and I promise I should not have disturbed you all if the matter were not so terribly urgent—"

"No trouble at all, miss! You are *always* welcome here," Woodcombe averred, his heartfelt utterance taking her and even himself off guard, it seemed, by the widening of his eyes.

With that, the old butler sealed his mouth shut, as though he suddenly feared he'd said too much.

She and Mrs. Brown exchanged a puzzled look before Felicity returned her gaze to the butler.

"Ahem, right. As I was saying," she continued, "the only reason I decided to come in person is that I *do* need an answer to my question."

"Shall I fetch Mr. Richardson for you, miss? He is His Grace's man of affairs. He is here even now, working on the household ledgers."

"Oh, that would be very fine, indeed!" she exclaimed. "But perhaps, Woodcombe, you may know the answer to this yourself."

"I shall be happy to try, miss. What is the question?" the dear old fellow asked, tilting his head attentively.

"I need to get a message to my brother. That is all. I-I know His Grace has him off in some jungle...or valley...or desert somewhere in the...general vicinity of the, um, Himalayas? But that does cover...quite a bit of ground, and since His Grace is the mighty, moving force behind the team's expedition, I just wondered if the duke might have a way, that is, some special means o-of getting in touch with my brother somehow?"

To her dismay, Felicity's eyes suddenly welled with tears. "I'm afraid it's a-a bit of a family emergency…"

# # #

Oh, bugger all. Muffled voices woke him, coming from somewhere below.

Frowning, Jason Hawthorne, the sixth Duke of Netherford, obstinately refused to open his eyes. What was the point? He always hated this moment. Waking up.

Back in Town…another useless day.

But the people mumbling downstairs wouldn't shut up, and then he became aware of the snoring harlot nearby.

No, wait—two snoring harlots.

God. With half a mind to blow his head off on any given day, Jason finally decided he had nothing to lose by admitting that he was awake.

He opened his bloodshot eyes—and promptly found the ceiling fresco staring down at him, a lush, gaudy mockery. All the coy cupids and tawdry, romping demigods and amorous goddesses up there, still selling the lie that the fleshly life was one big, nonstop celebration.

To be sure, it all might start in gaiety and wine, but he was by now intensely aware of the truth: that the end of this road only led to despair.

Which was where he now resided.

Self-disgust rose in his throat. Surely it was grotesque of him to lack for nothing and yet to feel so alone. He wouldn't have believed it, but despite his best efforts to the contrary, it was beginning to look like maybe money really *couldn't* buy happiness, after all.

Who'd have bloody thought it, he mused in cutting sarcasm. Surely he could've learned at least *that* little lesson from his rich and miserable parents.

Having just returned from his ancestral pile in the country where they—or rather, the servants—had raised him, his parents were on his mind, though both had long since departed from this earth.

Still irked at the voices coming from below, he heaved himself up to a sitting position on the divan where he must have passed out, and noted that his private party with the cyprians had never made it to his bedchamber last night.

The drawing room was littered with empty bottles and articles of clothing after his little welcome-home celebration.

Squinting against the golden morning sunlight and wondering what ungodly hour it was, he spotted his latest playthings, soon to be discarded.

He supposed they'd have been horrified if they could have seen what they looked like right now, sprawled and snoring, their mouths hanging open.

The room spun a little, but thirst consumed him, so Jason forced himself up from the divan. As he stood, he noticed he was still wearing the same clothes from last night, though these were unfastened. Well, the girls knew their trade.

Whoever the hell they were.

He did not recall actually having sex with them, though. If memory served, he'd had them both on their knees last night, taking turns at pleasuring him with their filthy red mouths, and then he'd enjoyed the show of watching them pleasure each other.

Same old.

He stepped over one prostrate, scantily clad form and then the other as he headed to the door to bellow for Woodcombe to bring him a pitcher of spring water, a glass of juice, and maybe a loaded pistol.

But on second thought, not knowing who the voices in the hall belonged to, perhaps a wee hint of discretion was in order.

On the way to the closed door of the drawing room, he glimpsed his own reflection in the pier glass on the wall and scoffed.

You look like hell, mate.

Indeed, he looked as debauched as he felt—tousled hair, eyes nearly as red as a demon's, body stripped half-naked by his latest pair of whores. He buttoned the placket of his trousers and then gripped the handle of the door, opening it a crack.

Who the hell's in my house at this hour?

Peering out discreetly, he looked down the staircase and saw three females standing in the entrance hall. A bony servant girl hung back behind the other two. A plump matron in a ghastly brown coat with a black feather on her hat stood protectively beside the third intruder.

This one—blond and slender—caught his attention.

His eyes narrowed with interest. Much too young and tasty to be clad all in black. *Ah, pretty young widow? My favorite. Hullo...*

She was angled slightly away from him so he couldn't see her face, yet she seemed a bit familiar...

Jason both stared and listened harder, the sleep and drink and dissipation slowly clearing from his eyes. It was the musical lilt of her voice that suddenly flooded him with shocked recollection, and whatever dying ember was left of his soul suddenly leaped to life within him.

Holy God!

His stomach flip-flopped, and his heart began to pound.

Felicity Carvel?

Immediately, he pulled back into the drawing room, out of sight, his blood throbbing in his veins. A tremor ran through him.

What in the world is she *doing here?* he thought as titanic shame filled him that she should find him thus. She had never set foot in his house before!

It had been a fortnight since he had last spoken to her, at her great-aunt's funeral. It was always difficult seeing her, but even more so under such sad circumstances. Felicity had lived with the dear old dragon lady ever since her mother's death several years ago.

With her father dead, too, and her brother away on his expedition, Jason had stood as near to hand as he dared during the funeral, feeling awkward, saying little, but loath to leave her side, for he was well aware she had no one left now. Well, no one in England at the moment. No one she was close to. She *did* have an uncle of some consequence and two cousins, but they were more or less idiots.

Not that he was much better.

On that hard day, Jason had done his best to remain present for her, though in the background. And he'd tried not to stare, but he had been impressed with her grace in the midst of her grief. He had to admit the little freckled menace had grown up into quite a lady. On the other hand, God knew she'd had enough practice by now at the grim ritual of putting loved ones in the ground.

All the *ton* had been sad to hear of Lady Kirby's passing, the old spitfire. She'd had a sharp tongue and mirthful naughty streak, with an eye for the young bucks. She often liked to prod them in the backside with her cane as they walked by, which was always rather startling. In short, most of the rakehells in the *ton* had quite loved the old girl.

Jason had been worried about Felicity ever since Her Ladyship's passing, naturally. Yet for all his concern over what would become of her after her aunt's death, at the funeral, he had remained—as always—afraid of venturing too close. Afraid of what it could lead to. He never knew what the hell to say to her. God, there was so much to say.

But he wasn't allowed to say it. Wasn't allowed to think it, or feel what he felt about that particular girl.

She was Pete's little sister, for God's sake.

Then it dawned on him that she wouldn't have ventured here today into his den of iniquity unless something was very, very wrong. He leaned again toward the crack he had left in the doorway, and, listening for all he was worth, heard a phrase that chilled him to the marrow.

Family emergency?

Jove's beard, was she crying? Had something *else* happened on top of her aunt's death while he'd been off attending to his business in the country? *Bloody hell. I wasn't here for her.* He felt sick at the realization.

He had just got back into Town last night after dark, and had immediately sent for the requisite female companionship. He did not, as a rule, go more than a few days without having some pretty creature see to his needs, but it was also his strict rule not to poach on the locals back at Netherford Hall. So he had waited until he'd returned to London to have a couple of girls brought to him from the Satin Slipper.

Too bad he had to drink copious amounts of liquor to drown out the protests of his conscience and his heart over his dubious choice of bedmates.

All vestiges of sleep fell away immediately, however, at the thought that Felicity might need him. Jason strode back into the drawing room and went over to the ice bucket, in which the several bottles of wine had chilled last night.

The ice was melted now, and he reached into the porcelain-lined urn and cupped his hands full of water. He splashed it on his face and shoved his fingers through his dark hair, smashing it into any sort of order he could make of it.

He quickly rinsed his mouth, pulled on his wrinkled linen shirt, and hastily tucked it in. Then he glanced around until he found his waistcoat, cast across the pianoforte. He put it on, as well, even though it was clearly eveningwear: She would know he had fallen asleep in his clothes.

Damn. Normally, he would not risk making himself look like any more of a colossal jackass than Felicity Carvel already must think him, but that phrase—*family emergency*—clanged in his head like a fire company's bells. And contrary to what she probably thought, he still felt more like a member of the Carvel family than he did his own. He had to find out what was wrong and see if he could help.

Fortunately, this time, the mirror gave him a slightly better report. Now he simply looked like a rakehell the morning after rather than a whore-mongering pervert.

He took a deep breath at the drawing room door and braced himself. With a quiver in his stomach, he shoved it open and walked out. To his relief, he quickly observed that she was not crying anymore. *Thank God.*

Alas, for his part, he had already started down the steps when he noticed that he wasn't wearing any shoes.

He rolled his eyes in frustration with himself. *Perfect.*

Well, a grown man could do as he liked in his own home, could he not?

His secretary, Richardson, was still talking to Felicity when she must have heard his footsteps, for she turned, lifted her glorious sea-green eyes, and saw him coming.

Time stopped.

As usual, with her.

Emergency or not, calamity or not, despair or not, Jason could not fight the tender, lopsided grin that formed on his lips at the sight of her.

No more than it seemed she could fight that particular, tremulous smile that he knew with his heart and his loins alike had always belonged only to him.

There was no other smile like it in the entire world.

It was daybreak and sunrise. Soft as rabbits' fur. As warm and sweet and homey as a mug of hot chocolate on a cold winter's night.

In short, it was torture.

And liar that he was, he refused, as always, to show how deeply that smile affected him.

"Felicity Joy," he greeted her matter-of-factly.

"Your Grace." Her cheeks turned pink as she dropped a slight curtsy.

"Don't you dare stand on ceremony with me," he warned as he joined them in the entrance hall. He propped his hands on his waist and pretended not to know she had been upset a moment ago, curious to hear what she had to say for herself, and rather determined to cheer her up, in any case. "What are you doing here, girl?"

Her virginal gaze skimmed over him with searing awareness, but she quirked a brow and pointed at his bare feet.

He shrugged. "I'm starting a new fashion."

"Ah."

"So what's afoot?" he jested.

She gave him a droll look at his pun. The maid behind her giggled, then coughed self-consciously.

Before answering his question, Felicity nodded at the older lady beside her. "Your Grace, you remember Mrs. Brown, my chaperone?"

"Ma'am." Jason bowed to her.

The portly matron nodded in answer, but pursed her lips and eyed him with the sort of scathing review he was well accustomed to from young ladies' chaperones. He offered the maid a brief, cordial smile, as well.

Felicity studied him with measured wariness. "I've been trying to find out for the past week, Jason, if there is any way to get a message to my brother," she said, a flicker of annoyance passing behind her eyes. "Did you not get my letters asking as much?"

"Letters?" He turned to his secretary, instantly simulating fury. "Richardson, why was I not informed of this?"

Actually, his staff *had* politely murmured something last night about a pile of mail waiting for him on his desk, but after a week's absence, that was to be expected for a man of his consequence.

Jason had been in no mood to deal with it upon walking in the door after two days on the road, penned up in his coach. He had figured he would simply go through each item in the morning.

But it seemed he and Felicity were suffering once again from their age-old case of bad timing.

Richardson stammered, well aware it was his job to take the blame from time to time for things that weren't necessarily his fault. "My humblest apologies, Your Grace. I-I was waiting until you returned from the country to bring the letters to your attention."

"Oh—" Felicity said abruptly. "I did not realize you were away." She furrowed her brow, looking slightly chastened after her obvious annoyance at him.

"Yes, well, apparently we had a fire at Netherford Hall," Jason explained. "A few of the peasant cottages and outbuildings burned down. But that is no excuse! Now, look here," he scolded his man of affairs, with great effect. "Miss Carvel is one of my oldest and dearest friends—"

"I am?" she muttered under her breath.

"Not to mention the sister of the man leading the expedition I am sponsoring! When someone this important has a message for me,

Richardson, I expect to be informed of it at once, do you understand?" he fairly bellowed, then turned to her. "Shall I sack him for you?"

"What? No, no! It's all right," she hastily assured both him and his sweating secretary. "All I wanted was to ask you if it's possible to send a message to Peter, wherever he is, then I'll be on my way. Please, there's no need to go sacking anybody, I implore you."

"Very well, if you're sure."

"Was anyone from the castle hurt?" she ventured, since, after all, she had grown up on the smaller estate adjoining his parklands.

"No, thankfully. A few sheep got their wool singed, is all, and several cottages will need to be rebuilt. Other than that, the people were mostly scared, and I felt it best for me to put in an appearance there. But I'm back now, and it's all sorted. So, ah, what is the message you wanted to send to Pete? The news of your aunt's passing, I presume?"

Her smoky gaze locked on to his uncertainly; he read her general wariness of him there, and it pained him. "Actually," she said, "there's a little more to it than that."

But she made no move to explain, and Jason's heart sank at her reluctance to share her worries with him. Of course, they were no longer as close as they had once been. He was not privy to her personal affairs anymore—and that, by his own choice.

He looked away with a judicious nod. *So be it.* "Well, I have good news for you," he managed, glossing over her reticence. "It was supposed to be a surprise, but—under the circumstances—I think you'll be happy to hear your brother is on his way home even as we speak."

"He is?" she cried, drawing in her breath.

Jason smiled wryly, pleased by her delight. "Their ship left India three weeks ago. Hard to reach him right now since he's at sea, but he'll be back before the Season's over."

She lifted her fingers to her lips. "Oh, that is wonderful news! I am so relieved! Thank you."

He nodded, slightly tongue-tied at this reminder of her unhesitating ability to love those she let into her heart.

It killed him to know he could've had that, once.

"Ahem, I'm sure when, er, your brother arrives, having family close will comfort you…in your loss," he finished lamely, cringing within. God, everything he said was sounding so stupid in his own ears.

Yet most ladies considered him wickedly smooth.

"It's not that," Felicity confessed with a rueful smile. "Not the grieving, I mean. I'm feeling better, actually. It's only been a fortnight, but a little time has helped, and after all, Aunt Kirby was very old. It was a shock but not a surprise, if that makes sense."

He nodded encouragingly, then she considered and told him more.

"Things have grown a bit complicated, is all, and I expect they'll soon get even more so." She shrugged. "I could really use my big brother's guidance on certain matters. You know how he is—always ready to take charge. I fear I'm a little out of my depth ever since we had the reading of the will last week."

"Oh?" *So that was it.* "Is there some problem sorting out Her Ladyship's affairs? Because if there's anything I can do... Well, I take it you have to find a new place to live now, for starters?"

Jason knew that, with her parents dead and her brother off first at university and then at the war, Felicity had gone to live with her great-aunt in Mayfair, along with the widowed Mrs. Brown. Both had served as companions and caretakers to the feisty old dragon, kept her amused, and helped look after her.

But Felicity was shaking her head at his question. "No, everything seems to be in order with the will, nor do I have to move out, for Her Ladyship left me her house. That's just it, Jason." She hesitated. "Aunt Kirby left me *everything*."

"Everything?" he echoed in surprise.

"Nearly." Felicity glanced at her chaperone. "Mrs. Brown got a portion of the Kirby fortune, too, since they were friends forever, but the lion's share went to me."

He furrowed his brow and stared at her. "Felicity, wasn't your aunt once married to some fabulously wealthy nabob?"

"*Yes*, Jason. Yes, she was!" She nodded emphatically. "That's what I'm trying to tell you!"

"Ha!" As understanding flooded in, Jason suddenly laughed aloud. "Felicity, you're rich!"

"Very," she admitted with a wide-eyed nod.

He clapped her roguishly on the shoulder, and Mrs. Brown's disapproving scowl deepened. "Well done, Felicity Joy."

"No!" she exclaimed. "It's not well done at all! This is a disaster!"

"What are you talking about?" he teased. "You just stumbled into a huge inheritance—"

"Yes!" she burst out. "And it's ruining my life!"

CHAPTER 2

The Rogue at Home

"Ah, so you mean to give the money up, then?" he shot back with a knowing wink.

"Well, I didn't say *that*," Felicity amended, her heart in her throat as her former idol laughed merrily, flashing straight white teeth.

"Good! I was worried for your sanity for a moment there," he drawled. "So, what's the problem, then?"

"Well, I've been trying to keep the news as quiet as possible, because I know it's going to lead to chaos. But, in fact, it's already started. My cousin Charles must've let it slip, for he was at the reading of the will, as was Cousin Gerald." She rolled her eyes at the mention of that rude bulldog. "That's why I'm glad to hear Peter's coming home soon. He's better at dealing with this sort of thing."

Jason smiled at her. "I want you to know I'll be happy to help you however I can. Er, until your brother comes back, of course," he added rather awkwardly.

She stared at him. "Really?"

"Of course!" he exclaimed. "Just tell me what you need."

Felicity stood tongue-tied. In truth, she could not help but feel a trifle breathless at his interest in her crisis and his supposed willingness to help. After the studied distance he had put between them for so long, his friendly demeanor this morning was as perplexing as it was delightful. Obviously, he was too rich for it to be about the money. His fortune was still far larger than hers.

To be sure, she had not expected this reaction from him, let alone the welcome revelation that he had a perfectly good excuse for failing to respond to her letters.

All she knew was that, somehow, being with him again was as magical as ever—even though she could tell he'd been up to no good last night.

That much was altogether plain.

Fool that she was, though, his wicked ways didn't matter anymore from the moment he had smiled at her, breezing down the grand staircase on his big bare feet.

Seeing them reminded her of lazy summer childhood days when they had gone wading in the brook between their family estates. Indeed, there were parts of Jason on display right now that she hadn't seen in years.

She could feel the scandalized horror pulsating off Mrs. Brown at his lack of all decorum, to say nothing of his absent shoes and cravat. But for her part, Felicity merely peeked at the curve of his neck, the jut of his Adam's apple, and the little notch at the base of his throat between his collarbones. She stifled a sigh. He was indeed a beautiful man, though in need of a shave. Yet the slight shadow darkening his jaw merely added to his appeal in its overt masculinity.

In spite of herself, she let her gaze drink him in with greedy fascination, devouring the lean, muscled length of him in his rumpled formalwear.

She still found it curious that she had to tilt her head back to meet his night-dark eyes, considering they had once been somewhat closer to eye level. But he'd grown into his stature like a tree, becoming stunningly handsome and imposingly muscled.

He towered above her at maybe six foot three, and his broad chest tapered down to a lean waist and hips. His wide shoulders still were not entirely even, the right slightly higher than the left because of that broken collarbone when he was eleven. She had been there, had seen him fall, had even heard the crunch.

Jason had been lucky he had only broken his clavicle and not his head. She had kicked her brother for challenging him to climb the old oak, for Peter knew full well that the neighbor boy could not resist a dare.

Sure enough, one branch had proved weaker than it had looked, and down the future duke went.

Papa had tanned Peter's hide for his role in that mishap, but, of course, Jason never got in trouble for anything.

Sometimes Felicity wondered how different his life might have turned out if his parents had bothered disciplining their son every now and then, or if his army of caretakers had ever risked raising their voices to His Little Lordship. Unfortunately, keeping their posts had been more important to the servants than the boy himself. The Carvel children had gaped at how the duke's heir told adults around him what to do—and how they usually obeyed!

The only one who had ever really laid down the law with Jason was her brother. One good punch in the face at the boys' first meeting and the two had become fast friends. *Peter* he respected, especially after he had killed a few of the enemy in the war.

She knew Jason had been bitter when her brother got to go off and fight Napoleon while he'd been forced to stay home, his father lingering at death's door. He had to be ready to take up the dukedom, and for that, it was his duty to remain unscathed.

Thinking back on it, it seemed like that had been the start of his descent into the debauchery he had pursued ever since he'd come into his title. As though he had nothing better to do and deeply resented it.

"Please," he was saying in a surprisingly serious tone. "Let me be of service to you in this. We've known each other for a very long time, and I'm quite familiar with the pitfalls you're about to face. Believe me, I'm used to being rich and all the bull—" He stopped himself. "Responsibility that goes along with it," he amended.

"Ah, yes, you're quite the expert on responsibility," she murmured with a smile, trying not to leap at his offer of help and support. "I can see that."

"When I make the effort!" he retorted, tweaking her nose.

She smacked his hand away, laughing. "That will do, Your Grace! I'm not nine years old anymore."

"No, you're not," he said softly. His subtle glance down the length of her body sent a thrill of pleasure through her every nerve ending.

Felicity fought off a swoon.

Jason looked away abruptly, silent for a moment. "Right, then. So I shall call on you later, Miss Carvel, and make sure everything's in order with your aunt's affairs."

"Oh, no, I couldn't possibly impose—"

"It's no imposition! Please, your brother would never forgive me if I failed to look after you in this. He'd want me to check in on you in his absence and make sure no blasted lawyers and such are taking advantage of you in your…inexperience." A shadow flitted across his face, as though the word pained him somehow.

"Oh, lawyers?" she echoed with a frown. "I hadn't thought of that."

Ruefully lifting his gaze from the floor, he smiled at her then with such protective, knowing tenderness, she could have fainted on the spot.

Truly, he was the most confusing man. He had barely said a dozen words to her for the past year, but now that she'd caught him in the privacy of his own home, here he stood, gazing at her like she was still dear to him.

But although she was bewildered, Felicity could not bring herself to believe he was merely toying with her emotions.

Not even he would sink that low. Not with her.

No, this show of kindness was merely down to his loyalty to her brother. She searched his chiseled face uncertainly, but all she could see was how weary he looked down to his very soul.

At the same time, his striking good looks made her wistful. Self-destructive maniac or no, he was comely.

His short, sable hair was damp, slicked back from his square, strong face. He had thick eyebrows, high cheekbones, a straight Roman nose, and a lovely chiseled jawline she had often dreamed of tracing with her lips.

Gazing into his melancholy, chocolate-brown eyes for that brief moment made her long to cup his cheek in her hand and tell him how much she missed him.

But, of course, such a move would have stopped poor Mrs. Brown's heart where she stood, and, more importantly, it would have sent Jason running for the hills.

He had never wanted her love…

Or surely he'd have taken it by now.

Just then, a tiny creak from the top of the stairs drew her attention.

Felicity glanced up and saw a couple of female faces with smeared cosmetics and riotous hair peering out of a white door above.

Her insides promptly turned to ice, and her throat closed. She dropped her gaze, swallowing an angry laugh of belated realization. *So that's what you got up to last night as soon as you set foot in Town again.*

Typical. She shook her head, well aware she had no business having an opinion on what the rakehell duke chose to do with his life or his time.

Or his body.

"We really should be going," she said in a tone of strangled politeness.

"Of course. I will call on you later, then," he said. "How does two o'clock sou—"

"No! Thank you," she said, rather more forcefully than intended.

He stopped, those big brown eyes looking wounded and confused.

"That won't be necessary," she tried again. "But thank you for the offer just the same. I'll manage fine until my brother returns. Come along, Mrs. Brown. Dorcas. Thank you, Mr. Richardson. Woodcombe," she added with a taut smile as she pivoted in a cloud of frost. "Let us leave the duke to his guests. Pardon the intrusion, Your Grace. I wasn't aware you were in the middle of entertaining after so recently returning from your travels. Good day."

She strode out and didn't look back.

# # #

Ah, bloody hell.

Jason stood in the entrance hall, slowly deflating from a momentary whiff of hope blowing in the window like the spring breeze, back to his usual state of deadened cynicism.

"Miss Carvel certainly left in a hurry, sir," Woodcombe said in the politest tone of withering reproach as he shut the door behind the ladies. "I wonder why."

"Oh, I think I have a notion," Jason muttered.

Sure enough, when he turned around and looked up toward the top of the staircase, there were his harlots, smugly preening.

"Netherford! We're hungry," the redhead called down.

Her friend rested an elbow on her shoulder, giggling. "We worked up an appetite last night."

He checked his rage and turned to his butler. "Woodcombe, see them fed and paid, and then kindly remove these creatures from my house."

"Gladly, sir. Humph!" Woodcombe marched off, sending Jason a bit of a glare, probably for bringing them here in the first place.

Laughing, the girls ran back into the drawing room when they saw his butler coming to throw them out.

Hating himself, Jason turned awkwardly to his secretary. "Sorry about all that. Blaming you."

"Not at all, sir." Richardson hesitated. "But I do fear the young lady was offended."

He scoffed. "You think? Ah, well," he mumbled after a moment. "It's always safer when she hates me, anyway. I prefer it, in truth."

"Safer?"

"For her. Nevertheless, we do have to help her, Richardson."

"Indeed, Your Grace. So, just to be quite clear, do I, er, still have my post?"

"Of course you do, ol' boy." Jason gave him a clap on the shoulder. "I only said that to try to spare her feelings. I wouldn't know what day it was without you, Richardson. What day is it, by the by?"

"Thursday, Your Grace."

"You see? Mind you, if she sends me anything else, bring it to me at once."

"Such as a bomb, sir?"

Jason chortled. "Couldn't really blame her if she did. Let me see those letters."

Richardson left for a moment and returned with the letters, passing them to Jason. Still barefoot, the duke sat down on the stairs to read. Quickly glancing over both urgent missives, he saw they did not contain any new revelations.

"Well," he concluded, folding up the letters and handing them back to Richardson as he rose, "it doesn't matter if she hates me. I still intend to look into this and make sure her best interests are protected. As her brother's patron—and the reason he's not here when his sister needs him most—I cannot help but see this as my duty. You realize, Richardson, that barmy old dragon aunt of hers was worth some twenty thousand pounds, if I'm not mistaken. And she had no children of her own."

"Egads, sir! That *is* a fortune," Richardson replied, glancing at the door through which the unexpected heiress had just marched in high dudgeon. "Truly, I am glad for Miss Carvel. She seems a fine young lady."

"The best there is, Richardson. But you didn't hear it from me."

"I fear she'll be besieged by fortune hunters," his man said gravely.

Jason nodded, narrowing his eyes. "My thoughts exactly."

"She is quite pretty, after all."

"Pretty? Man, are you blind? That girl is bloody gorgeous! And she has no idea of it. Which is just so charming that I…" His voice trailed off. "Never mind," he mumbled, his head pounding. "Come on, I want my morning tea. Let's go see what Hannah's cooking."

Richardson followed him back to the kitchen, where Jason badgered his motherly cook into pouring him a freshly brewed cup of tea. Hannah always fussed at him when he invaded her domain like he was still ten years old. *It's no place for a gentl'man!* she liked to say, but Jason didn't care. He found the lively, bustling atmosphere of Hannah's kitchen oddly comforting. It was such a relief to escape all the pretense of the *ton* now and then, and to be with real people.

"There you are, Mr. Richardson," Hannah said, her round face a wreath of smiles as she poured a cup for his secretary, as well.

Richardson thanked her, then turned to Jason, who leaned against the cabinets. "Er, Your Grace, not to be indelicate, but when you go to call on the young lady—"

"Call on a young lady?" Hannah burst out in spite of herself. "Wot did I miss?"

Jason attempted to give her a stern look and failed. The cook pursed her lips shut and turned away, bustling off to get the cinnamon pastries out of the oven.

Jason was well aware his entire household—especially old Woodcombe—wanted him leg-shackled and producing heirs for them to spoil.

"What I am trying to say," Richardson resumed, "is that there are certain concerns Society might have, were they to learn of your visiting Miss Carvel…under the circumstances."

"Ooh, the Carvel girl!" Hannah breathed, eyes widening.

"You mean my reputation," Jason said, pointedly ignoring her and her idle hopes of a match.

"Well, Your Grace would hardly wish to make the young lady an object of gossip."

"No, no, of course not," he said impatiently. "It's not like that at all. Crikey, man, she's Pete's little sister!"

Hannah's round eyes said it all as she listened to every word, but she kept her mouth shut, glancing over continually as she used her spatula to move the freshly baked cinnamon rolls off the baking sheet and onto a plate, where they could finish cooling.

Jason put his hands out, unwilling to wait; she tossed him one right off the spatula.

"Attagirl," he said as he caught it. It burned his hands slightly, but it was worth it as he licked the icing off his finger. "No, Richardson," he continued, "if you are implying that I would ever misbehave around

Miss Carvel, you are grossly in error. That particular maiden is on the highest of pedestals in my eyes and always has been."

"Is that so?" Richardson murmured, studying him from behind his rectangular spectacles.

"Mmm," Jason said, quickly scarfing down another bite of pastry and washing it down with a swallow of tea. "Oh, that's good."

"You're welcome," Hannah quipped.

"Trust me," Jason continued, "the fair Felicity is better guarded from me than the bloody Tree of Life from Adam and Eve, complete with killer angels wielding flaming swords. That, old chap, is what we call forbidden fruit."

"I see." Richardson fixed a piercing stare on Jason, then asked discreetly, "You gave her brother your word?"

"Long ago. Rue the day. He knows me too well. But," Jason said, "I can most certainly help our little heiress as a *friend*. Aye, whether she likes it or not," he decided, glancing at his servants. "I shall not stand by and watch a pack of fortune-hunting hounds tear my wee girl apart like a slab of fresh meat. Hell no!" He suddenly stood up straight, warming to his project. "I may have no purpose whatsoever in my life, but I do know this: her father's in the grave. Her brother's on a frigate in the middle of the ocean. Who else is there to keep the little widgeon out of trouble? I'm helping her whether she likes it or not."

Hannah stared at him in shock.

Richardson was slightly more direct. "I never knew you to play the knight in shining armor, sir."

"Ha! Yes. Well," Jason drawled, "first time for everything—God help us all."

CHAPTER 3

Family Matters

"*A*ctually, the word that comes to mind is *odious*," Felicity replied.

Charles, Viscount Elmont, laughed aloud at her words, but poor Cousin Gerald pouted.

"Am not! How now, coz! Honestly! That hurt."

"Keep your voices down, please," she chided. "My chaperone is sleeping."

Mrs. Brown's bedchamber was right above the parlor where Felicity had felt obligated to receive her two irksome kinsmen when they came calling.

The ladies had returned from Moonlight Square a few hours ago, but Felicity was sure that her chaperone would not have gone upstairs for her afternoon nap if she had known their dealings with annoying men were not yet over for the day.

This time, it was Felicity's two exceedingly silly cousins.

Charles Carvel, Lord Elmont, the heir to her uncle's marquessate, was a high-flying dandy, but the less objectionable of the pair.

Seated in a wing chair by the unlit fireplace, the lazy viscount took a pinch of snuff off his wrist and then sneezed prettily into his monogrammed handkerchief.

"You shouldn't be snorting that stuff into your lungs with your consumption!" Felicity chided.

"Oh, I know. My physician hounds me to quit, but what can I do? Hopelessly addicted. I like to think it is my only vice." Crossing his skinny legs in striped pantaloons, Charles looked over in amusement as beefy Cousin Gerald Carvel resumed badgering her as he paced back and forth across the parlor.

"I know it's not what either of us wanted, Felicity, but you must admit that keeping all that money in the family is the most practical solution. After all, the Carvels have always been an old and respected clan, but never one of the richest among our set. Till now," he added with a gleam in his piggish little eyes.

"Gerald, you're dreaming!" Felicity exclaimed, standing and folding her arms across her chest. "I am not marrying you. Besides, if the whole family argument were legitimate, it should be Charles whom I wed, anyway, not you. And *blech*," she and the viscount said simultaneously. "No offense intended, Charlie."

"None taken, dear," he said, for everyone suspected that his tastes ran otherwise. "Trust me, I'm quite happy with the fortune I possess."

"As you bloody well should be!" Gerald fumed.

Felicity shook her head in amusement. "As for you, coz, I didn't think *practical* was a word you even knew, judging by the gaming debts you've run up all over Town."

Gerald scowled. With a thick body and thin hair, he was not a handsome man, but he walked with a swagger that said he thought he was, and he was very proud of his mustache. His coloring was as light as her own; Gerald, however, had got the ruddy jowls of their grandmother's side of the family.

"If you ask me," he posited with a *harrumph*, "our marrying was probably what Aunt Kirby had in mind all along."

"And what on earth makes you think that?" Felicity nearly laughed, and could only wonder what stinging quip Aunt Kirby would've delivered in response if she could've heard this absurd claim.

The old woman's portrait hung on the parlor wall, the gleam in her watchful eyes brighter than the jeweled brooch that adorned her silk turban with its peacock feather ornament.

Do tell, Nephew, her shrewd stare seemed to say.

"Well, she had no children, except for that *thing*," Gerald muttered, pointing at Her Ladyship's longhaired cat, Daisy, with the jeweled collar. The cat looked on from the windowsill with an air of disdain, twitching her fluffy tail, collar sparkling in the sunlight.

"It makes perfect sense when you think of it," Gerald endeavored to explain, pausing in his restless march through the room. "There were only the four grandchildren in our generation for her to have chosen from as her heirs. Charles here is already handsomely well off, as the future marquess. Then there's Pete, who's more than able to fend for himself in this world, if he doesn't blow his own head off first," he added under his breath.

Felicity gasped. "How dare you?" she uttered, paling as she took a step toward him.

"I'm only being honest, coz! You know he came back from the war all wrong in the head. Demmed bloodthirsty, I hear. Even some of his regimental chaps say your precious brother started to enjoy the killin' just a little too *much*."

Her fists bunched at her sides. "That's a lie!"

"Gerald, really," Charles said with a frown. "Cousin Pete's a bloody hero. Charging the French lines and all that. We all know you're just jealous."

"He isn't here to defend himself, either," Felicity growled, the offended sister.

Gerald waved it off. "Then there's you," he continued, nodding at Felicity. "I, as the only child of our grandfather's *third* son, have less than all of you! That's my point here. It isn't fair!"

"You *do* have damned expensive tastes, though," the viscount muttered.

"So?" Gerald retorted. "Am I to live like a peasant? Hardly! I'm from the same lineage as you two."

"So find a rich lady to marry. Just *not me*," Felicity said, narrowing her eyes at him.

Charles sighed and looked at her. "Won't you just give in and get it over with, coz? You know he is a bulldog and won't let go once his jaws clamp down."

"That's right," Gerald said, folding his arms across his chest.

"Please, just humor him so I don't have to keep picking up his tabs whenever we go out on the town, hmm?"

"No!" Felicity retorted.

"Well, why not?" Gerald demanded. "And don't say I'm odious again! Lots of women find me charming, as it happens."

"Drunk women?" Charles murmured.

Tempting as it was, Felicity let that point slide and stuck to the topic at hand. "First of all, if Aunt Kirby had wanted you to have a piece of her fortune, she would've put it in her will. She did not."

"She forgot me! Senile old bat."

"No, Gerald. She thought you were a bully. And I assure you, her wits were sharper than yours."

Gerald ranted on, but Felicity looked at the ceiling, paying him no more attention than she would the throaty barking of a neighbor's dog.

Her thickheaded, thick-bodied cousin had always been exasperating, but at least he was honest about his intents.

Much worse were the other fortune hunters who'd been calling on her for the past few days, offering their phony sympathies. The stampede of eligible bachelors with empty coffers to fill had officially begun. They accosted her in the park or pestered her at the shops as the news about her inheritance spread. Some were polite, but others had the nerve to pretend they had long been acquainted in Society and *truly cared* what she was going through.

Ugh. Felicity wasn't fooled a whit. She scoffed at their compliments and even refused to learn their names, for they had scarcely bothered learning *hers* until she'd inherited her fortune. Their false praise was so unsettling that she was glad she'd have to be in mourning for a while, unable to dance with these would-be suitors at balls or even be seen too frequently in Society. Maybe by the time her somber observance was over, they'd have forgotten about her.

Just like Jason had…

These two, though, she had known all her life; as her relatives, it was harder to make them go away. Felicity glanced up at her aunt's portrait and wondered what she would've thought about this explosion of male attention suddenly directed her way.

Why, the old schemer would've probably relished it with her usual wicked amusement. Indeed, perhaps she had intended it to some degree, for Aunt Kirby had always hated how Jason's rebuff had turned Felicity into a willing wallflower. *You were never meant to be so prim and meek, gel! Stand up straight! Hold your head high.*

This had been a frequent refrain when Felicity had first come to live with Aunt Kirby after Mother's death. Presently, she could almost hear the old lady's sigh of impatience over this vexing visit from her cousins: *Just throw them out, darling. Go for your wicked duke if he's the one you really want.*

I don't! He's not! He's awful, she assured the shade of her aunt, as well as her own still-shaken heart.

After that trip to Netherford House, she could not erase from her mind the image of those trollops leering down at her from the top of the staircase. *He's horrid and debauched and thinks he's the center of the universe.*

Mm-hmm, Aunt Kirby seemed to say with that sly, knowing sparkle in her eyes.

Felicity shook her head discreetly at her aunt's portrait. As maddening as the old spitfire had been, she missed her dearly. It was still hard coming back into the house, knowing she wouldn't be here—although, sometimes, *hearing* Her Ladyship's blunt opinions hadn't been easy.

Thank goodness Mrs. Brown—the voice of reason—had also lived with them, for Aunt Kirby had loved urging Felicity to do something scandalous, disapproval be damned. Felicity had been aghast at some of her aunt's suggestions about daring things to wear, dodgy places to explore, and shocking things to say to people.

I'm not you, Aunt Kirby! she had finally cried. *I don't want to be the talk of the town! I don't care about excitement, and I want no part of adventure. That's Peter's territory!*

Indeed, there had been times over the past fortnight when she had rather wished her aunt would have left the money to her brave, wise brother, not her. But Aunt Kirby had held an opinion even on the subject of Felicity's obedient attitude toward her elder brother. In short, she hated it.

Felicity couldn't understand why. It made perfect sense to her. Upon their father's death, Peter, at age eighteen, had become the male head of their household. Once Mother had also passed away of a heart condition two years later, Felicity had viewed her then twenty-year-old brother in an even more parental light.

He was four years older than she was—the same as Jason—but more than that, Peter had always possessed an inborn air of authority, which no doubt had helped in his military career. He always knew what to do, had always been her protector. He charged at problems and sorted them out. Still, Aunt Kirby had had no patience for Felicity's general lack of rebellion toward her brother and his conservative ways.

Oh, stop waiting for your big brother to tell you what to do and think about everything, gel! He's no smarter than you are! Just because he is a leader doesn't mean you need to be a follower!

But how could someone like Aunt Kirby ever understand? Neither she nor Peter were scared of making mistakes. Felicity was. How could she possibly trust her own judgment anymore when she knew how very high the cost of a bad decision could be? With one wrong move, she had made a fool of herself and driven away the lad she had adored.

"Well?" Gerald demanded, snapping her back to the present. "Do you see now, from everything I've said, that Aunt Kirby meant for us to marry?"

Felicity sighed. "No, Gerald. That is not what she intended at all. Frankly, she did not hold you in the highest esteem. And you never even *tried* to get on her good side."

"Ha, like you did? I suppose you think you earned the loot, kissing up to her all these years!"

"Is that why you think I took care of her?" she huffed. "For your information, she was very dear to me."

"Oh, of course she was," he said.

"It's true! We were close, even before my mother died. And then she took me in and raised me as if I were her own."

Gerald narrowed his eyes and waved a finger at her. "Throwing your orphan status in my face isn't going to make me feel sorry for you. Are you really so greedy that you'd hoard the whole twenty thousand quid to yourself, just so you can swan about, acting like some top-lofty thing?"

"I do nothing of the kind!" she cried.

"You're not helping your case here, Ger," Charles observed, examining his fingernails. "The dragon always did look fondly on Felicity," he pointed out. "She tried to turn her into an Original. Not that it worked. Sorry, coz."

Felicity scowled. "I never wanted to be an Original, Charlie. Or a diamond or a toast. I only wanted to be me."

And blend into the background.

Pinching the bridge of her nose and striving for patience, she let out a sigh and looked again at her burly cousin. "You really must desist with this nonsense, Gerald. My answer is no, and if my brother were here, you know he'd put you through a wall for bothering me like this."

Gerald paused. "I've figured it out," he said, then leaned closer, glaring at her. "You know what you are? Selfish."

"Indeed? Well, frankly, I would rather drown myself in the Serpentine than marry you. No offense intended," she added sweetly.

Charles snickered, but Gerald feigned outrage.

"No offense?" he exclaimed.

"Oh, for heaven's sake! A lady picks a husband for his character," she snapped. "Do you fancy I've forgotten how you used to bully Peter and me before he outgrew you? Both of you!" she added with a scolding glance at Charles.

"That was just boys having fun!" Gerald scoffed. Impatiently, he turned away, shooing the cat off the windowsill. Daisy fled with an indignant meow.

"Me, you only called names," Felicity charged on, "but my poor brother? Why, the two of you used to gang up on him and use him for a punchbag—at least until he made friends with the neighbor boy and evened up the odds."

"Neighbor boy?" a deep voice drawled from the doorway just then. "Is that all I was? Why, Miss Carvel, you cut me to the quick."

All three of them looked over.

"Your Grace!" Charles jumped to his feet, but Gerald bristled when Jason appeared at the threshold of the parlor, hat in hand.

The butler looked a trifle worried as he showed the notorious scoundrel in. "The Duke of Netherford, Miss Carvel."

"So I see." Felicity stared at him in a shivery blend of wariness and pure thrill. *I can't believe he actually came.*

Fortunately, she remembered she was still annoyed at him.

"What are *you* doing here, Netherford?" Gerald grumbled as Jason drifted in, drawing off his gloves. "Obviously, you know Pete's out of town," he said, then muttered under his breath, "I swear, this one thinks he belongs to this family."

"Gerald!" Charles chided with an uncomfortable laugh, sending their blustery cousin a panicked look for insulting a higher member of the realm's hierarchy.

But Jason ignored Gerald's fuming with a telltale quirk of his brow—a signal that warned Felicity the rogue intended to enjoy this. "Why, I just popped by to congratulate Miss Carvel on her marvelous inheritance," he said, smooth as silk. He bent down, picked up the cat, and began stroking her. "What are you gents doing here? Already trying to wrest the blunt away from her?"

"Trying to talk some sense into the girl is more like it!" Gerald retorted. "Not that it's any of your concern, Netherford."

"Cousin Gerald believes that I should marry him," Felicity said wryly, setting her displeasure with the duke aside for now. "He doesn't realize I am well aware he lives with his mistress and is deeply in debt."

"You really *should* lay off the gambling, ol' boy," Charles offered helpfully.

"Can we not discuss this in front of him, please?" Gerald cried, his ruddy jowls growing apple red. "It's none of his business!"

"Oh, don't mind me." Jason leaned his hip on the arm of the sofa. "I'm just here to have a glance at all the legal papers. Make sure Felicity's best interests are *protected*." He gave the word a meaningful added emphasis. "For her brother's sake, of course," he added, "since Pete is still away. That is all."

"Well, if you have any influence over the stubborn chit, you should tell her that her best interest is to marry *me*! I'm sure that would be Pete's advice, too."

"How's that?" Jason inquired.

"Keep the fortune in the family! After all, I'm the one that needs it."

"Gerald expected to receive a share of our great-aunt's money," Felicity explained.

"I daresay many of his creditors were under that impression, too," Charles interjected. "Well, it's true, Ger."

"Very well, so I admit it!" Gerald exclaimed with a scowl. "My straits are…slightly dire. But that is easily amended if she'd stop being such a mule! What are you waiting for, anyway, woman? You're at your last prayer as it is."

Felicity's jaw dropped.

Jason glanced at her, his dark eyes dancing. "How can you resist a proposal of such sweeping gallantry?"

"Indeed," she choked out. "I am quite speechless."

Jason stood, turning to her. "Pray tell, do you have the papers from the solicitors, Miss Carvel? Won't you be a dear and fetch them?" The hard look he sent her from across the room left no doubt in her mind that he wanted a word alone with these two gentlemen.

Uh-oh.

"Oh, er, of course." Felicity gulped as Jason set Daisy down on the back of the couch, where the cat perched. Striding out into the hallway, Felicity strained her ears trying to hear what was being said.

Low murmurs were exchanged. Stammers from Charles. Bluster from Gerald, of course. And a flinty, cool tone from Jason in reply.

The sheer impropriety of eavesdropping suddenly made her lose her nerve. Why was it she lost all sense of decorum when that man was anywhere near her?

Wide-eyed, she pressed her lips shut and turned away from the doorway, heart pounding. She sped off to fetch the folio of legal papers from her chamber.

When she returned to the parlor, Gerald's face seemed redder than usual. Charles's bland smile looked brittle, and Jason leaned against the couch again, serene as the cat, who rubbed against his leg, purring noisily.

"Ah, here we are, then." Jason came toward her and took the documents from her, fully in control. The disheveled rakehell from this morning was nowhere to be found. "Well, gentlemen, Miss Carvel and I have business to discuss. If you don't mind."

Gerald's cravat suddenly seemed too tight for him. "And what if I *do* mind, Netherford?"

"Come, Gerald," Charles said, turning gracefully. "We are wanted at our club."

"Indeed," said Jason, his cold stare fixed on Gerald.

"Good afternoon, coz." Setting his hat at just the proper angle, Charles hastened out the door, but Gerald lingered a moment longer, bristling, his thick legs planted. He reminded Felicity a bit of a wild boar as his beady eyes shifted back and forth angrily between her and Jason.

"This isn't over," he informed them both.

"Oh, but it is, Mr. Carvel," Jason said softly. "Good day."

Whatever Gerald read in Jason's eyes made him back down, at least for now. He stomped toward the door, snatching his hat off the coat hook on the way. "You're as mad as the old dame was, Felicity," he muttered. "No wonder you're a spinster."

The front door slammed a moment later.

"Spinster?" she cried, turning to Jason, who scowled at her.

"Neighbor boy?" he retorted.

But staring matter-of-factly at each other, they both started laughing at the absurdity of the exchange.

Felicity shook her head and cupped her temples. "Why in the world would I want to marry Cousin Gerald?"

"Why would anyone want to marry him?" he countered.

"Good point," she replied. "That boor!" She sighed, then shook her head again with a chuckle, holding his gaze. "Remember the battles you boys used to have?"

"Do I ever. Hurling everything from rocks to mud pies at each other." He grinned. "Good fun."

Propping her hand on her hip, Felicity looked him up and down. "Well, you might have got rid of him for me, Duke, but don't think this changes anything. I am still cross at you. And rather shocked you actually showed up."

"Eh, don't get too excited." He gave her a sardonic look. "I'm only here to see the papers." He brushed past her, folio in hand. "Arrived not a moment too soon, though, by the look of it. Oh, what fun you have in store, Miss Carvel. If you think your cousin is obnoxious, wait till word of your inheritance really gets out. Trust me, you've entered a whole new realm of false friends and toadies. Welcome to my life," he added under his breath. "I need more light. This writing's tiny."

He stalked through Aunt Kirby's pretty stone house—or rather, *her* house now—as if he owned it, breezing out through the back door onto the shady terrace, where he headed for the wrought iron table and chairs.

Felicity followed. "I noticed that about the print on all those documents. Why do they make it so small?"

"Because they're hoping you will never actually read it." He pulled out one of the cushioned chairs for her and waited for her to sit.

Felicity fought not to get drawn in by his charm or the wonderful air of command that he was capable of when he chose to use it. "Is this really necessary?" she asked.

"You might show some gratitude," he said crisply, though his eyes still danced like the stars at night. "Do you think I would subject myself to the torture of reading legal jargon for just anybody?"

She tried not to smile at that.

"Chop, chop, girl, before I change my mind and leave you to the parasites and sharks."

"Humph." She plopped down into the chair while Jason sat down beside her in the shade.

He opened the leather binder and began turning the pages, assessing what was there.

"Why *did* Her Ladyship leave everything to you, anyway?" he asked as he skimmed another page, only glancing briefly at her. "It does seem slightly surprising."

Felicity smiled and propped her elbow on the table, resting her chin on her hand. "Aunt Kirby had rather particular ideas about the role of a woman in the world. That's why people called her eccentric. She loved being a wealthy widow because she didn't have to abide by anyone's rules."

"She didn't like her husband?"

"Oh, no, that's not what I meant. She adored him for the decade she had him, but he died so young. After that, all she had was his money. She told me once that she wouldn't have remarried for the world."

He eyed her curiously. "What if she fell in love?"

"Oh, she did fall in love. Lots of times. But she preferred to keep her independence." Felicity paused. "Did you know she took herself on a Grand Tour well before the French Revolution?"

He smiled. "No, I didn't. Sounds as though Pete's not the only adventurer in the family."

"That's true. Aunt Kirby said the fortune she'd inherited from her husband permitted her the freedom to live an extraordinary life. She wanted that for me, too." She heaved an unhappy sigh. "That's why she left me this ridiculous pile of money."

"I see." He closed the binder, studying her. "So what kind of extraordinary life do *you* envision, Miss Carvel?"

She looked at him for a long moment, a slight flicker of panic rising in the back of her mind at the question. Not a single answer came to her. Not a single dream dared present itself for her to chase, and that in itself frightened her.

Good God, was she really this boring? Or just locked in a cage of her own making?

No, she realized. Her heart refused to suggest any grand wishes because, deep down, she thought, *What's the point? Why let yourself long for anything when it'll never happen?*

She glanced at him. *That was the lesson you taught me, Jason.*

Floundering, she hid her teeming inner conflict from his searching gaze with a polite smile and just shrugged. "I hardly know."

"Well, you'd better think of something, because I don't recommend you spend it all. A wise schedule of investments will preserve it for future generations and help to make it grow. That is one reason it was wise of your aunt not to split the money up and dole it out among you and your cousins. Lesson one in being rich: a large sum is much easier to grow."

She tilted her head. "You actually sound like you know what you're talking about."

He snorted and leaned back in his chair, slanting her a wry smile, then he read on.

"You're looking better than before," she remarked after a moment, studying him.

"You shouldn't stare at someone while they are reading. It's considered rude," he said.

"Who were they?" she ventured in a confidential tone.

He went very still, but his glance shifted uncomfortably from the page to her face and then back again. "I presume you mean the girls."

"Yes."

He avoided her gaze. "They were no one."

"Which one is your lover? Or...surely not *both*?"

His cheeks actually colored a bit as he sent her a brief scowl. "Neither!"

"Don't lie to me. I'm not a child."

"I'm not lying! I wouldn't use the term *lover* for women of their sort," he mumbled.

"Oh. I see."

He shot her a glower and then looked away, clutching the papers in both hands as he stared very hard at them, sinking down a bit in his seat.

Wickedly, she was rather enjoying his discomfiture. "So...what *would* you call them, then?" she asked after a while.

He refused to look at her. "If you must know, they *told* me their names were Ginger and Velvet. So that's what I call them."

She stifled a snort of ridicule. "*Ginger* and *Velvet*?"

Jason eyed her, clearly hearing the humor in her voice and apparently relieved she had not fainted. He returned his gaze resolutely to the papers and mumbled, "I'd wager their real names are closer to Fannie and Jane, but, you know, I didn't really ask."

"You mean you didn't care," she needled.

"Obviously."

"Jason!"

"What?" he bit out, tossing the folio aside. "I suppose you want me to apologize for something that doesn't concern you. Fine, if it makes you feel better. I am sorry. Though for what, I am not sure."

"I don't want your apology!"

"What, then? What do you want from me, Felicity Carvel? Please tell me, because I've no blasted idea."

She knew exactly what he was talking about and shut her mouth abruptly.

He waited as though daring her to admit something she never would.

"I want you to be happy," she managed at last. "And sane. And to stop killing yourself bit by bit and racing full tilt down the road to perdition."

There. It was close enough to telling him that she still cared. And frankly, she'd been dying to say those words to him for years—tell him what she really thought of his wild mode of life.

"I see." He tapped the pencil he'd been using as a pointer through the legal pages on the table a few times, then chucked even that aside.

"See what?"

"You're going to sort me out, are you, my darling?" he taunted, the most cynical of challenges in his midnight eyes. "Do you know how many times I've heard this speech from well-meaning women?"

She looked at him for a long moment, taken aback by the tactic. What could she do but shrug and deny it?

"I'm not going to do anything with you, Jason. I tried that, as you'll recall. It didn't work."

"Oh, yes, I do recall. Your attempt to rob me of my honor. That, or get me killed."

She gasped at his accusation. "And here I thought you might've become a gentleman now that you're supposedly grown up!" Furious at him, she started to rise, meaning to leave him sitting there alone, but he grasped her forearm.

"Don't you dare say I was not a gentleman with you," he warned her, fire in his eyes. "You have no idea what that could have led to. None at all. You were *fifteen*."

"And you've hated me ever since," she said coldly, her insides turned to ice. "What are you even doing here?" She pulled her arm free of his hold. "You can't be after the money. So why did you even bother? Oh, wait. I know why. Because you're such a great *friend* to my brother."

"What's that supposed to mean?" he demanded.

She stared at him, amazed at how willfully obtuse he was being.

"What, you want to make me say it?" he countered. "Very well. I'm here because I care about you, Felicity. If that's wrong, I'm sorry. It's the truth."

She stared at him, dismayed to find that she believed him. She dropped her gaze, though she could still feel his scrutiny. "Well, you've got a funny way of showing it, all but ignoring me for the past eight years." She ventured a guarded glance, but to her surprise, he did not deny that he had done so.

"It seemed best to stay away from you," he finally admitted.

"And why is that?"

"Why do you think, Felicity?" he exclaimed, then looked away.

A moment later, he shoved the papers toward her. "Everything appears to be in order here. I should go."

"I do not understand you," she said.

"Obviously," he muttered again.

"If you care so much about my brother, then why did you send him off on this expedition? You should have talked him out of this whole daft notion, not *paid* for him to go! Must I lose my last remaining family member? Will you not be happy until I am left entirely alone?"

His angry gaze softened as tears rushed into her eyes.

She struggled to keep her composure, lowering her gaze. She shook her head. "I know Peter's always liked science and travel, but he barely just got home from the war, Jason. I worried about him night and day for *six years*. Why couldn't I just have my brother safe at home for a while? But no, you must always indulge yourself, living vicariously through him! Just like Aunt Kirby tried to relive her youth vicariously through me."

"Felicity—"

"Well, it's true, isn't it? You send my brother off to risk his neck while you stay at home playing with y-your Gingers and your Velvets!" she finished in withering contempt.

He stared at her, looking taken aback to hear anyone dare address His Grace that way, let alone to grasp the anger she had been carrying around toward him.

"Well," he murmured at last, "you *have* grown up, haven't you?"

She glared at him.

"Very well," he said. "I think it's time we had that conversation."

"What conversation?" she demanded, roughly brushing away the tear that had run down her cheek.

"Sit down. Please."

Begrudgingly, she sank down into her seat across from him. He studied her for a moment, as though unsure what to say.

Around them, the birds chirped in the garden, and through the screen of shrubberies beyond the fence, a carriage clip-clopped by along the quiet Mayfair street where she lived.

"My dear, you may be Peter's closest kin, but you're apparently as blind as everyone else was to his true condition."

"What are you talking about?"

He paused, watching her tenderly. "Felicity, your brother came back more damaged by the war than I think you realize."

Her stomach promptly knotted up. "What do you mean? I know he got shot and slashed with cavalry sabers a couple of times, but he healed up fine. He told me so!"

"I'm not talking about physical scars, darling. Surely you noticed he wasn't quite himself when he came back."

Gerald's words about her brother rang in her ears: *Not right in the head...*

"You knew about the nightmares?" Jason asked gently.

"Well, yes, but he said he was getting better."

"Of course he'd tell his sister that." Jason shook his head as he held her gaze. "You can't expect a man to hurl himself against the enemy continuously for years, and then toss him back into the streets of normal life as though nothing ever happened. Believe me, I didn't want him to leave, either. I missed him just as much as you did. He's the truest friend I've got. Which is precisely why I funded the expedition with the field crew and the naturalists and the artists and cartographers and the native Sherpa guides and the whole bloody lot. You think I *wanted* him to go? No. I feared what he might do if we didn't find some project to keep him busy. Something big."

"What he might...do? Surely you don't mean...?"

"Yes," he whispered in regret.

"Oh my God." The words that escaped her were barely audible. She covered her mouth and stared at him with the ghastly realization.

"Pete's a man of action. So I sent him on this adventure to the Himalayas and told him to make me a map. Name a mountain after me or a river or some such thing. Do you think I really give a damn about that sort of monument to my ego? No. I did it to save my friend's life."

Her voice fled, and his face blurred as tears welled up in her eyes.

Jason searched her face, then shook his head. "I'm sorry. You were never supposed to know this."

"My poor brother," she whispered.

"A man pays a price for being a hero. Which is why I generally stay away from it." When he saw she was too upset even to smile at his wry jest, he whispered, "Sweeting," and moved out of his chair and came closer.

Going down on one knee, he gathered her into his arms. Felicity was too dazed to protest. She fought not to weep outright as he hugged her and whispered reassurances.

"Don't worry. He'll be all right. This expedition was just the thing for him, I promise. Nearly a year in the wilderness will have no doubt helped your brother work out the savage part of him the war created. And who knows, maybe making this map will help him find his own way out of the maze he's in. If not, by God, I'll just send him off again. All right?" He took her by the shoulders and pulled back to gaze into her eyes. "I won't let anything happen to our lad, don't you worry. I'll tell him to go find me some long-lost temple or something. He'd probably enjoy that."

"And here I was, blaming you." Her mind was reeling. "I just wish he would've told me he was still in pain."

"Sweeting, he only told *me* when he was drunk. It's not the sort of thing a man admits. Especially one who's used to being fully in control at all times."

"Oh, Jason, he's *got* to be all right. I need my brother back in one piece. He's all I've got."

"I know. Try not to worry," he whispered, smoothing her hair. "He'll be much more himself again by the time he gets home, I'm sure. He sounded rather happy in his letter when he wrote to let me know they were on their way back to England."

"Really?" she asked with a sniffle.

He nodded. "I'll bring it next time I see you so you can read it for yourself. But I'm telling him it's your fault his surprise was ruined once he gets here, so don't blame me," he teased in a gentle tone, coaxing a smile out of her.

"Thank you," she whispered earnestly. "I am sorry for those accusations. I didn't understand."

"I know. It's all right." He rose and returned to his seat with a look of reassurance. "I don't want you to worry overmuch. He survived the war. He managed not to get eaten by any tigers in those tropical mountain forests, so I think it's safe to wager he'll make it across the sea in one piece and you'll have him back soon. Don't tell him what I told you, all right? He just needed a distraction for a while to help him readjust. I only suggested it because it seemed to me a spot of survival in the wilderness would make a good middle step for him between war and civilian life. And, of course, when we were children, he always daydreamed about seeing elephants in the wild."

"I remember that," she said with a rueful smile. "He hated seeing that one locked in its cage in the zoo. Well…" She wiped the last tear off her face. "At least in the future, now that I'm rich, I can pay for my brother's adventures myself if he needs to go off somewhere again."

"Excuse me, are you trying to steal my glory? I might have to fight you on that," he teased.

"Don't be greedy! Maybe I want a mountain named after me, too."

"You're much too pretty for a mountain," he said softly. "Maybe some species of orchid. Or possibly a waterfall."

They gazed at each other for a long moment.

"May I ask you a question?" she murmured.

His glance slid away from hers, and he sat back in his chair. "Hmm, I suppose. If you must."

"Why didn't you go with him?" she asked. "You don't seem very happy here. It might've been just the thing for you, too."

A shadow passed behind his eyes, but he hid it with a jest. "What, a duke sleep on the ground? With the insects and the snakes? Get dysentery? No thank you, madam." He feigned a shudder. "Not my idea of a holiday."

"You're lying," she whispered with a tender smile. "You'd have loved it. Just like you wanted to go fight in the war, too."

He arched a brow in surprise, but he did not deny it. He waited a thoughtful moment, then shrugged. "I have obligations here," he said at length. Secrets flickered behind his eyes, but he didn't share them.

He drummed his fingers idly on the table, playing the role of the wealthy scoundrel once again. "No, my dear, some men are born to go forth into the world and do great and interesting things, while others merely exist to foot the bill. That's me."

"You're bored, Jason," she murmured with a knowing shake of her head. "That was always when you got into the most trouble, as I recall."

He chuckled. "You know me too well." He rose from his seat. "I must be going."

He bowed to her, but she remained seated. "Jason," she said as he started to leave. "Thank you for coming to look at the papers. Thank you for what you confided in me, too. And thank you most heartily for what you did for my brother." She paused. "You're a good man underneath it all. I just wanted you to know that I *do* know that. And, yes, you were always a gentleman with me."

Unfortunately.

He was silent, absorbing her acknowledgment for a moment like rain on a thirsty field. But it was only a heartbeat before the next ready jest sprang from his sardonic lips. "Well, for God's sake, don't tell anybody. I can't have that sort of talk getting round."

She smiled wryly. "Your secret's safe with me."

He winked at her like the rogue he was and strolled away, but he paused when he reached the back door of her house. "By the by, when you receive an invitation to the musicale at Lord and Lady Pelletier's house in Moonlight Square, I hope you will accept."

"Lord and Lady Pelletier...? I don't know if I've ever been formally introduced to them." She furrowed her brow. "When is it?"

"Tomorrow night at eight p.m."

"Oh." Her face fell. "I did not receive an invitation."

"You will. And I hope to see you there."

"But, Jason, wait—I'm still in mourning for Aunt Kirby for at least another fortnight."

"That's why I suggested this occasion," he replied. "A private house concert should be decorous enough even for your esteemed chaperone."

Her pulse pounded as it sank in that he wanted to see her again. Soon. Tomorrow night!

She tucked her hair behind her ear and did her best to seem nonchalant. "Well, if Mrs. Brown does not object, and if you really think you can get me an invitation at this late date..."

"Child's play," he declared. "Until tomorrow night, Miss Carvel." Then he bowed to her once more and took his leave.

"Your Grace." The farewell left her lips on a whisper, as he'd left her breathless yet again.

But after he had gone, Felicity sat trembling for a moment and stared unseeingly at the garden, contemplating where his sudden attention might lead. Hadn't she hurt herself badly enough before, chasing after him? Suddenly, London seemed more dangerous than the jungles that her brother had just traversed, while Jason's words echoed in her ears: *Sounds as though Pete's not the only adventurer in the family...*

But she wasn't thinking of Aunt Kirby this time. No, to Felicity's dismay, it appeared that her brother's best friend was still the only adventure *she* craved.

She closed her eyes and shivered with a sense of impending doom, for she wanted him even now.

I am such a fool.

CHAPTER 4

Nocturne

*L*ord and Lady Pelletier's intimate musical evenings were always very well attended. About a hundred guests had crowded into the earl's impeccable home in Moonlight Square, but so far, none of them was Felicity.

Jason wandered restlessly among the crowd, starting to get a bit nervous over whether she was actually going to come. He nursed a single malt Scotch and watched the top of the staircase for her arrival. On the main floor of the house, the pocket doors had been rolled back, joining the drawing and music rooms for the occasion, so he had a clear view from the post he now took up on the far end of the space, near the ensemble.

A gleaming pianoforte had been rolled into place in front of a small chamber orchestra of about twenty musicians. The players were tuning up, chatting, checking their sheet music, and receiving a final bit of pestering from Herr Schroeder, the Pelletiers' very capable German composer, who would be debuting a new piece for the Season on this very night.

The recital would soon begin. For now, liveried footman scurried among the guests offering beverages. All around him, the elegant house was full of the sounds of people talking and laughing, glasses clinking, and friends meeting up, and he was feeling, as usual, slightly out of place.

This was caused, in part, by the several ladies sending him scowls and icy stares from around the room. Marriage-minded mamas dealt him expert snubs, but it was the trio of debutantes giggling at him from behind their fans that was making him feel the most self-conscious. What the hell was so funny?

He did his best to ignore them, turning his attention to his male acquaintances. Chaps he had last seen sprawled around the Satin Slipper had recovered and were out again tonight. The dandies were arguing over brands of pomade. The rakes were talking about who had lost the most at faro last night. The older gents were talking politics, which made Jason want to bang his head against the nearest column.

Sometimes it shocked him how much he did not fit in anywhere, really. Perhaps Felicity had been right. Perhaps he should have gone east on the grand trek with Pete.

But no. Even he possessed enough of a sense of family duty to realize that a duke could not go traipsing off into the jungles and risking his life until he had first sired an heir.

A legitimate one.

For, in truth, his title aside, there were two small but very important reasons he could not just go off risking his neck as his mate had, no matter how much he might like to do it.

Bored, he drifted over to talk to the musicians while he waited for Felicity. He had a genuine admiration for artists of all kinds. The musicians greeted him warmly, knowing who he was because of his patronage of that blasted good-for-nothing Italian, Leandro Giovanelli. But even as he chatted with them and learned that some surprise musical guest was to appear tonight, his mind stayed on Felicity.

If she did not arrive in short order, he supposed he should give up. Perhaps the weather had kept her indoors, he thought, already braced for disappointment. There was a steady drizzle tonight with gusts of wind and no stars.

Just then, the composer himself came bustling over to his ensemble again, tension apparent on his lined face. Jason greeted him with a smile. "Surely you're not nervous, Schroeder? I'm sure you'll dazzle us, as always."

"Ah, Your Grace is very kind. Actually, sir…I would be obliged if you would listen for the key change at the end and tell me later on if you like it. I'm not sure if I should keep it."

"My good man, that is far too much flattery for a dilettante like me. Believe me, I shall be listening with pleasure, but I am in no way qualified to advise you in your art."

"Ah, but sir, my friend Giovanelli would argue that. He assures me

Your Grace has an excellent ear."

"Humph." Of course, Giovanelli would say anything to keep the money flowing. Sometimes Jason even wondered if the bleeder was faking his Italian accent. But curse him, he was just so amusing that Jason could never quite bring himself to toss the man out on his backside.

"Tonight, sir, you see, it is the reaction of an educated audience member with taste that I desire most at this stage, not the critiques of my rivals," Schroeder said confidentially.

"Well, if you think it would help you, I shall listen intently and give you my honest opinion. Speaking of your rivals," Jason added, "I am grateful that your piece was ready for this evening. I know the Pelletiers pride themselves on unveiling new music for the Season at this annual concert night of theirs. Giovanelli's new string quartet was to have been finished in time for tonight, but he cried off at the last minute. Claims the muse is not cooperating."

"Ah, we have all had to wrestle the angel now and then," Schroeder answered with a sympathetic shrug.

Jason did not say as much, but Giovanelli had quite embarrassed him by missing his deadline. He feared the flamboyant Italian had a work ethic that was even worse than a duke's.

There was no getting around it. The contest among aristocrats for the honor of attaching one's name to real talent through patronage was fierce, and in Herr Schroeder, Jason glumly had to admit that his neighbors had got the good one.

He left the German to his mission with a smile. "Best of luck, ol' man. I'm sure it will be splendid."

Schroeder bowed. "Thank you, Your Grace."

With an encouraging nod at the orchestral players, Jason withdrew, not wishing to pester them as they prepared for their performance. They had more important things to do right now than humor him.

When he turned again toward the doorway, at last, his vision was rewarded with the sight of Felicity.

She was just walking in alongside her chaperone, her cheeks still pink from the tossing of the wind outside, her golden blond hair fetchingly tousled.

The sight of her nearly stole his breath.

He was still slightly in knots over their conversation yesterday on her terrace. The merely friendly visit he had meant to pay her had taken a far more serious turn than he had expected. He couldn't believe that she didn't know how he really felt about her.

But how could she? To him, his desire for her had been like a thorn stuck in his paw for years. He was constantly aware of it. But to her, all she saw was his pointed effort to stay away from her. As he'd always known he must. He had a frightfully low resistance to temptation. Best just to stay away. So why had he asked her to come here tonight?

When she caught sight of him from across the room and sent him a little wave, the doubts and questions fled. He smiled at her, quickly striding over to her side to make her formal introductions to their hosts, since he gathered she did not know the earl and countess personally. Though Felicity had been out in Society for a few years now, they hadn't seen much of each other—partly by design on his part.

On those occasions when they had even attended the same balls, Felicity and Lady Kirby had either been on their way out or had already left when he was just arriving. After all, rakes of a certain stature did not go out before eleven, and dowagers of a certain age did not stay up much past ten.

It had frustrated him sometimes that they were always missing each other, but it was probably just as well.

Of course, current circumstances had changed the situation. Felicity needed him now, and being needed was something Jason secretly craved. His life of pleasure and luxury left him starved for a chance to be of use and do something—anything—that really mattered.

Helping his darling girl had given him a much-needed mission. One he'd complete, whether she liked it or not.

Upon joining her, he introduced her and Mrs. Brown to their hosts and their daughter, Lady Simone. As greetings with welcomes and thanks for the last-minute invitation were exchanged, Jason noticed Mrs. Brown looking rather less than pleased to see him.

"Do take your seats, ladies," the glamorous Countess of Pelletier said, relishing her role as the grand hostess of the evening. "They'll be starting any moment now."

"You see? You got here just in time," Jason said fondly to Felicity as they drifted into the joined concert rooms side by side.

"I wasn't sure we were going to make it at all," Felicity confessed as they put just a little distance between the two of them and her chaperone.

"Well, I'm glad you're here. You look beautiful," he added.

She laughed off the compliment, glancing around at all the brightly garbed ladies. "I feel like a lump of coal in the midst of a rainbow!"

"Well, at least you're not the only lump of coal here. I wore black, too, so I could match you. See?"

She chuckled. "Maybe we're just two diamonds in the rough."

"Ah, me, no doubt. But you, my dear, are already *very* much a diamond."

"Such charm! And directed at me, of all people! Are you feeling all right?" she asked pertly.

"Of course I am. I just don't want you to feel out of place on account of your mourning attire. Lump of coal, indeed. It's not the clothes that determine a woman's beauty, anyway."

"You would know."

He ignored the jibe. "Besides, very soon, you are going to blossom like a flower into beautiful color again, and then you will outshine every woman here."

She squinted up at him. "I really am going to call the physician if you keep saying things like that. Do you have a fever?"

"I'm just glad you came." He gave her a rueful smile and offered her his arm.

She took it, her gaze intrigued. "So am I. The invitation arrived, just as you predicted."

He smiled at her. "The Pelletiers are good friends of mine. They were dying to know why I wanted you here."

"So am I, frankly."

"What? To cheer you up in your mourning, of course. Why else?" he drawled. "Anyway, word has it there's going to be a special guest for tonight's grand finale," he confided as he led her toward the orchestra, ignoring the stares as people watched him with Felicity, a young lady who, despite her beauty, had somehow managed to stay in the background of Society for the past few years.

As if she did not want to be noticed, hiding behind her eccentric dragon of an aunt.

As if some part of her was ashamed of herself. Or at least, did not trust herself.

And that was all his fault.

Oh yes, deep down, Jason knew how he had hurt her by rejecting her adorable, kittenish advance on him eight years ago. He'd had no choice. She was too young, too tempting, and at nineteen, he had been in no wise ready to take a wife, which was what the situation would have demanded.

Why, at that age, he hadn't even known yet who he was, other than a randy young buck who wanted sex all the time, but good God, not from her!

Thankfully, he had discovered he at least had some semblance of morality that day, to his relief, and had walked away from what she had offered, turning his back on the girl that he knew worshiped him for some ungodly reason.

He had even told her brother what she had done, feigning mere concern about his little sister's fast behavior. But in truth, he simply had not wanted her trying to tempt him again. He wasn't *that* good.

Nevertheless, he ached to know how hard she had taken his rejection. No wonder all that anger had flashed out at him yesterday afternoon from under her smooth surface. She had reason.

At the moment, though, things were friendly between them, almost like the old days of childhood, before the little widgeon had decided that she wanted to marry him when she grew up. He had laughed at that when she was eight, scowled about it when she was twelve, and run like hell from it from the moment she had sat down on his lap.

"So who is this special musical guest supposed to be?" she was asking.

"They haven't told us," he replied. "It's a surprise. Can I get you something to drink?"

She said she'd take a glass of white wine, while Mrs. Brown opted for a lemonade. Jason told the nearest footman and sent the fellow scurrying.

"How are you this evening, Mrs. Brown?" he asked politely.

"Humph," was all the lady said, turning away to chat with an acquaintance.

Jason arched a brow at Felicity, then bent to murmur in her ear. "I take it she's cross with me for coming over to see you yesterday?"

"No, she's cross with me for not ordering the servants to wake her so she could sit with us. I got quite a tongue-lashing after she awoke."

He winced. "Sorry I got you into trouble."

"Nonsense. I assured her you were barely half an hour at the house, and besides, I've known you longer than I've known her. I did not argue with her, but I didn't apologize, either. And why should I?" she whispered. "You came to help me. That is all. We did nothing wrong. Frankly, after talking to you, I realized maybe you were right."

"About what?"

"Perhaps I've been the obedient companion long enough. I've done what they've told me. I've followed all the rules. But now, maybe it's time I start taking hold of a little of my aunt's independent spirit, since that was the whole point of her leaving me her fortune in the first place. Don't you think?"

"I couldn't agree more," he said in amused approval.

"As dear Cousin Gerald pointed out, I'm not getting any younger. It's not as though I'm a chit fresh out of the schoolroom anymore, like some of the debutantes here are, the sweet little things." She glanced around at the sixteen- and seventeen-year-old girls clustered here and there, looking terrified, but if there were other females in the room, Jason had not seen them.

There was only her.

After a brief check with her chaperone, Felicity beckoned him closer. He leaned down breathlessly to catch her whisper in the noisy room and tried to hide his shiver of longing when her warm breath tickled his ear.

"Anyway, I have a sneaking suspicion that the real reason Mrs. Brown is annoyed is because she missed the chance to see my cousin Gerald."

Startled out of his trance by this information, he straightened up with a roguish grin. "Really?"

Felicity nodded, her eyes dancing with wicked mirth. "She quite fancies him," she mouthed, nodding at her chaperone's back. "What we see as bluster, she views as strength. Decisiveness. She told me so once, and said Her Ladyship simply didn't understand him."

Jason laughed aloud, causing several folk to look at him strangely. "There's your solution to the cousin problem, then."

"Exactly. If Gerald hopes to avoid the sponging house, let him redirect his attentions to a lady who'd enjoy them, for I have no interest in the creature."

"I see. And has any inspiration struck yet on what you might do with it in the interests of expanding this *freedom* your aunt intended you to enjoy?"

"Not yet. But I'm pondering the possibilities," she said shrewdly.

As am I, Jason mused rather wickedly. Charmed by the sparkle in her eyes, he watched her take her wineglass from the footman, who had returned with the drinks he had requested.

Jason lifted the lemonade off the tray and offered it to Mrs. Brown with a penitent smile, but though she accepted it with a terse "Thank you," she still eyed him with as much disapproval as any other matron in the room.

Ah, well.

"Cheers," he said to Felicity as she lifted the wineglass to her rosy mouth.

Those lips...

"Cheers, Your Grace. To old friends," she added meaningfully, and tapped her glass to his, holding his gaze as they each took a sip.

Her lips glistened, damp from the wine, and Jason flinched, forcing himself to look away. "Come," he said, trying to emulate a breezy manner, "I saved you a seat. Best in the house."

"You did? That was very thoughtful."

"Unfortunately, I do not think it would be wise for me to sit with you, however." He looked askance at her.

"Ah, I understand." The grateful look she gave him said she was well aware that scandal tended to follow him. Though, honestly, it was never his intention.

He showed her to the seats he had reserved for her and Mrs. Brown in the front row. His gloves were on one chair and his hat on the other. He had chosen for himself one of the chairs on the side, where the U-shaped row curved around opposite the pianoforte. The players would be in profile from his vantage point and the sound would've been better in the middle, but what mattered to him was that he would have an unfettered view of Felicity.

Which was all he had really wanted.

Taking leave of the ladies, he went and sat down.

He quickly found that Azrael Chambers, the Duke of Rivenwood, had ended up beside him.

They were both members at the Grand Albion, which, in addition to the exclusive gentlemen's club on the ground level, contained the famed Assembly Rooms on the *piano nobile*, as well as a few luxurious hotel suites on the top floor.

Though Rivenwood was not really a member of his set, they got on well enough and occasionally played cards. Still, Jason had to admit the highborn loner was endlessly mysterious. He seemed a haunted man, and struck Jason as, well, just a little damned strange.

At first, Jason had assumed they'd had the same idea—to watch the ladies rather than the concert—but then it occurred to him that, with Rivenwood, you just never knew what was going through that head of his. Rivenwood, the enigma, had a tendency to watch everyone and everything, but mostly kept his conclusions to himself.

Of course, he was pleasant enough, and rich as Croesus, but as for reputation, where Jason was called *scandalous*, Rivenwood was viewed as rather eerie. The rumors that surrounded his family were considerably darker than the merely adulterous tales of Jason's own. Word had it he had seen his father murdered as a boy, but nobody in memory dared speak to him about it.

Rivenwood even *looked* mysterious, with his long, straight hair as pale as moonlight pulled back into a smooth queue. He was a tall, elegant man in his early thirties, with high cheekbones and strong, symmetrical features, but his intense eyes were the ice blue of a glacier.

What sort of father names his child Azrael, anyway? Jason wondered as he nodded to his acquaintance and took his seat. To be sure, the odd name fit.

Apparently, the previous Duke of Rivenwood had had some fixation with the occult secrets of antiquity and had thought it a fine idea to name his son after the archangel of death.

Poor beggar. And I thought my childhood was bad.

"Netherford," his fellow duke said as Jason joined him.

"Rivenwood." Jason flipped the tails of his coat aside as he sat down, then tugged his white silk waistcoat into place. "Evening."

They sat in silence for a moment while the rest of the audience snatched up fresh drinks before settling into their chairs for the first hour of the recital.

"So who's the young lady?" the archangel of death drawled under his breath.

Jason looked askance at him, briefly wondering about the reason for his interest as he met the man's wary, pale blue eyes.

"That's Felicity Carvel," he conceded.

"Ah. The Kirby heiress I've been hearing so much about?"

"Yes."

An idle pause while he contemplated her. "And who is she, exactly?"

"Do you know Major Peter Carvel?"

"Heard of him. Gentleman soldier turned explorer. You're funding his expedition, no?"

Jason nodded. "Great friend of mine since boyhood. That's his sister. Known her all my life. I'm keeping an eye on her for him while he's away."

"Now there's a pleasant task." Rivenwood was now studying Felicity intently through narrowed eyes. "What is her lineage?"

"Why do you want to know?" he asked, forcing a tone of amusement, though his thoughts were otherwise.

Don't even think about it. You're too damned strange.

Now, now, he scolded himself. The attentions of multiple dukes would help any girl in Society. Even dukes known as scandal hounds and spooky quizzes.

Rivenwood waited.

"She's the niece of the Marquess of Bellingham," Jason told him.

"Ah, so she's Elmont's cousin."

"Yes." They exchanged a knowing look, having both heard the stories about that particular dandy.

Rivenwood furrowed his brow. "If Elmont doesn't sire an heir, isn't Major Carvel next in line for the title?"

"Yes. Lord Bellingham only has the one son."

"Hmm," said Rivenwood.

Thankfully, Lord and Lady Pelletier stood up in front of the orchestra before his friend asked any more probing questions about Felicity. Jason found himself wanting to keep every luscious detail about her all to himself.

Their hosts were all smiles as they faced their two roomfuls of guests to introduce the evening's entertainment. Egads, they were holding hands in front of everyone.

Jason furrowed his brow, slightly embarrassed for them. It was ghastly unfashionable how in love they were, despite having been married for more than twenty years. Pelletier did not keep a mistress, and not even Byron had succeeded with the lively countess. They were that rare thing in the *ton* called *faithful.*

Lady Pelletier was the real music aficionado, as Jason knew from the friendly tug-of-war they'd had over Herr Schroeder. Alas, Her Ladyship's charm had won out with the German over Jason's money.

Their hostess welcomed everyone to their home, thanked them all for coming, and reminded them of the light supper that would be served at the end of the recital. The earl said nothing, just stood there beside his wife, gazing at her with a doting look that said, *Ain't she clever?*

"And now I give you our dear Herr Schroeder," she finished. Then she and her lord skipped off to their seats.

The German bowed to the audience, then took his seat at the pianoforte across from the other two members of the trio, on violin and cello. The rest of the ensemble waited in the background for their cue.

Schroeder looked at his fellow soloists, and all at once, they launched into the Sonata in G major by the crowd-pleasing Ignaz Pleyel.

It was a smart way to start off the performance and warm up the crowd before unveiling his new piece, Jason thought. The light, charming composition showcased the famous Austrian composer's hallmark sweetness.

Jason watched Felicity enjoying the music and felt an idiotic glow of warmth stealing into his heart. The entire atmosphere of the room had changed for him with her arrival.

The sense of drifting through Society unanchored had vanished, and he congratulated himself on his foresight in placing her well in view.

That girl wants out of mourning, he thought with a private smile. Her head was bobbing to the music, and she sent him a big grin, as though delighted with her excellent view.

So was he.

He had offended several people by reserving that seat for her, but it was worth it to see her happy, especially after all she had been through of late.

She was clearly enjoying the music, but then, everybody liked Pleyel. It was popular, uncomplicated music that everyone had surely heard before at some point, and did not ask much of its hearers.

Jason didn't mind such stuff, but as a discriminating aficionado, he reserved the full measure of his admiration for the wild, moody brilliance of Beethoven. He had read that the famed composer's London publisher had just released the sheet music for a new piano concerto fresh from the maestro's pen. Jason had not yet heard it played.

The tempestuousness of Beethoven's music comforted his own stormy soul, but what he liked best about the master on the whole was how Beethoven did not try to please everybody. In that regard, at least, Jason felt he had one small thing in common with the genius. Then he thrust the towering figure out of his mind, as it wasn't fair to Schroeder to make comparisons with the man's own efforts next on the program.

There was applause after the third and final movement of the Pleyel sonata, and then Herr Schroeder's moment came.

His fingers alighted on the keyboard, unleashing a delicate, arpeggiated cantabile, full of the feeling and tenderness common to the nocturne form. As the single movement developed, gathering intensity, soon Schroeder's hands were racing up and down the keys with passionate force.

Hmm, Jason thought, impressed. *Didn't know he had it in him.*

He glanced over at Felicity to get her impression. She was staring at the performance, tapping her toe in time with the tempo…and Jason somehow became fixated on watching that dainty, slippered foot bobbing up and down.

The wicked drift of his imaginings was, in his defense, not intentional. He barely noticed it at first, paying more attention to the music than the impulses forming in his brain.

Well, not his brain, exactly. Other regions of his person.

Watching that lovely little foot rocking up and down, he imagined sliding his finger into her shoe, tickling the arch a bit, guiding it off her, perhaps. And then his mind flitted further into forbidden territory as he realized he could just make out the slim line of her ankle each time her foot lifted with the rhythm.

The hint of ankle made him inevitably think of her silk stockings. Were they black to match her mourning? Or virginal white? Or pink, perhaps? With lace? His wonderings filled his fancy with an alluring fascination. He pondered skimming his fingers up her calves to touch her ribbon garters, which he decided would be blue.

His body began to feel hot as he imagined untying them with his teeth. A faint sweat dampened the back of his cravat as the mental picture of her elegant knees only made him want to part them. And then…

His heart was now pounding, but music apparently *was* the food of love. Or at least lust. Because he could not stop—and didn't try very hard, in truth—from imagining what happened next between them.

The room had disappeared and all the people, her chaperone most especially. His pulse hammered as he stared, unmoving, at this woman he'd wanted for so long. In his fantasy, it was only the two of them and a plush piece of furniture atop which she reclined on her elbows, watching his every move with the same fire he had seen in her eyes so many times when she had looked at him over the years. For he might pretend not to notice, liar that he was, but he was well aware she wanted him, too. Had wanted him for a long time. This understanding was not born of arrogance but of torturous self-denial. He'd known he would only hurt her if he gave in to it. But in his nocturne fantasy, Jason had yielded completely. He set those pretty feet on his shoulders as he knelt down before her, lifting her black skirts and kissing his way up her thighs.

He was nearly panting where he sat, legs crossed to try to hide his swelling member. Mentally cursing the current fashion of tight pantaloons, he watched her ravenously in real life, flinched when she licked her lips, then went on teaching her pleasure in his mind's eye.

He was horrified at himself but past caring. He had never claimed to be a good man.

All the same, he was relieved—and extraordinarily frustrated—when the piece ended. No wonder some said the new Romantic music was dangerous, the same claim they'd made of the poetry and the novels.

Thankfully, the emotional intensity of Schroeder's new piece backed off when the ensemble took up J.C. Bach's Piano Concerto no. 5 in E-flat major. The cooling logic and light, orderly elegance from "the London Bach" helped Jason scrape his wits and his one shred of decency back together.

By the time it ended, he was no longer throbbing.

Now he just felt guilty. Not only had he mentally deflowered his best friend's little sister, yet again, he had failed to pay the proper attention to Schroeder's key change, as the man had asked.

Damn.

For the final performance of the first half of the concert, they rolled the harp forward, and a popular tenor of the London stage stepped up to perform several of the *Irish Melodies* by Lord Byron's friend, Thomas Moore.

One could never fault an Irish folk song, Jason conceded, but he personally could have done without all the melancholy crooning.

The first song moaned with sorrow over some green valley back in Ireland, where the singer's young beloved had been buried.

Why was it everyone died tragically in Irish songs? he mused. English as he was, it seemed to him that in their music, the Irish, for all their charm, were always either homesick or ready to get into a fight. And indeed, next came the patriotic war song, right on schedule, though, of course, being of the tragical persuasion, "The Minstrel Boy" died, too.

The third piece was different—a touching musical reassurance from an old husband to his aging wife that he'd still adore her even if she lost her looks.

And after all this naked sentimentality, thank God, the singer livened things up to close the first act of the night with some cheeky Irish humor.

A few bouncy bars introduced the well-known favorite "When Love is Kind."

> When Love is kind,
> Cheerful and free,
> Love's sure to find
> Welcome from me.
>
> But when Love brings
> Heartache and pang,
> Tears and such things—
> Love may go hang!

"Hear, hear!" a few young bucks in the room agreed, applauding between verses. Laughter rippled through the room. Even the rakes knew the words, Jason thought in amusement, for such rollicking fare often served as tavern songs. Verse two proceeded.

> If Love can sigh
> For one alone,
> Well pleased am I
> To be that one.
>
> But should I see
> Love giv'n to rove
> To two or three,
> Then—goodbye, Love!

Felicity looked over at Jason meaningfully and arched a brow.

What? he mouthed at her, feigning innocence.

Her knowing smile reminded him of certain Gingers and Velvets of his acquaintance. *Humph.*

He heeded verse three.

> Love must, in short,
> Keep fond and true,
> Through good report,
> And evil too.

Else, here I swear,
Young Love may go,
For aught I care—
To Jericho!

Enthusiastic applause burst out and the tenor bowed. Then came the intermission. Jason longed to rush over to Felicity's side, but still suffering the pangs of a guilty conscience after his delicious little fantasy, he was all the more cognizant of the likely result should he seem too attentive.

In the interests of not causing a scandal—and for the sake of that rare virtue *prudence*—he hung back, thinking he would let a little time pass before he sauntered over.

Alas, his reticence proved a mistake.

Within moments, the lovely and highly eligible Kirby heiress was swarmed with introductions to a dizzying array of bachelors, all moving in en masse to make her acquaintance.

He was annoyed, of course, but he couldn't help smiling about it in spite of himself.

Good for you, girl.

After weeks of grieving and what truly had to have been long, tedious years of meekly attending the bossy old dragon, at last she was getting the chance to come out of Her Ladyship's shadow and stand in the sun. Add to that all her worry about her brother and she deserved the pleasure of all the admiration suddenly pouring her way.

When she happened to catch Jason's eye, he lifted his glass to her in a silent toast. *Let her enjoy the attention,* he thought. He could always see her later. If he knew women, nothing cheered a girl up more than being told she was beautiful by eligible men.

Which this one absolutely was.

Ah, well. So much for his hopes of playing her knight in shining armor. It was oddly depressing to see she didn't need him at all, really. The papers he'd looked at yesterday were perfectly well in order, her cousins had been easily scared off, and she didn't need his help in Society, since it looked like everyone suddenly wanted to meet her, even though she was not new to the *ton*.

The bleeders just hadn't quite noticed her until the twenty thousand had dropped into her lap.

Thankfully, the dour presence of her chaperone, along with her black mourning clothes, seemed to restrain the bachelors who had now walled her in, at least somewhat. Jason still monitored the group, protectively keeping watch over her from a distance, even as he and Rivenwood got up to stretch a bit and hunt down another drink.

"Miss Carvel has become quite popular," his fellow duke remarked.

"Yes. Would you like to meet her?"

He shrugged. "Why not."

But before he could take the tall, tow-headed peer over for an introduction, the man got to chatting with some others, and then Jason had to nudge him.

"There is a young raven-haired beauty by the wall who's been staring at you all this time," he informed him discreetly. "Who the deuce is she?"

"Oh, not again." Rivenwood turned around and spotted the girl, who flicked her fan as though to hide her face and spun away the moment she realized she'd been seen. "This is really getting rather tiresome," the other duke grumbled. "I do wish she'd stop spying on me."

"Who is she and what does she want with you?" Jason persisted, intrigued.

Rivenwood arched a brow. "Well, we have never been formally introduced, but to the best of my knowledge—and this is but a guess—that is Lady Serena Parker."

"And?" Jason prodded.

"And I suppose she has recently discovered that we were once betrothed."

"*What?*"

"As children. Ah, it doesn't signify," he said with an elegant wave of his hand. "The thing's long since been nullified. It was arranged by our parents, and as you've probably heard, the lot of them were quite mad."

A trill on the high notes of the pianoforte summoned the guests back to their seats for the second half of the night's entertainment.

"Your fiancée?" Jason remarked as they sat down again.

"Ah, not since I came of age—she was just a child then, herself. I have a feeling she only stares at me out of morbid fascination, to ponder the fate she barely escaped." Rivenwood shrugged in amusement. "Beyond that, I cannot fathom why she's started stalking me of late. She's got another beau by now, in any case."

"I'm not surprised to hear it," Jason said, intrigued.

Then Lady Pelletier bustled back to her spot before her guests and cheerfully hushed them for the next portion of the musicale. As they settled in, people were murmuring curiously to one another about the surprise performer, soon to be revealed.

But first, up to the pianoforte went their daughter, the decidedly mousy Lady Simone, who had made her debut the year before but still looked terrified of everyone. She curtsied to the audience, wide-eyed, then sat down at the bench and played a couple of short, charming sonatinas by Muzio Clementi to demonstrate her accomplishments to any and all possible future husbands present.

It was over quickly, and the girl seemed relieved. She shot to her feet, sketched another pink-cheeked curtsy to the applauding guests, then fled, leaving the rest to the professionals.

This was followed by the obligatory Haydn for the night, one of the impeccable *Erdody* Quartets, a masterwork with forty years of experience behind it. In fact, Lady Pelletier had selected Jason's favorite of the lot, no. 3, known as "Emperor" in a tribute to the Habsburg crown.

The crowd sat quietly, basking in the rich elegance of that worthiest of masters, known as "the composer's composer," for Haydn had taught both Mozart and Beethoven their art, among others.

In the tender serenity of the second movement, Felicity sent Jason another kind of smile, subdued and gentle, sharing in the beauty of the piece with him. His very heart stirred as he gazed into her blue-green eyes from across the candlelit distance between them and found himself thinking, *If I could ever be truly capable of love, my darling girl...*

But by the time the agitated cadenzas of the fourth movement unfurled, its high-strung tension reminded him of what touching her could cost him. The friendship of a man who was like a brother to him, not to mention his own self-respect.

And then, at last, it was time for their surprise guest. He shoved his grim fears aside and focused on the moment at hand.

They heard the diva before they saw her, for the lady sent out a melodious trill from behind the curtains that framed the front of the music room.

"Can you guess who it is?" Lady Pelletier playfully asked her guests, standing to the side.

But unwilling to let anyone ruin the surprise for the others, the mystery guest did not wait. Jason's eyes widened as the famous soprano

Bianca Burns wafted out to the front of the ensemble to stand, preening, beside the pianoforte, as she was wont to do.

Oh no. He folded his arms across his chest and began sinking down guiltily into his chair, hoping somehow to go unnoticed.

Was it too late to hide?

CHAPTER 5

Serenade for a Scoundrel

*A*s she swanned out into view, the voluptuous Bianca Burns moved her hands in a graceful arc, presenting herself. She smiled grandly, accepting the enthusiastic burst of applause from the many who had recognized her even before she showed her beautiful face.

With only a few brief bars of introduction from the chosen flautist who had stepped forward, she launched into a medley of well-loved songs by the English favorite Thomas Arne.

Her rapturous voice enchanted the whole room as she opened her performance with a Shakespeare song from *The Tempest*, "Where the Bee Sucks, There Suck I."

Aye, and very well, at that, Jason thought wickedly, then he shoved the lecherous memory away with another stab of guilt.

The music carried Bianca on nimbly into the second tune in her Arne medley, the infamous cuckoo song from *Love's Labour's Lost*, "When Daisies Pied," a warning to all husbands about springtime adultery from their amorous wives.

Jason had heard her sing both before, for God knew this was one art he had explored thoroughly. Indeed, it was the diva's many pointed repetitions of "Come hither, come hither!" in the lyrics of the next song, "Under the Greenwood Tree," that he had once heeded all too well.

When the striking blonde finally noticed him there, sitting off to the side and slumping down in his seat to try to make himself smaller, a gleam came into her playful, sparkly eyes.

Uh-oh. Heart pounding, he prayed Felicity didn't notice that they were acquainted, but when, next, she performed "O Ravishing Delight," he couldn't help thinking it sounded remarkably like some of the noises she had made in his bed.

Unfortunately, considering the unceremonious manner in which he had ended their brief but torrid affair, Bianca must have been inspired to dedicate her next song to him. She turned around and murmured something to the orchestra, and they all flipped a few pages in their Arne songbook.

She spun about to face the audience again with a wicked smile stretching from ear to ear.

Oh, please, don't.

Inwardly cringing, Jason refused to betray any outward sign of chagrin, but he held her frank stare as the soprano drifted toward him, took a deep breath, and then had at him, bursting into lively song: "Monster, away!"

Knowing male laughter rumbled through the rooms.

Jason didn't flinch, merely arched a brow and looked askance at the other men, his lips pursed as he ruefully took his comeuppance. Still, he sincerely doubted he was the only chap in the room who had enjoyed her favors.

At one point, she leaned down and sang the words blithely in his face, just to make sure everybody got the point.

> *Every creature,*
> *Fierce by nature,*
> *Harmless is*
> *Compared to thee!*

Even Rivenwood chuckled beside him. "What did you do to her, man?"

"What didn't I do to her," Jason muttered, folding his arms across his chest, though he kept his chin high.

She sang on, having her fun with him with an air from the Arne opera *Artaxerxes*.

> *Paths explore*
> *Where lions roar,*
> *And devouring tigers lie!*
> *Monster, away!*

"You enjoyed it," he chided politely for his pride's sake over her singing, which only made people laugh more.

Mrs. Brown wasn't laughing, however. And though Felicity would hardly be surprised to learn of this dalliance, he still couldn't bring himself to look over at her while his ex-lover publicly serenaded him on what a beast he was.

Literally.

But having given him his deserved punishment, Bianca came back over, laughing, bent down, and kissed him on the cheek, letting bygones be bygones.

"Miss me?" she whispered.

He narrowed his eyes at her. She smiled, straightened up, and, while turning away, winked at Rivenwood—rich as he was. Always on the lookout for a new keeper, her sort.

Then she flounced away to resume the program as planned. As she returned to her spot, the sustained cheering and applause from the female segment of the audience, rewarding her for taunting him, was quite loud.

Jason finally scraped up his courage to glance over at Felicity. She shook her head at him with a chuckle, looking at once amused and rather irked, but far from shocked.

He sent her a shrug.

To conclude Bianca's performance at the Pelletiers' famous annual musicale, she quieted things down with one of Arne's most charming, melodic confections on the subject of love, "O Come, O Come, My Dearest."

> O come, o come, my dearest,
> And hither bring
> Thy lips adorn'd
> With all the blooming spring...

Sitting very still, Jason pondered the lyrics just enough to wonder what an innocent love of the sort the song described would be like. Something sweet and clean rather than something deliberately dirty.

> ...Heal me with kisses,
> Or else I die...

The Pelletiers' house fairly shook with applause when she finished. Then came the true test of his nerves…

It was not going to be an easy thing to face Felicity after that, but he was determined to brazen it out.

He rose from his chair, still feeling like a fool, and went over to Felicity before she was swarmed by all her new admirers.

"Well, that was lovely," she declared as he approached, still dreading her disapproval. He could barely hear her over the din of the crowd. "They are all so talented! Thank you for securing me an invitation."

"Absolutely," he blurted out, startled by her lack of reproach. "Er, where's Mrs. Brown?" he asked, feeling slightly disoriented.

"She went to say goodbye to a couple of her friends."

He tried to hide his disappointment at the news that they were leaving. "You're not staying for the supper?"

"Alas, Mrs. Brown has had enough. And I think it's probably best that I withdraw now, since I'm still in mourning."

"Maybe I shall go home, too," he said with a sigh.

"Early night for you, I'd imagine."

"I've had enough humiliation for one night, thanks," he said dryly.

"Humiliation? On the contrary, Your Grace. I think every man here is jealous of your conquest." She paused a beat. "I could do with some air. Will you walk me out to wait for our carriage?"

"Gladly. Ladies first." He gestured to her to walk ahead of him, and they both ignored the curious glances as they left together, going down the grand staircase to the ground floor.

He glanced uncertainly at her as they stepped out in front of the house, where some other guests had taken refuge in the damp night, having a stretch, or getting some air. A few men were lighting up cheroots, while several women tugged their paisley shawls around their shoulders.

The wind had died down but the streets were wet, reflecting the gleam of the lanterns and streetlamps lining Moonlight Square. Across the street, raindrops dripped from the leaves of the trees in the garden square.

Felicity sent a servant running to tell her driver to bring her carriage round, then she turned to him. They exchanged a smile and waited.

Jason tried not to stare at her overmuch. "You caused quite a sensation here tonight, you know," he told her in a low tone.

She smiled idly. "It doesn't signify. It's not me they want; it's Lady Kirby's fortune."

"It's both," he warned, though in her brother's absence, he had already made up his mind to monitor possible suitors for whatever designs they might have on her.

She shook her head. "I doubt it. I've been here all the time and they never even noticed me." She paused, clutching the handle of her reticule with both hands. "Do you know any of those gentlemen?"

"Some."

"Hmm." She nodded and gazed off down the street, then eyed him shrewdly. "You'll have to warn me which ones to avoid."

"You'd trust my judgment?"

"Of course. Why?"

He floundered, the polite smile fading from his lips. "What must you think of me," he ventured.

"Ah, you mean the little serenade?"

He sent her a penitent nod and dropped his gaze.

She smiled almost tenderly and shrugged the matter off, much to his amazement. "*She* may think you a beast, Jason. No doubt you gave her cause. But you've never been that way with me, have you?"

He nodded his thanks at that much-needed acknowledgment, but being Felicity, put on this earth to torture him, of course, she couldn't leave it at that.

A mischievous glint danced in her eyes as she flicked a speculative glance over him and added, "Would it were not so."

He nearly fell over, then averted his eyes, his heart pounding. He risked another wary look her way once his sardonic mask was firmly in place again, arching a brow as he tried to read her, but damned if he knew how else to respond.

Felicity laughed, blushed, and quickly changed the subject, as though remembering belatedly how things had gone the last time she had tried to flirt with him.

That was eight years ago, however, when she had been a budding little nymph instead of the ripened beauty now standing before him.

His lust rose fiercely in him again without warning, but Felicity had dropped her gaze, fleeing back to being demure after that quick flash of letting her desire show.

"Speaking as a friend, merely out of concern for you, of course, I don't approve of your womanizing ways," she admitted hesitantly. "But you are a grown man. It's your life, and the lady is old enough to know what she's doing."

He was silent, his head rather spinning with the intensity of whatever this was between them. Something far more delicate—and complicated—than what he was used to with women.

Felicity lifted her head and passed a glance of cautious study over his face, and then a half-smile curved her lips. "You look shocked, Jason," she murmured. "Did you expect me to have a fit of the vapors and faint over that little musical reminder of how many paramours you've had? Even after I caught you with those two unspeakable females the other morning?"

He could barely speak. "I'm…not sure what I expected, actually."

"Come, I have known you all my life, don't forget. I know your flaws. And your virtues," she added with a decisive nod.

He simply scoffed. "Virtues."

"Oh, they exist, beneath the roguery, I daresay," she said in soft humor. "You're kind and loyal and generous, and you have a measure of humility, where most in your position would exhibit only arrogance. But don't worry. I shan't tell anyone." She patted him on the arm, while he stood there in tongue-tied confusion at her praise. "Your reputation as a rake of the first order is in no danger. Mrs. Brown, for her part, still thoroughly disapproves of you, if it helps to soothe your vanity."

"Humph. Yes. Good," he said in wry distraction. "She'd better. I worked hard to earn my dreadful reputation."

"Oh, I know!" she said, laughing.

Just then, a wheedling voice called to him from the darkness. "Your Grace? A-begging your pardon, it is I, Giovanelli."

Jason looked over in surprise as the Italian stepped into view, dressed as though he had just come from the opera, in a showy blue velvet coat and white breeches. But he humbly clutched his flattened bicorne hat in both hands.

"Hmm. Good evening, Giovanelli," Jason said, moving toward him. "Didn't expect you to show your face here tonight."

The sardonic greeting made the poor fellow wince. "*Si,* but I only came to learn how Herr Schroeder's nocturne was received and to offer Your Grace my apologies once again. The muse, she is a-so difficult. I so hope the evening was not ruined?"

"Never fear, Herr Schroeder saved the day," Jason drawled.

Giovanelli clapped his hands together as in prayer. "*Maria*

Santissima, I am so relieved to hear this! He showed me the sheet music. De nocturne, it is enchanting!"

"We thought so, too," Jason replied.

"I am glad. But, still," the Italian said, wincing, "I know how disappointed Your Grace must be in me. I am unworthy—"

"Now, now, don't start that again, my good man. You know I've no patience for groveling. I am sure you will dazzle the world in due time."

Giovanelli looked astonished at the leniency he was being given. Frankly, the Italian had Felicity to thank. For with Miss Carvel present, Naughty Netherford was always on his best behavior. It was just an old habit he'd formed long ago. To avoid her brother's shooting him.

Jason turned to her. "Miss Carvel, allow me to present the composer, Leandro Giovanelli. I'm sure you've heard his music. A minuet of his was all the rage last Season. He had all London dancing."

"How do you do," she said with a smile.

The Italian beamed in the presence of a beautiful lady. "Did you like-a de music tonight, *signorina*?"

"It was wonderful."

"When-a my new string quartet is ready, I do hope you will come to hear. His Grace has been a-so very generous to me. He is a great man!"

"Oh, I *know*," she agreed rather too emphatically.

Jason narrowed his eyes at her in mock indignation.

"*Si!* De duke, he cares about de beauty."

"In some things more than others." She nodded, clearly referring to his infamous appreciation for the female form. "Am I to understand that the duke is your patron, Mr. Giovanelli?"

"*Si, signorina!* He has supported my humble efforts for de past two years."

"Is that right? And here I thought my brother's expedition was your only current project," she said, glancing over at him, looking impressed.

It was Giovanelli who answered before Jason could speak. "Oh no, *signorina*! There is me with-a my music. And de painter, Omero Caradonna, and the great sculptor, too, Vitale Sanfratello."

"One must have Italians for the art," Jason murmured sardonically to her alone.

"Ah," she said.

"De house where His Grace lets us live and work is like a-being back at home in Firenze. Well, except for the presence of de grumpy Scottish person, Mr. Sloan. But Grumpy Scot is indeed a genius," he conceded.

She looked at Jason again in amusement. "What does Grumpy Scot do? Brew your whiskey for you?"

"Now, now, Scots happen to be excellent inventors, if you hadn't heard," he informed her in a lofty tone. "Atticus Sloan builds all manner of odd contraptions. It wouldn't surprise me if one of his inventions changes the world someday. Indeed, the house in Bloomsbury where I've put them up is quite a hive of nonstop, ingenious creation. I should take you there sometime," Jason said. "It's rather fascinating."

"*Si!*" Giovanelli seized upon this chance to redeem himself in his patron's eyes. "Sir, if you bring de young lady, we should all be happy to give her a tour of our works! Grumpy may not speak to you too much, *signorina*. He is— How you say…?"

"Eccentric," Jason supplied, grateful for the opening. He looked at Felicity. "I was thinking of calling on these fellows tomorrow, as it happens. Having a look at everybody's progress. Care to join me?"

Her lovely face lit up. "Oh, could I?"

"Of course." He was almost abashed by her delight at his suggestion. "You and Mrs. Brown both."

"*Signorina*, you must come! You love it! Omero's paintings, they are so beautiful, and Vitale's marble goddess…she almost seems to breathe."

"How wonderful. If you're sure I wouldn't be intruding—"

"Not at all," Jason said at once.

The Italian charmer had done well by thinking of the idea, and if the other resident geniuses didn't like their visit, well, Jason paid for their existence. He bloody well ought to be welcome to call on them whenever he dashed well pleased.

Within reason, of course.

His respect for them was actually immense. He did not give a fig that they were lowborn. Leonardo da Vinci himself, after all, had been the illegitimate son of a housemaid.

"Oh, I'm so excited!" Felicity clapped her hands daintily, beaming. "I've never been behind the scenes of an artist's studio before."

The appearance of Lord and Lady Pelletier in the doorway of the entrance, talking to some of their guests, made Giovanelli look over anxiously. "I should go before I am seen," he said with an apologetic frown. "I have already embarrassed de dear lord and lady of this house enough for one night."

"Don't worry. They're not angry at you, far as I can tell," Jason said, feeling generous now that he knew he would see Felicity again as soon as tomorrow.

Still, the flamboyant Italian could barely drag himself away from the *signorina*. He clasped Felicity's hand between his own and bent to place a flowery kiss to her knuckles. "It has been a-such a pleasure meeting you, *bella signorina*."

"Likewise, Mr. Giovanelli."

The composer bowed to Jason with a courtier's flourish. "*Buona sera,* Your Grace. Until tomorrow."

"Good night," Jason replied.

Then the fellow whisked off with a flap of his cape and disappeared into the shadows.

Standing side by side, Jason and Felicity exchanged a twinkling glance of amusement at his dramatic exit.

"What a charming fellow." The arch smile tugging at her lips made him want to throw her in her carriage—which was rolling down the street toward them now—flatten her on the squabs in there, and kiss her senseless.

Unfortunately, her chaperone was on the way.

"Until tomorrow, then," Felicity whispered, discreetly capturing his hand by her side and giving it a squeeze while they were still alone.

He curled his fingers around hers. Her hands were warm and soft, and he wanted them on his body. He leaned down to whisper in her ear. "Think you can talk Mrs. Brown into it?"

"It'll be easy," she breathed in his ear. "All I have to say is that I'm going with or without her."

Jason shivered, wondering what would happen if that were possible, if she really could spend one day alone with him. She seemed to be asking herself the same question as she pulled back, gazing hungrily into his eyes.

Intoxicating prospect. But there was only one way to accomplish that and still preserve her reputation.

Marriage.

Egads.

And yet what scared him most was that the thought *didn't* scare him anymore, not as it should.

God, she was a lovely little menace.

He cleared his throat a bit and stepped back from her. "Right, then. I'll pick you up tomorrow at, say, three?"

"Sounds perfect." She smiled intimately at him as her frowning chaperone marched toward them down the few front steps. "I'll see you then," Felicity whispered.

Then Jason shooed away the footman and got the carriage door for the ladies himself.

"Mrs. Brown," he said cordially as he handed the older woman up. "I hope you enjoyed the music."

"Humph," she said.

Wicked mirth twitched about Felicity's mouth at her chaperone's disapproval as he then handed her up into the coach. "Your Grace," she said in farewell.

"Miss Carvel." He shut the door for them, then stood there on the pavement for a long moment, watching their coach rumble off down the street.

A fond smile still lingered on his lips after she had gone, his mind exploding with possibilities that he had long since forbidden himself to consider.

Maybe, just maybe, it was time to change the rules.

CHAPTER 6

Patron of the Arts

*F*elicity almost expected Jason to forget about the plans they had made. She wasn't sure why. Years of being ignored and forgotten had probably made her more wary of him than she had realized.

But sure enough, when three o'clock came, a knock promptly sounded on the door.

Why, he was even on time!

Mrs. Brown was still finishing getting ready, but Felicity rushed into the parlor and arranged herself neatly on a chair to receive him as the butler got the door.

Her heart started pounding from the instant she heard Jason's voice as he asked for her, and then his footfalls as he followed the servant into the house.

"Miss Carvel," the butler intoned a moment later from the parlor threshold, "the Duke of Netherford."

"Your Grace," she started, welcoming him with a polite nod, but she and Jason took one look at each other, dressed in matching colors as they had been last night, and both burst out laughing.

"Not again!" he said.

"How did you know?" she exclaimed at the same time he added, "I see you've decided to venture into half-mourning."

Last night, they had been two black-clad lumps of coal; today they were both wearing brown.

For the first time since the dowager's death, Felicity had donned a chocolate-colored walking dress with black piping. The hat she meant to wear today would still be black, however, as were her gloves and shoes.

For his part, the duke looked marvelous in a fawn-brown afternoon tailcoat and tan trousers. His waistcoat was beige, pinstriped with light blue, and his smart neckcloth was navy. Having handed his beaver hat and walking stick over to the butler, he was the very sketch of a gentleman about Town—and devastatingly handsome.

"Well, I think we look smashing," Felicity declared as he crossed the room to her.

"*You* certainly do." He took her proffered hand, bowing over it with a warm smile.

"Ha. You like the brown? Just wait until I venture into the lavender next week. Maybe even white."

"How daring, Miss Carvel!"

"They are both acceptable colors for half-mourning, my modiste assures me."

"Just be sure and let me know the day, so we can coordinate it again."

She chuckled at his playfulness in delighted amusement. "Hullo, Jason."

He gazed into her eyes. "Hullo, Felicity."

"You're looking well rested this morning," she said fondly, thinking of the haggard state in which she'd first found him earlier that week. "Did you leave the Pelletiers' early last night, as you thought you might do?"

He nodded, lowering himself onto the ottoman in front of her chair. "It was boring after you left. I ate some food, then went home and went to bed."

"What? Not all alone?" she teased in a brazen whisper, since her chaperone had not yet arrived to spoil their fun.

"Very much so," he whispered back. "Pity, no?"

"Hmm. You should try it more often. A good night's sleep keeps a person healthy, you know."

"Yes, Mother," he said sweetly.

She gave him a sardonic look. "Now, now, don't compare me to the duchess. With all due respect, your mother was even wilder than you are."

"I came by it honest," he agreed. Then he gave her a guarded smile. "Thanks for caring, though."

I've always cared, she thought.

Suddenly looking a little self-consciousness, Jason cleared his throat and glanced around the room. "So are both of you ladies ready to go?"

She nodded. "I'll go call my chaperone."

"Do," he said with a meaningful hint of deviltry in his glance. "No telling what could happen if we're left alone too long."

Aunt Kirby's portrait above the mantel almost seemed to nod mischievous encouragement on that point. With no intention of misbehaving, Felicity nevertheless sent him a grin and rose, trailing a hand fondly over his shoulder on her way to the door.

The fleeting touch of his solid form sent a thrill through her body, as did the gratifying knowledge that he had resisted the temptation of another night with Bianca Burns. In Felicity's view, the songstress would not have bothered scolding him in public and making it so obvious they had been lovers if she did not want her name attached to his again. The kiss on the cheek the diva had given him at the end of her flirtatious musical rebuke had said it all. Having punished him a little, the singer seemed to be signaling that she'd be willing to take him back.

And no wonder. What a grand triumph it would be for a woman of her ilk, what a rose at her feet, to upbraid the Duke of Netherford in front of Society and then bring him to heel again as her keeper.

Love was all just a game to such people, just a sport, Felicity thought as she went into the hallway. It was rather sad.

Not that someone like Jason would know any better. His parents had been the exact same way, married by arrangement in their youth, with nothing in common except their ever-growing disdain for each other. She had seen it for herself. Neither duke nor duchess could seem to stand to be in the same house together, so they had each fled to their own pursuits, leaving their son a bit of a lost boy to be raised by well-paid servants. And now here he was.

In truth, how could he be otherwise?

Deep down, she had always wondered if Jason had any idea at all what love even *was*.

When she came upon her butler, she sent him to tell Mrs. Brown that His Grace had arrived to take them on their outing and it was time to go. Upon returning to the parlor, she found that Jason had risen from his seat and was sauntering idly across the room. "What's with all the flowers?"

"Oh..." She blushed. "A few of the gentlemen I met last night sent them."

He arched a brow at her. "Indeed?" He leaned toward the nearest bouquet and read the name on the card. "I told you that you caused a sensation, didn't I? It's like a garden in here."

She smiled, feeling shy about her sudden popularity. "Invitations have been showing up, too."

"I'll bet," he murmured as he furrowed his brow and went to read the rest of the cards, as though making a mental note of all the senders.

She took one off the silver mail tray where the butler had left it. "This one's for the ever-coveted subscription ball at the Grand Albion Assembly Rooms two Thursdays from now. Mrs. Brown knows the patronesses, and they've been thoughtful enough to send us a voucher. Will you be going?" she asked hopefully. "You live right there."

He looked over in distraction as she brought him the sumptuous, engraved summons that had arrived earlier that afternoon. "I'll even be done with my half-mourning by then. You don't think six weeks seems too short for a great-aunt who leaves you a fortune, do you?"

"No," he said absently as he unfolded it and skimmed the invitation.

"Mrs. Brown and I debated it at length, and asked many of her friends what they deemed appropriate. The rules aren't entirely clear in this case."

"Oh, we wouldn't want to break any rules," he drawled softly.

She ignored his teasing glance. "If Aunt Kirby had been of my direct bloodline, like a grandmother, it would have to be much longer. But for a great-aunt by marriage—and a person over eighty—not to mention it is the Season and a girl only has so many of those before she's on the shelf, the ladies I consulted all agreed that four weeks in black and two in half-mourning seemed just right."

"Well, thank God that's settled."

"Jason!"

"She's dead, love. She isn't going to care. Knowing her, she wouldn't have cared while she was alive."

"True. Actually, free spirit that she was, and all those years that she spent widowed, Aunt Kirby hated black bombazine. She always said it made people look like crows."

"Or lumps of coal?" he reminded her.

She beamed at him.

He nodded, tapping the invitation against his opposite palm. "Aye, I got one of these. I can go. It's not like I have anything more important to do, well, ever." He let out a disgruntled sigh.

She tilted her head and studied him. "You're bored witless, aren't you?"

"Not at the moment."

She frowned. "Still, that worries me."

"Why?"

"Because when we were children, it was always when you started getting bored that you ended up landing in a scrape of some sort. We shall have to entertain you somehow."

"No," he said. "That's just it. I'm so bloody sick of entertainment I could shoot myself." The words slipped out, seeming to take even him by surprise. "So to speak," he added, dropping his gaze.

Felicity gazed at him, intrigued. "So you want something serious, then. Something that matters."

He glanced cautiously at her from under his lashes and shrugged, looking very much at a loss. "I don't even know what's left to try."

Her heart clenched to find that somehow, under the hard, polished gleam of all his worldly sophistication, he was still her lost boy.

But she looked away and nodded briskly. "Don't worry, my friend. I shall think on it for you. I promise I'll come up with something meaningful for you by the night of this ball. Meet me there and I shall give you your instructions."

He snorted. "Oh, indeed?"

"Yes, indeed!" she countered. "You will come, won't you? *You* may be fed up with fun, but I've spent the past several years of my life looking after an old lady! You think *you're* bored? Humor me!"

"Very well," he said in a long-suffering tone, laughing when she smacked him in the arm to jolt an answer out of him. "All right, all right! You don't have to beat me, Miss Carvel. I said I'd come."

"Good! Because I am going to have the most glorious gown made just for the occasion and I am going to be...magnificent!"

"Well, then, this I truly must see." He sighed. "I suppose you do have to start spending all that blunt of yours. By the way, if any of these flower boys gives you any trouble, just let me know and I'll thrash 'em for you."

The offer took her aback. "How sweet."

"Eh, don't flatter yourself. It's only for your brother's sake, Felicity. Honor and all that rot."

"Ah, right, of course," she answered, matching his tone of mock gravity. "I'm sure they won't perturb me, anyway. But you know, if it ever came to that, you wouldn't necessarily have to do the thing yourself.

You, being a duke and all. Perhaps you could become the patron of a skilled assassin next."

"*That* is an excellent idea. It's not like any woman's worth getting punched in the face for."

"Absolutely not!"

"Not even the one who followed me around pestering me since she was old enough to walk."

"Mm, there's no accounting for taste. And besides," she said, "what if you fought my suitors and one of them broke your nose? Let's be honest, Jason. You really can't afford to get any uglier."

He grinned. "Hold on. I'll think of a snappy rejoinder any minute now."

"You see? This is what happens when you dull your wits with liquor every night."

"Don't scold me, you minx."

"Somebody has to."

They were both still grinning at each other over their exchange of playful insults when Mrs. Brown appeared in the parlor doorway.

"Ahem." She glowered at the easy, romping warmth that filled the room, then greeted him with a wary nod. "Your Grace."

"Mrs. Brown. Ahem." The great rakehell stood at attention and gave her a very correct bow.

Felicity smiled at the woman. Nothing could dim her mood now. "Are you ready to go and imbibe from the well of the muses, Mrs. Brown?"

"Just let me get my parasol," she said with a last suspicious glare.

After she had bustled off, Jason leaned down to murmur in Felicity's ear. "'Tis my mission today to get on her good side."

"Good luck with that."

"Watch and learn," he whispered.

A few minutes later, they left the house and walked out to his extravagant black town coach. Then, as they set out for the artists' house, he proceeded to work his charm on the older lady.

He attempted first to draw her out by asking her about her hobbies. Mrs. Brown was reluctant to engage in conversation with him, but resisting the Duke of Netherford was easier said than done. He had been conquering female opposition of all kinds with that devilish smile since the day he was born.

Felicity watched the two of them in amusement, helping him just enough to point out that Mrs. Brown was a fabulous hand at cribbage and produced impeccable embroidery.

Steered onto the right path, he was soon wearing her down. Why he bothered, Felicity scarcely knew. She was rather annoyed at her chaperone, herself. All Felicity had been able to think about for the past two days was Jason, but Mrs. Brown wanted her to direct her interests elsewhere. Anywhere but toward him.

"I doubt he has any interest in marriage," Mrs. Brown had said with a sniff earlier that day. Felicity had to admit the woman had probably been right.

In truth, she did not know how she had let herself get swept up in him so quickly once again.

I'm only setting myself up to be hurt, she thought.

But she couldn't seem to stop. It was dizzying, how connected to him she felt once again, despite the time and distance that had passed between them. Their old bond had instantly returned, as though they'd never been estranged. Being with him had always left her rather breathless as a girl. She would have hoped that part of her would have outgrown him by now, but apparently not. Even to this day, all grown up, she was as excited to be near him, as drawn in by his magnetism as she had been in the past.

Perhaps this time she could at least refrain from crawling onto his lap and trying to kiss him...

All she knew was that, for once, her brother wasn't there to come between them, to pull her back and reel him in.

For once, at last, deliciously, she finally had Jason all to herself.

The question was, what was she going to do with the opportunity?

She considered it as she sat across from him in his elegant carriage, studying him discreetly. He really was a pleasure to look at. As she watched him pretending to be interested in hearing Mrs. Brown describe her latest sewing project, she found herself wondering why he went through so many lovers.

Boredom? Ego? Or did his hunger go deeper? It was as though he was constantly seeking something he could never find. In her heart of hearts, she knew what it was and the blasted man was looking in the wrong place, consuming the wrong thing. Gorging himself on what would never slake his hunger. A man at sea could drink all the water in the ocean and still die of thirst.

With everything in her, Felicity felt—had always felt—that *she* could give Jason what he needed. Satisfy him completely. A dangerous thought.

For her to try had always been her riskiest impulse, her parents' occasional worry, and her brother's greatest fear.

She was not blind to the fact that the effort could end in her destruction. Maybe he had been wise to stay away, she thought with a sigh. For heaven's sake, she did not wish to be the cause of some hideous Greek-style tragedy with him and her brother shooting each other at twenty paces at dawn.

But it didn't have to end that way. Not if she could make him love her.

Nakedly admitting that desire to herself took even Felicity by surprise.

The carriage soon rolled to a halt before a handsome middle-class sort of residence in bustling Bloomsbury, home to the British Museum and to countless bookshops and coffeehouses frequented by poets and artists. The redbrick house had a green-painted door, three windows per story, and a wide but shallow balcony running across the width of the second floor.

As soon as his footman got the carriage door for them, Jason stepped out and handed the ladies down. They began walking toward the front door of the house when it swung open before them.

There stood a handsome young man with tousled black hair and romantically disheveled clothes, which immediately identified him as one of the resident artists.

If this had not sufficed, of course, his Italian accent would have done so. "Your Grace! Welcome, signore! Ladies, *benvenuto!* Come in, come in!"

"Allow me to present the sublimely talented painter, Mr. Omero Caradonna," Jason said as they stepped into the small entrance hall. He then gave their names to the beautiful lad, who bowed to the ladies with a sweeping continental flourish.

"I am a-so happy you have come! Giovanelli told us you might honor us with a visit today, Your Grace. Alas—" Caradonna winced. "He, himself, is not here at the moment."

"Ah. Of course he's not," Jason said dryly.

"He is a-very sorry. He forgot that he has to teach the pianoforte lesson to the young daughters of de Lord and Lady Edgecombe."

"I think he's hiding from me," Jason murmured in a mild tone.

Caradonna politely pretended not to hear. "But it would be my honor to give your guests the tour, sir! Ladies, if I may, h-here is the parlor," he said with obvious eagerness to please as he gestured to the doorway behind them. "If you like to see, I have a-dozens of my paintings in various stages of drying all over the walls in here. Come, come!"

As they joined him in the cozy front sitting room, they were soon ooh-ing and ahh-ing over the dizzying array of his artwork on the walls.

"A few of these, of course, are Sanfratello's. He is mainly a sculptor but also paints from time to time. But not as good as me," the young Italian added with a jolly little half-smile.

Felicity glanced at him and would have wagered that his sparkly black eyes won him a lot of female hearts. Caradonna answered their casual questions about what inspired him, how long such impressive paintings took to make, where he had studied, and so forth. In due time, they stepped back out into the entrance hall as their tour continued.

"Across from us is a-the business office," Caradonna explained, "and back here are the rooms Giovanelli uses as his musical conservatory."

They followed Caradonna as he strode farther into the house, waving them cheerfully into the room behind the parlor. "This is, in truth, de dining room. We still eat here some nights, but Giovanelli has claimed it."

He glanced around at the ceiling. "He says it has the best acoustics. Ah, the sideboard used to stand over there, but as you see, now it is reserved for de maestro's pianoforte."

"The room is very spacious," Mrs. Brown remarked. "But it is a pity Mr. Giovanelli could not be here himself. I daresay it's rather disrespectful of him."

"Is this the piece he's been working on?" Felicity inquired, glancing over the hand-scrawled pages of a musical score that had been laid out across the large dining table.

A metronome sat in the center, acting as a paperweight.

"Ah, I am not certain, *Signorina* Carvel." Caradonna gestured toward the doorway. "Giovanelli has also taken the library across from the way. You like to see?"

They went.

Though the library walls were lined with bookshelves, the furniture had been shoved back to make room for a quartet of plain wooden chairs and music stands, clearly a place for an ensemble to practice. Stringed instruments perched upright on stands. Woodwinds rested on the desk. Jason strummed his fingers lightly over the strings of a large harp in the corner as he drifted past it, but without the resident composer on hand to comment, they grew restless and soon headed upstairs.

"The servants' quarters are on the top floor. These are our bedchambers, but here, in the front of the house, *this* is my domain." Caradonna flashed a grin over his shoulder and then led them to a bright, airy drawing room. "Because of de balcony, this room gets de best light— and de best ventilation. The turpentine odor sometimes bothers the others. Me, I don't even smell it anymore."

He smiled at his patron, then, hand on heart, told them, "I am very happy here and very grateful for all His Grace has allowed me to create, as this is de passion and de purpose of my life."

Felicity smiled at Caradonna and nearly swooned herself, then she glanced at Jason, who was looking slightly abashed by the Italian's heartfelt thanks.

"And you think what you do doesn't matter," she said softly, only to him.

He looked over and his gaze locked on to hers. It was a lovely thing he had done here, making it possible for these artists to express their genius, creating works of beauty for the rest of humanity to enjoy.

"It does seem like a perfect artist's studio," Mrs. Brown remarked as she walked over to the French doors that let out onto the balcony.

Above them were large, arched windows through which the spring sunlight poured. There were easels and paintings everywhere; half-built frames; around the walls hung sketches of everything from faces to still lifes to architecture. Rural landscapes in pastels, city scenes in charcoals. Drying brushes were neatly laid out on rags beside paint-stained palettes.

"My goodness," Felicity murmured as she walked slowly through the room. "You really are amazingly talented, Mr. Caradonna."

He folded his hands behind his back, beaming at her praise. *"Grazie mille, signorina."*

"Explain this one to me," Mrs. Brown said, pointing at a blurry rendition of what looked like St. James's Palace. "That is…what does it *mean*?"

While Caradonna attempted to explain to her chaperone that it didn't actually *mean* anything, that he had just liked the lines and the ominous look of the place that night, Felicity leaned closer to gaze at one of his works in progress.

In it, two plump, apple-cheeked children flopped in a large wing chair side by side. The older boy—about four years old, if she had to guess—had his arm around a wee girl, probably aged two.

Felicity smiled, barely noticing Jason, from the corner of her eye, watching her intensely. She was about to ask if the children's portrait was a commission or just Caradonna's own pursuit when the very frank sketch of a nude woman draped across a couch startled the question right out of her head.

Egads, the couch in the drawing was identical to the one right over there by the wall. Which could only mean the drawing had been done right *here*.

She colored at the realization, casting a furtive glance toward the piece of furniture where the naked model had lounged. It dawned on her that, obviously, some rather risqué things went on around here…supposedly in the name of art.

But then, looking closer, it was not just the couch Felicity recognized. She had *seen* that woman in the sketch before. She suddenly remembered where.

It was the same face she had seen peering down at her from the top of the staircase in Jason's house the other morning! Her jaw dropped, but she recovered quickly from her shock and turned with a low huff, instantly blushing. *So which one is that?* she wondered in disdain. *Ginger or Velvet?*

"Ahem, shall we, er, continue with our tour?" Jason suggested, perhaps noticing how quiet she had become. "Caradonna, would you lead the way to the coach house?"

The artist obliged, leading them outside to the garden, and explaining on the way that both the inventor's lab and the sculptor's studio were situated in the coach house, which had been converted into work spaces for them.

"Sanfratello's marble blocks are so heavy the floor inside the house itself would not support them," Jason elaborated. "The coach house floor is made of flagstone, and of course it has no steps to get in, like the house does."

"*Si*, this way, de finished sculptures can be moved onto wagons and transported to their new homes more easily," Caradonna chimed in. "As for Mr. Sloan's laboratory, His Grace deemed it best to put it out there, as well, i-in case of any explosions."

Mrs. Brown stopped midway down the garden path. "Did you say explosions?"

"Mr. Sloan likes to play with chemicals," Jason said. "They can be volatile. As can he."

"Are you sure it's quite safe?" the older lady asked, frowning anew.

"Very safe, ma'am." Approaching on the right side of the coach house, he gave a casual knock on the open door of the inventor's lab. "Sloan?"

The red-haired, bespectacled inventor was younger than Felicity had expected. As Atticus Sloan greeted them absently, she arched a brow at the small whiskered face—a white ferret—peering at them out of the pocket of the inventor's tatty coat.

"Er, one minute, please," the inventor said, waving them through his laboratory and on to the sculptor's studio with an impatient gesture. "I've almost got it. I'm terribly sorry, but I-I really must finish this equation before I…"

He never did finish the sentence, staring off into space.

"Of course," Jason said in amusement, apparently used to him. "Ladies, this way."

He beckoned them through the doorway that led into the sculptor's studio in the other half of the coach house. As they walked through the laboratory, Mr. Sloan seemed oblivious to their presence. Ignoring his patron and guests alike, he whirled around, mumbling to himself and his ferret, and resumed furiously scribbling out a long equation on his large chalkboard on the wall.

Odd fellow. How he could even concentrate with all that banging coming from the other side of the building?

Once Felicity stepped through the doorway into the sculptor's workshop, however, it was like entering a fairyland. A white stone forest of tall marble statues waited ahead, beckoning to be explored…

Heroic figures captured in the midst of dramatic action.

Rearing horses.

Goddesses on pedestals.

Centurions with spears.

Busts of a wrathful Zeus stared down from the shelves, as though the god were tempted to hurl lightning bolts at any intruders.

A life-sized Hermes with winged hat and shoes posed in midflight, off to deliver some message between the gods.

She walked among the statutes in wonder, looking each one up and down, while Jason trailed a few steps behind her. The banging grew louder as she reached the main work in progress in the center of the studio. She tilted her head back and stared up at it in amazement.

It was a massive composition of two figures, male and female, erupting upward in a frozen moment as they contested with each other, larger than life, in three dimensions.

Perched on the scaffolding beside it, chisel in hand, was a short, swarthy man in his forties with thick, hairy forearms and powerful hands. He wore an apron over his clothes and a tool belt around his hips, and his thinning black hair was coated in white dust.

When he saw them, he jumped down off the elevated platform and came around to greet them, wiping off his hands. Felicity was mystified to think that such sublime alabaster fantasies should issue forth from such an ordinary-looking, earthy, little man.

But she liked him at once. Vitale Sanfratello was warm and gracious—and devoid of pretension—as he welcomed them to his studio as though he were just another hardworking craftsman, not a genius of renown.

As soon as Jason did the introductions, Felicity could not hold back. "Mr. Sanfratello, may I just say this statue is remarkable!" she said, staring agog at the marble duo on which he had been working. "What do you call it?"

He just smiled at her, then glanced at Jason, who answered for him.

"It is called *The Seduction of Hades*. That's Hades." He pointed to the musclebound male, then the lithe female. "That's Persephone, and they're going into the entrance hall of Netherford Hall as soon as they are done."

"Ohh." Wide-eyed, she looked up at it again. A randy Hades was in the middle of pulling his resisting young bride onto his lap.

But the sculptor had turned the Greek myth on its ear by posing the virginal goddess with just a hint of coyness in the way she looked over her shoulder at her ravisher. Instead, the suggestion was there, in stone, that it was she, the springtime goddess, who was in fact luring the dark and dangerous god of the underworld under her spell, even while Hades *thought* he was the one capturing *her*.

"It's magnificent," she said.

And a little shocking, apparently.

Mrs. Brown gasped when she saw it, then mumbled an excuse, and fled back into Mr. Sloan's laboratory, even as the Scot called begrudgingly to them through the open door that he had solved the equation and was ready to give them a demonstration of something to do with voltaic current.

Jason and Felicity lingered behind, exchanging a glance as her chaperone rushed off to the safer territory of mere possible explosions.

Sanfratello took one look at them, and with a knowing glint in his eyes, followed Mrs. Brown into the scientist's lab, taking Caradonna with him, to give his patron and Felicity a moment alone.

"What do you think?" Jason murmured, leaning closer.

"It's very…stirring, isn't it?"

He nodded. "To me, as well. The sketch alone was what made me take on patronage of Sanfratello. From the moment I saw the drawing, I knew this sculpture simply had to be made. I'm not sure why it speaks to me so much," he mused aloud, staring at the pair. "It's amazingly lifelike. You can touch it if you like."

"Are you sure it's all right?"

"You're not going to break it. It's stone, you know. Very hard." He ran his hand slowly and deliberately up Persephone's gauze-draped thigh to demonstrate. Then he looked at Felicity with hunger in his eyes. "Go on," he whispered, "touch it."

She bit her lip and then took the dare, since nobody else was watching. Reaching up, she laid her hand boldly on the muscled thigh of Hades.

Jason watched her trail a naughty, gliding caress all the way up to the statue's alabaster groin. She cupped her hand around the contents of his fig leaf.

"You're right," she murmured. "*Very* hard."

Shock registered in his eyes as he held her gaze for a second in ravenous fascination. Then the wickedest half-smile she had ever seen flashed across his face. "You have no idea."

She withdrew her hand from Hades's marble crotch and, feeling brazen, settled it against Jason's stomach. "Then why don't you show me?"

As she fingered a single button on his waistcoat, she could feel his chest rising, falling quickly, and she could see in his eyes that, at last, he was considering it.

Considering *her* in the way she had always wished him to.

Her mouth watered for his kiss, but the surest way to make him run had always been to push, so she somehow found the strength to turn away, and coyly headed for the scientist's lab. Strolling toward the doorway, she could feel his fiery stare devouring the curves of her body. Before she drifted out of the sculptor's studio, she sent Jason a beckoning glance over her shoulder. He was standing stock-still, watching her with searing intensity.

A thrill ran through her at his palpable desire.

Then she stepped through the doorway and went to stand obediently behind the scientist to view a demonstration involving lots of wires and batteries made from oversized jars.

It was a long moment before Jason joined them.

But by then, she had made up her mind: she had to have him. The thought pounding in her brain rather scared her, but the day had yielded one conclusion.

You're mine, Netherford. And you always have been. Fight it all you like. But you've sown your wild oats long enough, my love.

The time had come for her to claim him.

But how?

On second thought, stealing a sideways glance, she caught him studying her with a taut expression, as though he were a little in pain, and she smiled to herself. Maybe her quest would not prove too difficult, after all.

Hiding her want of him as best she could, she watched the demonstration politely. The sparks from Mr. Sloan's big, jar-shaped batteries showered and popped, but they were nothing compared to the currents of fiery attraction running between her and Jason.

Yes, Felicity decided, acutely aware of the tall, strong, needy man beside her. She had his full attention now.

It was only a matter of time.

CHAPTER 7

Rearranging the Furniture

*T*his is all *very alluring,* Jason mused the next day in a state of distraction, his mind and senses still full of Felicity. *But I wonder what she'd say if she knew about the children.*

Sporting with demimondaines was one thing; siring illegitimate children on two different such women was quite another.

And yet, when Jason looked into the sweet little faces of his *indiscretions,* not for the world could he bring himself to regret either one…

Even if the little bastards didn't like him, he thought wryly.

It had been three weeks since he had visited the two separate households where his natural children lived—about a mile apart—in Islington. Indeed, the artists' residence was not the only place for which he was responsible. He wasn't much of a father, he supposed, in terms of guidance and paternal wisdom, but he did his duty by his little ones, and cared for them more than he dared admit or even knew how to show.

At least he was smart enough not to show up without an offering of some kind—a toy, trinket, or sweet. It was the only way he could get his four-year-old son not to run away and hide under the bed when he arrived just to be difficult.

So like his sire, Jason feared. What the boy's glamorous actress of a mother told the tot about him in his absence, Jason did not even want to imagine.

She wasn't there much. Simon was mostly being raised by carefully chosen and highly capable servants. Jason supposed if there was one advantage in how little Chloe could be bothered with her own child, it was that, at least, she wasn't present to poison the boy's mind against his father more frequently.

Jason really did not know why the redhead complained. She had done very well for herself by managing to get pregnant by him about five years ago. At the tender age of twenty-three, she had got herself an income for life.

Unfortunately, she was more beautiful than ever and still relished the adulation and male attention of her previous existence. She was still considered very fashionable to bed, but now she didn't have to do it for the money. No, now she simply did it for fun, and whatever sparkly presents she could pry out of her wealthy admirers.

As long as she kept her men out of sight of their child, Jason didn't care. He had frankly given up trying to make her stop. He had yelled at her about her titled paramours several times, had even made financial threats that he would cut off support.

But she knew full well he wasn't cruel enough to carry out the threat, and in the end, she always shut him up easily by pointing out the hypocrisy of "Naughty Netherford," of all people, ordering *her* to behave.

Ah, well.

Perhaps it was just as well that his two past concubines did not pay loads of attention to their offspring. They were not the best influences on children, anyway.

As if *he* was.

Poor tots. Some examples you've got for parents. With a frown, he pulled the high-stepping pair of bays hitched to his flashy curricle to a halt before the quaint pastoral cottage he had bought for his wee daughter, Annabelle, to grow up in.

The little stinker was as cute as a whole jar full of buttons and had him wrapped around her wee finger, but as he set the brake, he doubted that his daughter's sheer adorability would matter much to Miss Carvel.

Felicity could flirt with him all she liked—God knew he had enjoyed it. Craved more of it with every fiber of his being. But she had no real idea what she was getting into with him and all the untidy baggage of his life as a notorious rakehell.

In truth, Jason wasn't even sure what was happening between them—or if anything *should*—but he was fairly confident she'd back out fast if she knew about his babies.

Her brother knew. Hell, Pete was Simon's godfather, and his

awareness of Jason's little by-blows was part of the reason his friend did not want him courting Felicity.

"It would be different if you ever meant to change," Pete had confided to him in slurred tones one night when they had been out drinking. "But let's be honest, man. Simon and Annie are probably just the first of many."

Jason had been annoyed at this charge. "I could change if I felt like it," he had slurred back at his friend.

Pete had laughed. "You don't want to!"

"I don't even know why you're saying this to me. Godssakes, man, I have no designs on your sister."

"Just saying she might have designs on you. She worships the ground you walk on, mate."

He had snorted. "Felicity's just a schoolgirl with a little infatuation. It'll pass." Uncomfortable with the conversation, he had shouted to the barkeep over the pub's noise to fetch them another round.

After that, Jason had made a hobby out of staying away from Felicity out of respect for her brother, and from the simple fact that he did not really believe his own claim that he could change.

People didn't change, much. Or if they did, it was usually for the worse. But even if he could somehow mend his wicked ways, there still remained the fact that matters of the heart baffled him.

He had plenty of experience with sex, but love, on the other hand, bewildered him—a fact he masked, as a rule, with cynicism and scorn. In reality, he was terrified of ever opening his heart and letting himself be vulnerable, for what if his love was not returned?

Wouldn't that be poetic justice for a scoundrel, after all? And what then? How would he react to not getting his way when he always got everything he wanted? He was not sure he wanted to learn that degree of truth about himself. But so it was with love.

His money couldn't buy it. His power couldn't enforce it. His title could not procure it for him. Love was a gift freely given or it was nothing at all. And that meant if he let himself need it, he could end up totally helpless to seize the thing on which he knew his very survival could come to depend.

And if he were denied the one he wanted, why, then he would probably have a temper tantrum of epic proportions.

Just like his little boy.

Was he prepared to let Felicity reduce him to that? To what he had once been? A crazed child howling in fury at the top of his lungs for the comforting embrace of someone who wasn't coming, who simply wasn't interested, and forgot about him the minute the front door closed once again.

Out of sight, out of mind.

His parents had been too busy hating each other and escaping each other to bother loving him. He was naught but a reminder to them both of their mutual distaste, and neither of them had ever really claimed him.

The only true family he had ever known was when he'd found a brother in Pete.

With a grim set to his mouth, he went and knocked dutifully on the cottage door, only to learn that Annabelle was sleeping. He immediately cursed himself for managing to come right at his daughter's naptime. Helen, Annie's nurse, offered with obvious reluctance to wake the girl up, but Jason shook his head. Not even he was that much of a selfish boor. He had learned by now that the midday nap was vital for a tot. If he threw Annie off her schedule, she'd be fussy all day.

"I'll come back later," he whispered. "How's she doing, anyway?"

They chatted for a minute in low tones on his little daughter's progress.

"She hasn't climbed out of her crib again in the middle of the night, has she?" he asked.

"Oh, no, sir. I think she learned her lesson after she bumped her head."

Helen reported that Annie's growing insistence on doing things herself continued apace, no matter if the simple tasks, such as washing her hands or putting on her shoes took three times longer without adult assistance. Jason grinned to hear of his daughter's independent spirit. Of course, on a louder note, the two-year-old still resorted to angry shrieks of frustration when she found she did not yet have enough words to communicate her wishes. At other times, she made up new words entirely, mystifying everyone around her, the little charmer. Jason shook his head fondly, glad to hear that all was well.

"She keeps me on m'feet, that one," Helen said with a fond chuckle.

"Thanks for all you do for her." He slipped the woman a few pounds as a token of his appreciation. She looked her surprise. The vail was quite unexpected, since she was already quite well compensated. "You know to contact me if you ever have any problems with the babe, or her mother, yes?"

"Yes, Your Grace. And thank you very much, sir!"

He smiled and took leave of her with a nod, still feeling guilty that he did not even know his own daughter's daily naptime.

It had him feeling like a failure even before he arrived to visit the little barbarian, his son.

In the second, cozy, whitewashed cottage a mile away, all was in neat and tidy order, just like the first. Bright blooms burgeoned in the flowerboxes, and delicious smells floated from the kitchen in the back.

The housekeeper let him in with a wreath of rosy smiles. Hat in one hand, the expected tithe of a toy in the other, he stepped into the parlor and waited for his son to be dragged in to see him.

Simon soon marched in, his dark mahogany hair smoothed to the side and his wee cravat straightened, steered by Nurse Jane's hand planted on his shoulder; the four-year-old glared at him, this large, unwanted intruder who had dared interrupt his playtime yet again.

Jason, for his part, couldn't help smiling in spite of the boy's scowl. "Hullo, son."

Nurse Jane gave him a nudge. "Be polite to your father."

"Sir," Simon answered with a begrudging little bow.

"Come and sit with me." Jason headed for the sofa. "Tell me what you have been doing since I saw you last."

Simon neither came near nor answered. He stuck his finger in his mouth and looked up at his nurse.

"Why don't you tell him the joke you told me the other day about the numbers?" Jane urged.

"I forget it," Simon mumbled around his finger.

Jane bent down and whispered something in his ear, then the boy grinned.

"Why was six afraid of seven?" Simon blurted out.

This was good, Jason thought. "Hmm. I have no idea. Why?"

"Because seven…ate…nine."

Jason laughed. "Ah, that's a good one."

Simon looked exceedingly pleased with himself.

"Sounds like you've been working on your numbers as well as your jokes. What about your letters?" Jason ventured after a moment.

"Oh, he's been getting very good at his penmanship, Your Grace," Jane offered. "Would you like to see?"

"Please."

The nurse reached into her pocket and pulled out a folded piece of paper on which Simon had written his name. She handed it to Jason.

"Well, this is very good!" he said, his heart clenching at the backward letters S and N in Simon's autograph.

He'd get there.

"I can tell you must be working hard on this," he added.

The boy eyed him skeptically, then glanced around Jason's feet, searching for the expected toy.

Jason had placed it on top of the cabinet by the wall, knowing what would happen as soon as he gave it to him. He'd run off with it and that would be that.

"It's a nice day out," Jason said. "Would you like to go play ball in the garden?"

For some reason, the invitation seemed to annoy the child. "I already did, with Nurse Jane! You weren't here," he said reproachfully. "Where's my toy?"

"Simon!" Jane scolded.

"I don't want to!" he sassed her.

"That's no way to talk to your father. Apologize at once!"

"It's all right," Jason mumbled. "I can see he is annoyed with me." *As usual.*

"We don't have to play ball if you don't want to, lad. I'm sure we can find something else interesting to do."

Simon didn't answer. Having stuck the dagger of his indifference into his father's heart, he had taken cover on the couch and was hiding his head under a throw pillow, watching Jason from underneath it.

Feeling increasingly inept, Jason cast about for anything that might impress his son. "I know! I could take you out for a drive in my curricle. I'll make the horses run fast…"

Simon perked up at this, lifting the pillow off his head with guarded interest, but Nurse Jane winced and shook her head.

"Er, sir…? I'm very sorry, Your Grace, but an open carriage really isn't safe for a small child. It would be too easy for him to fall out."

"Aw, Nurse Jane!" Simon whined.

Even Jason wanted to argue, but when he thought of the sleek, open chassis of his favorite driving vehicle, he realized she was right. The flashy vehicle was a gentleman's toy, meant for adults. With nothing to restrain him, the tot would probably tumble off the seat and under the wheels if they hit a bump.

"Of course," Jason mumbled, feeling more and more like the worst parent on earth by the second.

Nurse Jane gave him a sympathetic frown, as if to say that at least she could see he was trying.

"But I *want* to go!" Simon insisted.

"Nurse Jane's right, son. It's not safe. I'm sorry I suggested it. When you're bigger, I promise you we'll go. I might even let you drive it."

"But I *am* big! Mama says I'm the man of the house now."

"No, you're not. You're just a little boy," Jason said impatiently. "Now, stop whining! I am your father and you will listen to me whether you like it or not. The answer is no."

Simon pressed his lips shut abruptly, unaccustomed to being reprimanded in such a firm tone. He blinked, staring back at Jason with brown eyes so like his own.

And then his lower lip started trembling.

"Oh no, you don't…"

Brilliant, he scolded himself acidly. *You're here ten minutes and already you make the boy cry. What a wonderful father!*

"I brought you something. Want to see?" Feeling rather desperate, he rose to get the present. "Close your eyes."

The prospect of the expected gift halted Simon's tears before they started.

He must've learned that trick from his mother, Jason thought. "Go on, close 'em."

When Simon had done so, Jason reached up and took the toy off the cabinet and hid it behind his back. "Now open them. Which hand?"

Simon actually smiled. He rolled off the couch and came over to him with a finger tugging shyly at his mouth. The hip-high boy leaned to the right and the left, trying to see behind Jason's back, but Jason moved away with a grin, preventing him, and trying with all his might to show the son who considered him little more than a stranger that he wasn't all that bad.

"Hey!" Giggling, Simon kept trying to get it, and Jason kept eluding him.

"What's wrong? Can't you find it?" he teased.

He did not want this small, sweet moment to end, for he knew from experience what would happen as soon as Simon got his hands on the gift.

Sure enough, when the boy finally seized the wooden pull toy in the shape of a horse, he snatched it out of Jason's hands and ran off without so much as a thank-you.

"You're welcome!" he called after him, but his son pounded off, clutching the offering.

Simon slammed the door to his bedchamber, either to play with the toy by himself or merely to toss the latest trinket onto the pile with all the other useless baubles and amusements that were, in truth, no substitute for what the child really craved.

"I'll go get him," Nurse Jane said in distress.

"It's all right," Jason said, crestfallen. "I'd say that was one of our better visits, actually. At least this time he didn't kick me. Let's not spoil it."

He made sure Jane had everything the boy required these days, asked where his mother was, and learned that Chloe had trundled off to Brighton on the arm of Lord Hayworth, of all people.

Jason nearly choked at this news, but apparently, the rich, drunken, older marquess had finally found the perfect way to get back at his cheating wife for her many affairs. His taking up with a voluptuous young actress was sure to annoy even the infamous Lady Hayworth, and perhaps give her pause in her endless pursuit of younger men.

But, damn it, Jason did not want the mother of his son getting caught in the middle of Lord and Lady Hayworth's disastrous marriage. The boy was already confused enough about couples and families...

Gritting his teeth, Jason soon walked out, feeling powerless and utterly depressed by the visit.

His exasperation with Chloe aside, his heart ached for his lonely, angry, disappointed son. Simon surely didn't understand why his mum was never there, why he wasn't allowed to live with his father, nor even his baby sister, and he was too young to have the ways of the world explained to him quite yet.

Even Jason knew it would have given both children a greater sense of family and stability if they could've at least lived under the same roof. But their mothers had always been rival courtesans in the demimonde, and would not hear of sharing a house with the enemy.

They despised each other even more than they both despised him. Moreover, each woman felt that having given the Duke of Netherford a beautiful, healthy child, a nice house of her own was the least she was entitled to.

Jason couldn't really argue with that. They always knew how to stifle his protests with tears and reminders that he wasn't the one who'd had to go through labor, anyway.

In short, he kept his mouth shut and his coin purse open, and gave his former concubines whatever they bloody well wanted. It was all he really *could* do, considering that at the end of the day, he had no idea how to be a proper, loving father. Where would he have learned this mysterious art?

His own father had been as much of a stranger to him as *he* was to Simon—and Jason had been the legitimate heir!

Instead, the only pattern he had to follow was the one he had received from his own cold sire—distance and formality—and he hated it. But he somehow couldn't figure out how to do it differently. How to bridge the gap.

All he ever felt regarding his by-blows was guilty, and the guilt made him want to stay away.

Feeling like hell, he decided to comfort himself by paying a call on Felicity.

Just thinking of her made him feel somewhat better. He wondered what mischief the chit was getting up to today...

When he arrived at her Mayfair address, he jumped down from his curricle and led the horses into the passage to the mews behind her house. He hitched his team to a post there, out of sight. He didn't intend to stay long, but he did not wish to cause any undue gossip with his repeated visits.

After leaving his carriage out of view, he headed toward the front entrance again, but just as he stepped past the corner of her house, he spotted a phaeton buzzing down the street toward him.

On it sat two of her new admirers from the night of the concert. At once, Jason ducked back and pressed himself against the wall until they had driven by.

The two bachelors continued on around the corner, gawking at her residence as they passed, their intentions clear. They, too, meant to call on her.

Damn. Jason did not feel like sharing her just now. Scowling in the shadows, he waited until the interlopers had passed before striding quickly to her front door.

He believed her would-be suitors had merely driven around the corner, circling the house while they worked up their nerve before coming up to knock on the door.

Idiots.

He did so with no such compunctions. But while he waited for her butler to answer, he glanced around hurriedly, impatient to be let in before the fools returned.

Still no one answered. He furrowed his brow, however, for he could hear voices from inside. Then he heard banging. He knocked again, louder this time, and waited only another moment before grasping the handle and letting himself in. He was, after all, an old friend, and suddenly, he was a bit worried by the noise. Was something wrong in there?

"Hullo?" he called as he stepped into the foyer, taking off his hat. "Anybody home?"

There was no sign of the servants, but as he shut the door behind him, he could hear a commotion coming from down the hallway. "Miss Carvel?"

Venturing into the house, he found the parlor all aflutter. The butler and footman were moving furniture back and forth to Felicity's impatient specifications, while the maid was up on a stepladder banging a nail into the wall.

Ah, he thought, still rather bemused. At least the hammering explained why nobody had heard him. But he still wasn't sure what all was going on here. On the center table, furniture catalogs lay open, along with a loop of fabric swatches.

"No, that's too far." Felicity waved the footman and butler to the right. "Go back. No, not too much. There! Now for the cabinet."

When the maid stopped tapping the nail into the wall, she hung up a small botanical print beneath the nature sketch of a butterfly's cocoon.

"Does that look straight, miss?" The maid glanced over her shoulder to consult with her mistress and suddenly saw him. "Oh—sir!"

"Good day," Jason said politely.

Felicity whirled around on her heel and suddenly saw him. "You!"

"You," he countered, raising an eyebrow at this peculiar greeting.

The way her face suddenly lit up with delight at his arrival chased off much of the gloom that had settled over him. At least *someone* in the world was glad to see him. Jason hung his hat on the coat tree. "What's all this, then?"

"Come in, come in!" Felicity bustled over, taking his hands. "You're just in time to help."

"I am?"

"The fellows here can't get the cabinet to budge. Roll up your sleeves, Duke, we need your help."

"Miss!" The butler nearly dropped the oil lamp on the footman's toe, so aghast was he to hear the young lady ask—well, order—a duke to exert himself. To say nothing of the poor chap's apparent horror over his own failure to answer the door. "Oh, Your Grace, I am so dreadfully sorry, I-I didn't hear your knock."

"Quite all right, my good man." Jason nodded over his shoulder toward the foyer. "I just let m'self in. Hope you don't mind."

"*Vous êtes ici chez vous,*" Felicity replied brightly with a welcoming gesture about the room.

"*Merci,*" Jason replied, holding her gaze just a moment too long in amusement. "You might like to know, however, that you are about to receive more visitors."

Felicity groaned. "Not again!"

"Afraid so. There are two nincompoops driving around and around outside your house. I think they are trying to decide if they dare approach."

She winced. "Did they see you come in?"

"Certainly not. I eluded them with the utmost cunning," he said dryly.

"Clever fellow! There were a few others trying to barge in an hour ago. I had Foster here tell them I was not at home."

"Oh…" Jason suddenly felt awkward. "If this is a bad time, I can show myself out just as easily—"

"No, no, don't be silly! That doesn't apply to you." She slipped her hands through the crook of his elbow and beamed at him. "Old friends are always welcome. Especially ones that I can put to work."

The butler shook his head at Jason with an agonized look of apology, but he didn't mind at all. Indeed, he decided on the spot that he quite adored being a part of all Miss Carvel's domestic hubbub.

Just then, an eager knock pounded at the door, and this time, everybody heard it.

"Warned you," Jason said with a grin.

Felicity laid her finger over her lips to hush everyone, then waved her hands in front of herself to the butler, shaking her head to make it plain she was not at home.

Foster nodded resolutely and pivoted, marching off to carry out her orders.

"Go and back him up in case they insist on waiting until I am available," she whispered to her footman.

"Aye, miss. We'll get rid of them…again."

"Thank you. Such a nuisance. Oh, and, er, I won't require either you or Foster for a bit when you're through."

The footman seemed startled by this pointed request for privacy with her caller, but he dropped his gaze, sketched a slight bow, and followed the butler.

Jason turned to the lady in charge. "Right. So what are we doing, then?"

Felicity pointed. "Moving this piece of furniture from here to there."

"Again," the maid said under her breath with cheeky humor.

"Dorcas! That will do, you saucy thing. Why don't you run along and fetch us some refreshments. Jason, wine?"

He shrugged. "Whatever you're having."

"White wine, and something small to eat," she told the maid, giving her a look that said, *And take your time about it.*

"Yes, miss." Dorcas climbed down off the stepladder and trundled off to her task.

As soon as she had gone, Jason turned to Felicity with a speculative gleam in his eyes.

Alone at last.

CHAPTER 8

Just Once

F or a long moment, they just stood there gazing at each other, drinking each other in with a warm and intimate smile.

Coming here had been a good idea, Jason had to admit. But it took everything in him not to reach over and cup that lovely face and kiss those pink, beguiling lips...

Felicity tilted her head, studying him. "What's wrong?"

"Hmm?" He came back to earth and shook his head. "Nothing. Why?"

"You looked a little glum when you came in."

Blast it, she was too perceptive by half. He smiled ruefully. "Well, I'm feeling much better now."

"Because of me?" she exclaimed, eyes twinkling as she stepped back and lifted her chin.

He narrowed his eyes. "Don't let it go to your head."

"Never. Now help me, would you? Here, take off that handsome coat so you don't rip it."

"Undressing me the moment we're alone, Miss Carvel?" he murmured as she moved behind him and peeled his snug merino wool tailcoat off his shoulders.

"I know. Aren't I incorrigible?" she purred.

He thrilled to the feel of her hands running down his shoulders and then gliding, for no particular reason, down his biceps through the thin, crisp linen of his shirtsleeves.

He liked her touch a great deal. She withdrew to go and lay his coat over the back of a nearby chair.

He turned around to face her and gestured at the chaos in the room. "So what's all this about?"

"Oh, it's so exciting!" She dashed back to him and took his hands, pulling him toward the sofa. "Remember how you told me I needed to figure out ways to spend some of my money? Well, it came to me this morning! Look!"

"I thought I was moving furniture."

"In a moment, yes, but look first." She tugged him down onto the couch beside her. "I decided to begin my new life by making this house I've inherited, you know, more my own. Put my own stamp on it. Not to be rude, but the decor is out of date and, well, frankly a little…old-ladyish, if you will. I want to make it fashionable and new. It's a wonderful house, in all. It just needs some freshening up. So I've decided to redecorate!"

"Is that so?" he murmured, ridiculously pleased she had taken his advice.

"That's good use of my money, isn't it?" she asked, waiting innocently for his answer.

He nodded.

"I had a fine cabinetmaker here today to talk about some new furniture, or at least new upholstery on the pieces I inherited. He left these books for me to look through. Chairs, tables, sideboards… And these fabric swatches are just some of the selections I can choose from for the chairs and couches. Isn't it exciting?"

"Thrilling," Jason drawled. "Now, if you need any help choosing a new bed…"

"Naughty!" she scolded with a happy little gasp, blushing as she slapped him lightly on the thigh.

Which took him aback and delighted him at the same time.

She seemed to have surprised herself, also. "Ahem, as I was saying," she continued, "I want it to be nice and bright and airy in here, and I need to get rid of all these knickknacks. They only gather dust and make me sneeze." She tucked a lock of blond hair behind her ear as she chattered away. "You must give me your opinion on several of my choices."

He watched and listened to her, entranced.

"After all, you have an excellent eye, Jason. There's no point denying it, now that I have been to your artists' house. I had fun yesterday, by the way," she added, elbowing him fondly.

"As did I."

Odd, he thought. Miserable as he had felt just a short while ago, now all was right with the world again. And once more, his gaze strayed down to Felicity's sweet lips.

So very tempting.

He swallowed hard, dragged his stare away, and loosely clasped his hands to keep from reaching for her, resting his elbows on his knees.

"Where's the Brown today?" he asked, striving for levity despite his rather strangled tone. Craving the ripened, charming woman beside him, he stared blindly at the printed booklet of various chairs for sale.

"With the ladies' altar guild. They're planning their next charity effort."

"Ah."

"What have you been doing today?" she asked pertly.

He shook his head. "Not much."

He did not like lying to her, but she seemed to read in his eyes that he didn't want to talk about it.

"Very well. So tell me which of these two fabrics you like better, then. Don't mock, this is serious business! For you see, you've inspired me with a marvelous new quest, Jason."

"I have? That one," he added, pointing at the subtle, pale brocade.

"Oh, good, that's the one I like, too!"

"What quest?" he inquired.

"Aha, well, once I've brought my house up into the first stare of fashion, I mean to begin holding salons and musicales here, much like the Pelletiers, only on a much smaller scale, of course," she hastened to add.

He studied her in wonder. "Really?"

She nodded eagerly.

He pondered this, thunderstruck, for despite his love of the arts, he had never contemplated such a notion before. All of a sudden, it seemed wonderfully obvious, a tiny glimmer of what was possible if he were married someday.

To the right lady.

He and his duchess could arrange pleasant evenings for their friends, just like Lord and Lady Pelletier did...

"Oh, dear. No response." Her face fell. "You hate my idea? Is it too presumptuous?"

"No, it's brilliant. Can I help?" he asked, giving her a boyish bump with his shoulder.

She looked delighted. "Certainly, i-if you like! You could host it with m— Oh, but I suppose that would be too shocking for Society. They'd take it wrong, wouldn't they? Especially with…you being, well, *you*."

"Mmm," he admitted in dismay.

"You do know they call you the Duke of Scandal, right? Naughty Netherford?"

He twisted his lips at the nickname, dismayed she'd heard it, though God knew he'd earned it.

She laughed at his rueful expression. "It doesn't bother me! You'll just have to be my silent partner, then. My right-hand man. Nothing official, nothing for people to gossip about. But your job will be to help lure important guests to my grand occasions! Before you know it, I'll be all the kick."

"You already are, love."

"That's not me, that's the money. But thanks anyway."

He shook his head and smiled. "Count me in."

She held his gaze for a long moment, then looked away, adorably pink-cheeked. "That reminds me of something else I wanted to ask you about. Do you think your *Signore* Sanfratello would make me a small statue or figurine to fit in the alcove over there? Nothing excessive, of course, I just have the perfect spot for it." She pointed toward the left wall of the parlor. "I would love to have one of his works here to admire all the time."

"Then you shall. It will be my housewarming gift to you."

"Oh, you don't have to do that!"

"I'm his patron and your friend. And I'm happy for you, getting this inheritance. It seems like it's rather changed your life. Though, to be honest, I daresay it's a lot of trouble to go to, remodeling this place, when I doubt you'll live here very long."

She cocked her head. "Why do you say that?"

"Suitors banging down your door. Half of London angling to snare you. Mark my words, you'll be wedded and bedded and living elsewhere by the time the Season's over. And then I won't get to visit you anymore or people will talk," he said in a studied tone of wry humor to mask his dismay as the realization unfolded. "They'll say we're having a tryst. Then your husband will call me out. And it'll all end in tragedy, and perhaps they'll make a musical about it."

"No doubt. Unless I marry *you*," she blurted out cheerfully.

He arched a brow.

"Or not." She turned red and immediately dropped her gaze to the catalog, turning a page. "I mean, it does seem a good solution at first glance, so we could both be a part of my little project. But you're right. Being married to the Duke of Scandal sounds very inconvenient, and besides, nobody's life turns out the way they planned at eight years old. That's just silly."

She flashed a blithe smile, turning to him, and her wicked gaze dipped to his lips. "Well! Since it seems the clock is ticking before—as you say—I'm married off to some *very* lucky man and the two of us are not allowed to play together anymore, I suppose we'd best enjoy it while we can, hmm?"

"Yes," he said warily, his pulse thundering. He had not expected that vixenish answer.

To be sure, his friend's little sister was all grown up now and very much a woman. In truth, his head was rather spinning at the deft circles she was running round him, emotionally speaking.

What the hell is going on?

And what exactly was she suggesting when she'd said *we should enjoy it while we can*?

And what of this other claim, that being married to him would be too "inconvenient" for her? What was that supposed to mean?

He was suddenly unsure if he was offended or relieved, but he was certainly confused.

"Oh, have I shocked you, Your Grace? You must think me very naughty," she whispered, laying her hand on his thigh.

He looked down at it, and then at her, instantly on fire. The minx was toying with him, and he found her utterly irresistible.

For a long moment, he sat stock-still, fighting what he wanted and panicking slightly to feel the chains of his resistance falling away. He wasn't sure he was ready to let them go.

"Felicity," he said in a strangled tone.

"Yes, Jason?" she breathed.

"You shouldn't be touching me."

"I've heard that song before. It didn't work then, either. Did it?" She began inching her hand slowly up his thigh. Just like she'd done to the Hades statue. "You want me to believe that you prefer me as a good girl...all prim and proper?"

You little hellion. His heart slammed in his chest.

"Stop me if you don't like it," she whispered, daring him with those stormy sea-green eyes.

Passion blazed through his body; the need was too strong. When he dragged his gaze up from the pretty hand creeping up his thigh and looked at her again, the impulse got away from him.

Suddenly—not sure what he was doing but past caring—he leaned in and claimed her mouth with years' worth of ravenous need.

# # #

Finally. Oh God…

Having only just saved the situation with a change of subject—namely, some brash flirting to cover up her blunder of mentioning marriage to the consummate rakehell—Felicity barely dared move, treasuring the wild, fevered caress of his lips taking hers.

At long last.

When a person dreams of a thing for years, yearns for it with every inch of her body and every beat of her heart, it is easy to be overwhelmed when the moment finally comes to exquisite fruition.

Jason's kiss was that dream for her, and it nearly made her fall apart. Its sudden crashing into reality made her body throb like the white-hot birth of a star.

Her heart raced with the impossible thrill of knowing that, in this moment, she finally had her idol's *full* attention. She wanted to slow time and savor every second of it, but crazed want pounded in her veins, and Jason's kiss was frantic. He wrapped his arms around her and pulled her onto his lap while his tongue plunged into her mouth like he would consume her.

Felicity clung to him in trembling excitement, overwhelmed with pleasure. God, he could've had her right there on the couch in the middle of the daytime if he wished it.

It shook her, facing how much she really craved him. Because deep down, she feared this still meant nothing to him. That she would ultimately prove just another female to him, or worse, he would suddenly find his little conscience once more, push her away completely, and break her foolish heart a second time.

And yet, even knowing the danger she was in, she couldn't make herself stop kissing him back.

She wanted this too badly. She slid her hand around his nape and opened her mouth for him, following his lead.

He groaned her name with such despair amid the deep, delicious licking of his kiss that, with one arm draped around his neck, she melted against his big, muscled body. Every inch of her had gone sweetly heavy with desire, yet with her other hand, she stroked his face in reverent longing as he went on kissing her.

I love you so much.

As her trembling fingers molded the angle of his chiseled jaw and explored the warm smoothness of his clean-shaven cheeks, she did not want to admit it to herself. But there was no getting round it. There had never been anybody else for her and there never would be. If Cousin Gerald was right in calling her a spinster, it was all Netherford's fault.

As his tongue swirled in the depths of her mouth, he gently pressed the small of her back, pulling her closer still, gathering her to him. She went eagerly as he guided her astride him, moving onto her knees to straddle his lap, her hands planted on his broad shoulders.

He hitched her skirts up a little to make it easier for her to move. "Are we really doing this?" she panted, staring into his eyes. They had darkened to midnight with desire.

"It would seem so," he said in a gravelly voice.

"Thank God."

"It's been a long time coming, hasn't it?" he whispered.

She lowered her head in answer and claimed his mouth with the utmost enthusiasm. Perhaps she was acting fast, but he seemed to have no problem with it, welcoming her without a word to do as she pleased to him. He leaned against the back of the sofa, thighs sprawled, his hands molding to the curve of her waist.

She kissed him fiercely, oblivious to anything but his mouth, his hands, his skin. She had him pinned down now, all to herself, and he wasn't getting away. With her tongue in his mouth, she reveled in the delicious taste of him, not caring about propriety, not even listening to the soft footfalls as the maid returned.

The footsteps stopped outside the doorway; the door creaked and then clicked closed to leave them their privacy.

Jason moaned, apparently taken off guard by her wanton response. On her knees across his lap, she was delighted to feel his strong, smooth hands sliding down her back. He grasped her hips, then she drew in her breath sharply as he gripped her backside hard through the fluffy layers of her skirts and petticoat.

He gave both cheeks a roguish squeeze. She laughed breathlessly, rocked against him. He nuzzled her breasts, and then used his lower position to start kissing her throat.

He made her dizzy with delight. "Oh, Jason."

She clung to him, quivering as his lips roamed up the curve of her neck to her earlobe.

"You taste so good, my darling Felicity," he whispered as he licked and kissed her neck. "Better than I dreamed."

She ran her fingers through his sable hair, loosening the light, stiff hold of the clean-smelling stuff that he used to slick it back. But this was only fair, since he had messed up her hair, too. He now brought it tumbling around her shoulders as he stole the combs that had been holding it up. With a slight, expert tug, he even robbed her of the ribbon serving as her headband. She countered by likewise untying his cravat.

"There. That's better," she whispered, undoing his top button and then sliding her hand into the intriguing region of his neck usually hidden by the collar of his shirt. It was lovely. She bent and kissed it.

He cradled her head against the crook of his neck, clearly enjoying this as much as she was; however, having loosed her hair, and certainly her instincts, he pulled back just a little to admire her with her hair down.

His stare was intense as he studied her, as though for the first time. "You really are *so* damned beautiful."

She dropped her gaze modestly.

He smiled at her blush and then pulled her down for another kiss. She did not know how the man could be so calm. She was going out of her mind with tingling sensations she had never experienced before, feelings that made her want to ride him like a horse. He did not seem at all surprised by this; indeed, the gentle pressure of his hand at the small of her back welcomed her without a word to do so. It guided her down to rest astraddle him, their bodies flush.

For his part, he sat up straighter, kissing her sweetly, nibbling her lips, and teaching her the marvelous results of what happened in her body when she moved against him just so.

"Oh *my*." The dizzy whisper escaped her.

"God, Felicity," he uttered, clutching her to him. "You're so sweet. So innocent."

"Jason."

She was so swept up in the tantalizing pleasure throbbing in her mound that she gasped in surprise when his left hand cupped her breast and then began rhythmically squeezing it.

Meanwhile, his right had begun roaming up her thigh beneath the drapery of her skirts. She felt his fingers curl around her garter like he wanted to tear every stitch of clothing off her.

She did not think she would have minded one bit.

She loved the scoundrel. Trusted him. God help her, she still believed in him, too. And if he wished it, she would gladly give herself to his pleasure right now in glorious abandon.

"Lie down, sweeting," he panted, but he was already helping her do so, switching positions with her, and slowly laying her on her back on the sofa. He moved atop her and leaned between her thighs, running an expert hand down her bared right leg to her bent knee.

She slid her arms around his neck, a little scared, but utterly excited to see what he might do next. Her lips burned, swollen as his own. His dark eyes gleamed with seductive knowledge.

"So many things I want to do to you. Show you," he breathed.

"Do them, Jason. Show me." Her voice was but a sigh.

"So willing?"

"You've always been the one. Haven't we both wanted this for ages?"

He eyed her in stormy defiance, unwilling to admit it even now.

She smiled in spite of herself. "Very well. I'll play along if you prefer it thus. We're just *friends*." Then she pulled him down to kiss her once more, and did some exploring of her own.

Unbuttoning his waistcoat with trembling fingers, she pulled his shirt out from his trouser waist and slipped her hand boldly underneath, moaning with admiration as she fondled his sculpted abdomen.

The hard, chiseled muscle and velveteen warmth of his skin drove her wild with twofold hunger. She ran her hands up his smooth sides, caressing his stomach and trailing her fingers across his muscled chest.

She laid her palm flat over his heart and felt it pounding as he kissed her.

The heart whose devotion she craved.

"Felicity, my darling." Braced on his hands above her, he shook his head gently. "We have to stop now."

"No, we don't."

"We do," he murmured in regret. "This has gone far enough."

"I want more."

"No. This can't happen."

"It already *is* happening, Jason. Mmm, you're harder than Hades."

He flinched and closed his eyes with a look of agonized pleasure when she cupped his rigid manhood through his clothes, just as she had done to the marble god.

"You heartless tease."

"I'm not teasing. You feel much nicer than that cold statue. Yours is hot. And pulsating."

"Yes, I know," he said through gritted teeth. "Please stop." Then he groaned, making no effort at all to pull away.

"Such a liar," she taunted.

"I didn't mean for this to happen."

"Well, I did."

"Felicity, no."

"Jason, don't start something you're not prepared to finish."

He looked down at her in astonishment, his hair tousled, his clothes undone as he lay between her legs, with her skirts hitched up around her hips.

"'Sblood, what am I doing?" He suddenly wrenched backward, shot dizzily to his feet, and turned away, looking routed. "I have to go."

"Don't you dare!" Felicity came up onto her elbows, glaring at him. "You choose *this* moment to go all virtuous on me? No. You cannot be this cruel to me again. Get back here, Netherford."

As your future duchess, I demand it, she thought, staring boldly at him.

But she was not mad enough to utter this aloud. That would send him running for the hills.

Standing a few feet away, weaving slightly on his feet, he seemed to struggle for sanity. "You don't know what you're saying. One of the servants already saw us."

"I don't give a damn," she said politely. "And neither do you. Not really. Now, you come back here, you naughty man, and finish what you started. Or else."

"Or else what?" he retorted.

She gave him angelic smile. "Or I'll tell big brother."

His jaw dropped.

She crossed her legs enticingly and waited.

"Oh, you little *devil*," he whispered, but as he shook his head at her, she could see that, somehow, he was perversely intrigued that she would use the threat of blackmail to force him into doing what they both wanted.

She bit her lip to stop herself from caving in to propriety.

"And here I thought I was the scandalous one."

"Oh, stop complaining," she chided in amusement. "You know you want this. Besides, it's only fair." She shifted the angle of her legs and let him stare at them. "You've done this with nearly every other woman in Town, so why not me?"

"Because you're the one that matters," he replied.

Felicity went motionless, and Jason seemed to have startled even himself with his own soft words.

He looked away while she hid her astonishment. "Of course, I had no idea you were such a naughty thing."

She shrugged, fascinated, but on her guard. "Maybe you just bring out the bad in me, hmm?"

He eyed her over his shoulder. "I rather like the bad in you."

"Don't run away," she whispered, holding out her hand to lure him back.

His eyes gleamed as he glanced at the clock. "When do you expect Mrs. Brown to return?"

She shrugged. "Not yet."

He took a wary step toward her, and when he came to stand by the arm of the sofa, his hand descended to pet her head. She savored his gentle touch, nestling against his palm. She looked up at him with almost unbearable yearning, and he seemed to reconsider.

Taking pity on her. Enjoying his control.

He walked around the sofa, trailing his fingertips down her leg as he came alongside her. "If we do this…it'll only be the once. I mean it, Felicity. It's not going to happen again. But…I suppose I can't just leave you in this state."

Whatever you say. "I knew you weren't that cruel."

"Yes. And if it's just to be this once…I suppose I ought to make it worth your while. Something to remember me by." He slowly lowered himself to kneel beside her on the floor.

Felicity trembled with raw anticipation. He kissed her bent knee, still holding her stare. "Because it all ends when I walk out that door. Understood? I won't be back."

Yes, you will, she thought, but she just stared at him, panting with desire.

"And, very well, I admit it. I suppose I've been a bit curious for a long time now." He pressed her legs apart.

"Will it hurt much when you take me?" she whispered. "They say—that is, I've never—"

He silenced her with a finger over her lips. "I'm not doing that to you. I don't care how you beg. I can give you what you need in other ways. Lie back now, there's a good girl."

Pulse slamming, she obeyed, and tried to relax as he kissed his way down her body. He pushed her skirts higher, nuzzling her thighs.

She watched him in nervous sensuality, but then closed her eyes with a silken tremor that ran the length of her when he gently touched her core.

"Ohhh." She blushed scarlet when he pressed his finger into her drenched passage. She could not help but move her hips as he began to stroke her, in and out. But she gasped in scandalized delight when he lowered his head and started kissing her mound of Venus, exactly as he'd done to her mouth. So warm, so shocking.

So *Jason*.

She rested her hand atop his head, petting his sable hair while he pleasured her with expert skill.

Felicity was in raptures. Contrary to her maiden fears, it didn't hurt *at all*. Between the intoxicating thickness of his middle finger penetrating her, and the wet, lusty glide of his tongue's wicked play at her mound, it was only moments before she climaxed with a series of violent shudders and a muffled shriek of blissful release.

He swooped up to capture her frantic moans on his tongue before they faded away completely. She could taste herself on him, which was strange, but what Jason had just done to her seemed to have almost as potent an effect on him as it had on her.

His hand shook as he pulled her touch to his member through his clothes.

My goodness! She marveled at the size of it. Ecstasy had left her reeling, but she immediately squeezed it to oblige him.

"Do you want me to kiss it, too?" she asked breathlessly.

He jolted where he knelt. "Oh God. Stop." His hand clamped down on her wrist like a manacle. "No," he said hoarsely.

"Why? I'm game. That was wonderful. Just show me how to give you pleas—"

"For God's sake, Felicity!"

He pulled away from her almost angrily, his eyes ablaze, his brow furrowed with a general look of dazed need.

"What? What did I do?"

"Be quiet!" He rose and turned away, then visibly strove to get himself under control.

There was silence, but for his panting.

He stood with his hands on his hips, head down, his back to her; she could see his shoulders moving as his chest heaved.

"Jason?"

No answer.

The spring breeze tickled the window, and the clock tick-tocked.

She sat up, watching him with an anxious little flutter in the pit of her stomach. "Why are you so angry at me?"

"Not at you!" He turned around and looked at her incredulously, as if it was the stupidest question he had ever heard. "At myself—because I shouldn't have let this happen!"

For a heartbeat, his anger almost scared her back into being prim and proper, but thankfully, she was shrewd enough to realize that she was finally getting somewhere with him. The bold approach had really worked thus far, so she vowed to stay the course.

"Oh. Is that all?" she said, pleased to sense that the balance of power had subtly shifted between them—in her favor for once. She laid her head on a throw pillow and gazed at him. "Well, I, for one, am glad it happened. I must say, it was worth the wait."

He cast her a glance full of dark longing and shock at her frank answer, clearly resenting that everything that had existed for so long between them was now fully out in the open, whether he liked it or not. Perhaps he had preferred the safety of self-deception, ignoring their attraction. He shook his head.

"Little fool," he muttered under his breath as he hurried to fix his various garments.

"Yes, probably so." She laughed idly, holding to her chosen path of brazening this out. Indeed, she found it oddly liberating. "A fool for you, my dear. I don't deny it. I love you, Jason. And I always will."

When she raised herself up onto her elbow, he looked at her like he wanted to devour her all over again.

Instead, he turned away, shaking his head. "I am leaving, Felicity. And I won't be back."

She let out a sigh and collapsed onto her back again. "Suit yourself."

This was apparently not the answer His Grace had anticipated. He paused in the middle of tucking his shirt in and arched a brow at her.

She slanted him a wry look. "What did you expect from me, tears? Pleading?" She shook her head. "No. Do as you please. You always do, anyway. You know how I feel about you, and that is sufficient."

"You're deluded," he muttered.

"If you think that, then *you're* the fool, Jason." She sat up again and pinned him with a challenging stare. "Do you think I would've ever let you touch me if I were not in love with you?"

He stared at her, mute.

She let out a sigh. "Yes, yes, I know. You don't want to hear it. Well, I really don't care if you love me back or not, as it happens. I'm not going to *die* without you like some brainless miss. So, go. Run away, just like you always do. Nobody's forcing you to stay. Get out of my house if you don't want to be here. Frankly, I'm tired of your games."

"*My* games?" he nearly shouted. But he snapped his mouth shut on whatever else he might have wanted to say and merely glared at her.

Turning away, he dragged his hand through his hair in a useless effort to tame it, snatched his coat off the chair where she had placed it, and marched to the doorway. "Farewell, Felicity. It's been fun."

"Come back anytime, Your Grace," she taunted, refusing to wince at his callous barb. "We both know this isn't over yet."

He scowled at her, then huffed out of the parlor.

Though his angry reaction to her declaration of love made her wince, she managed to laugh softly as she heard him go slamming out the back door into the mews. *Ah, why, of all the men on the earth, did I have to lose my heart to that beast?*

But her hopes soared, for he had said with his own lips that *she* was the only one that mattered...and the way he'd said it, she believed him.

So she refused to be daunted, refused to get angry, refused to give up. Not now, when she finally saw she was getting to him. *That's just my Jason. The scoundrel of the earth.*

Monster, she thought with a fond chuckle, remembering the diva's song to him. *He'll be back,* she thought with a shiver of lingering delight. But Lord, as bad as he was, he was certainly good at some things.

Letting out a delicious sigh, she fell onto her back again, cast her forearm across her brow, and wondered in amusement what she could do to torment the rogue next.

CHAPTER 9

A Losing Battle

*H*ow could I be so weak? Why did I give in to her? I can't believe I let this happen!

Jason fled out the back door of her house, shaken to the core. *I'm playing games?* Why, the little lunatic. She did *not* behave like any other female *he* had ever dealt with—neither lady nor whore.

Get out of my house if you don't want to be here? he marveled, confounded. *I don't really care if you love me back?*

What the hell was that supposed to mean?

He did not understand what she was after, and with his mind a scarlet vortex of sexual frustration, there was obviously no hope of puzzling it out until he got to come. He resolved to go at once to his favorite brothel, and paused outside the back door of Felicity's house.

There, with hands still shaking, he put his clothes back into some rough semblance of order before striding over to his carriage.

As he untied his horses and then jumped up into the curricle, he could not believe she had blackmailed him into pleasuring her with the threat of telling her brother. Wicked little vixen.

She was shameless.

And he utterly adored it.

Just when he thought Felicity Carvel could not get any more fascinating, any more alluring, she turned his world upside down.

If you are wise, his survival instincts warned, *you will never go near her again.*

Well, of course he would stay away from her. He had staked his pride on doing so, making his big, manly pronouncement that he wouldn't be back.

The thought of it already made him sick to his stomach. Indeed, a weak, sniveling, craven part of him wanted to go racing right back to her and throw himself at her feet, tell her he hadn't meant it and beg her to forget he had ever said it. That what she had "made him" do to her was exactly what he had longed to do. God, what was wrong with him?

Thank God for harlots, he thought as he drove hell-for-leather to the Satin Slipper. You paid them and then they went away. Nice and easy. No mess. Unless, of course, you got one of them pregnant...

With a growl under his breath, his blood still hot with fever, Jason did not want to think about that. He opened the small hidden compartment in his carriage where he locked up his personal effects and reached for the condom, slipping it discreetly into his pocket.

He did not have a civilized word for the proprietress as he stepped inside the infamous, expensive bordello. Well known there, he showed himself to the drawing room and looked around at the selection of bored girls waiting for the evening crowd.

He snapped his fingers at a blonde about Felicity's size and felt somewhat gratified by the way she jumped to her feet at his demand.

Some women at least knew how to obey.

The girl beckoned him toward the hallway with the rooms.

But it soon became apparent that it wasn't going to happen.

Jason shut the door behind him, clasped the woman, and dove his face into her bosom, pulling down her dress without so much as a greeting. He wasn't paying her to talk. She was obliging enough to whatever he attempted as he grasped her hips through her gaudy skirts and moved her around the room. She fondled him against the wall, by the bedpost, and then tried to pleasure him sitting on the chair, to no avail. His body refused to cooperate.

Shocked, the great cocksman told himself that clearly he was just too damned distracted. For some bizarre reason, he kept picturing his little son sitting cross-legged on the nearby chest of drawers, watching him intently. *What are you doing to that lady, Papa?*

Oh, for God's sake. He blocked out the irksome apparition as best he could, but by then, it was too late. Because the thought of his own child had him wondering if the harlot doing her heroic best to satisfy him had any children of her own. Bastards sired by thoughtless rakehells who did as they pleased without a care for the consequences to anybody else.

And, suddenly, the guilt was enough to make his member go well and truly soft.

Thus the party ended before it had even begun. Jason looked at the ceiling, mortified. Never mind the fact that he knew full well he shouldn't even be there.

"Well, then. Thanks, anyway," he said tautly. "It would seem my mind is elsewhere."

"No matter, Your Grace." She pulled up the strap of her chemise and politely looked away while he continued mentally cursing himself and righted his clothes for the second time within the hour.

Bloody *hell!*

"What's her name, love?" the harlot asked softly, leaning against the bedpost as she studied him, trying not to smile.

Jason snorted but supposed he owed her that much. "I personally like to call her Lady Catastrophe."

The woman's eyes danced. "Aw, she can't be that bad if she can win the likes o' you."

"Trust me, she's worse. She could wreck my life. Even get me killed. But you know the most pathetic part of all?" He paused. "She'd be worth it."

"Then what are you doing here?"

He sighed. *Running away.*

"What, she's married?"

He shook his head.

"Family won't allow it? She's not of your station?"

"No, it's not that. She's perfectly suitable."

"And you love her."

"No! Not like that. She's…like a sister to me."

The blonde arched a brow. "Lord Byron's kind of sister?"

Everyone had heard those rumors.

Jason shrugged. She smiled at his look of abject misery, then reached for his hand. "You want to try again?"

"No, I think I'll just go shoot myself," he muttered dryly.

Better he do it than leave the job for Pete.

"Thanks, anyway. You were sweet," he whispered, and gave the girl a large amount of money, mostly as a bribe to keep her quiet about his failed performance, then he left.

Outside, the sunlight helped to clear his head. He looked up and down the street, wondering what next.

Right. It's over, then.

Felicity Carvel had grown up into a lovely young woman. A passionate temptress of a woman, and a medicine to his soul. But it did not signify.

One little secret dalliance between them was not the end of the world, he assured himself. No one would find out. He liked her, she liked him, and that was all it was, all it had ever been. A flirtatious little friendship, which he had just wound down, for prudence's sake.

Marriage was out of the question, no matter what she said. He was a bad man, a terrible father, and would likely be a sorry excuse for a husband, too. All he'd ever do was hurt her in the end. He knew that. And then he'd lose his best friend and his self-respect.

So, no. Felicity deserved someone who knew how to love. And she would eventually find that man.

For him, it was time to move on and forget her, just as he had done so many times before.

Unsuccessfully, his heart pointed out, to his annoyance. He scowled at the reminder.

Yes, of course, his feelings for her always seemed to come back like a fungus or a mold growing in the cellar. Dirty and black. So wrong. But no matter. He'd simply wash them out with bleach to kill them off again and find another outlet for his lust.

Because, frankly, what that beautiful innocent offered — that bright star in his dark sky — terrified him beyond measure.

# # #

Alas, avoiding Felicity proved easier said than done, because from that day on, for the next week and a half or so, the chit was everywhere he went.

It was possibly the most miserable ten days of his life. Every time he had nearly scoured her from his brain, there she was. Smiling. Laughing. Knocking him back to the starting post in his quest to forget her, while she went on living her life with or without him, just as she had said she would.

She didn't even have the decency to hate him, which would've made life so much easier.

She was everywhere, looking as beautiful as ever, even in the ugly colors of half-mourning — black and lavender, black and brown, black and white.

At the horse races, she picked the winner, while he lost twenty quid.

At the garden party, she played croquet with a pair of fops whose necks Jason wanted to break, and ate ice cream, while he watched from a distance, longing to be licked.

He even went to church on Sunday morning and panicked the fiends of hell that they had lost one of their best recruits, but they needn't have worried. It was not the sermon that interested him. He was only there so he could catch a furtive glimpse of that damned woman from several rows back.

When he saw her singing a hymn in a beam of morning sunlight, he wished Caradonna could've captured her just like that, looking like a golden-haired angel.

To his chagrin, she caught sight of him in the church and audibly stifled a laugh to find him there, of all places. As if she grasped at once the real reason he was there.

He scowled at her from his pew, but didn't wait to talk to her afterward. He stomped off, wondering if he should go touring on the Continent to escape her.

Trouble was, the only thing worse than seeing Miss Carvel everywhere was not seeing her at all.

That night, he decided this had gone far enough. He got very drunk at home alone and then sent for the two courtesans who had been with him the morning she had invaded his house.

Unfortunately, when the obligatory Ginger and Velvet arrived, he took one look at them and feared there'd be a repeat of his humiliation at the brothel. Word might start going round that he had lost his manhood, and it would all be Felicity's fault.

Dreading such rumors starting—and the vengeful laughter especially from the female populace of London—he told his doxies in slurred tones that His Grace wished to play cards with them tonight. That was all.

Cards, for God's sake! What was happening to him?

At least it was naked cards.

For every hand he won, the girls had to take off one article of clothing. Those were the rules.

But even when he had trounced them and they both sat there shivering in nothing but their stockings, he still couldn't work up the proper interest for their usual sport, so he told them to get dressed and sent them home, baffled.

And then, on day eleven, as he sat at his desk in a state of black despair, staring into space, his butler knocked.

"Enter." Jason could barely find the strength to lift his gaze in question as Woodcombe walked in, bringing a note on a silver tray.

"This just arrived for you, sir."

He grunted his disinterest.

"Ahem, it is from Miss Carvel, if you please."

"What?" He nearly fell off the chair in his scramble to grab it off the tray, then dropped the letter and bumped heads with the butler as they both stooped to reach for it. "Ow."

"Terribly sorry, sir!"

"Not your fault, Woodcombe. Are you all right?"

"Oh—yes, sir. Thank you. And you?"

He did not attempt to answer that complicated question. "Leave me. And shut the door."

Woodcombe obeyed.

Jason braced himself as he went and sat in the window nook to read Felicity's letter, his heart pounding as he slowly unfolded it. Everything in him needed to know the information it contained. And everything in him dreaded it.

Had she written to tell him exactly what a devil he was? Or worse, what if she had given up on him?

As well she might, "monster" that he was.

He had the most awful feeling she was writing to tell him she had accepted some idiot's proposal. He had seen how the young bucks all over London had worked themselves into a frenzy over her. Taking a deep breath, Jason forced himself to face it.

> *Dear You,*
> *Don't forget the ball at the Grand Albion tomorrow night. You said you'd go, remember? I'll finally be out of mourning. You* must *see my new gown. It is magnificent, as promised.*
>
> > *Love anyway,*
> > *Me*

He stared at the paper. Furrowed his brow. He turned it over to see if the expected rant was on the back, but it was blank. He turned it over and skimmed it again, confused.

That's it? he wondered, his heart pounding at the reprieve. No calamity yet? No knife in the heart? No "happy" news?

There was, however, a postscript.

> *Postscript: Have you spoken to Sanfratello yet about the sculpture we discussed for my parlor alcove? I have some ideas about what I might like. Unless you are reneging like a bounder.*

What the devil? Jason was astounded as it finally sank in that she really, truly forgave him, and was opting to pretend as though everything was normal and nothing untoward had happened between them.

Neither her near-ravishment nor their falling out.

You bullheaded girl…why won't you let me go?

But still more waited from the confounding creature:

> *Post-Postscript: Speaking of bounders, I have been matchmaking between Mrs. Brown and Cousin Gerald. I'll tell you all about it when you dance with me at the ball. You see? Perhaps there really is someone for everyone. Present company excepted.*

Ha-ha, Jason thought as a wary half-smile crept across his face, but she wasn't done teasing him in her letter, and the last part was the most pointed comment of all:

> *Post-Post-Postscript: Miss me yet?*

A rueful smile spread across his face. He shook his head. *Cheeky.* Almost as if she knew somehow that he'd thought of little else for the past week and a half.

Relieved as he was not to have to wish her congratulations on her engagement, he knew he could not afford to waver. He had done the right and proper thing by pushing her away. Time to break the bond fully now.

With a sad sigh, he walked slowly to his desk, sat down, and pulled a sheet of paper toward him. He picked up a pen, dipped it in ink, and wrote a short answer that he hoped would finally bring Felicity Carvel to her senses.

And show her that only a fool would try to love him.

Dear Me,
Regret to say am no longer going to that ball. My plans have changed.
The company there is tiresome. Wear your new gown or go starkers
for all I care. Either way, you'll be magnificent, I'm sure. But recall,
this is none of my concern.

Yours indifferently,
You

Postscript: See? I told you I actually do read my mail.

He almost wrote a second postscript to answer her final question with a no, he didn't miss her, but he couldn't bring himself to do it.

Not even he was that great a liar.

Instead, he called for his butler to take his disappointing reply to her at once, before he lost his nerve. *In for a penny, in for a pound.* He couldn't quit now, when his addiction to her was almost truly broken.

He had stayed away from her house. He had kept his distance, barely greeting her every time their paths had crossed in Society since that day. He had hung back, drawing on herculean self-control while other men had crowded around her, making sure none of them got too close.

Of course, he could still taste the sweet nectar of her body on his tongue and feel her caresses running up and down his sides. It did not signify.

The echo of her laughter haunted him like a ghost, but he wouldn't break. Not even when his whole body ached to feel her arms around him. To let her love enfold him and fix all the things in him that were so broken.

She deserved better than him.

Still, he couldn't help wondering how she had reacted upon reading his cold reply. With any luck, she hated him by now.

Then life could go back to normal.

That night, certain he was finally rid of her for good, Jason walked out to the garden park in the middle of Moonlight Square and stood in the gazebo, cloaked in shadows.

He gazed up at the white, jagged horns of the crescent moon and felt as alone as the last man on earth.

Swallowed up in darkness.

CHAPTER 10

Butterfly

*W*hen the night of the ball at the Grand Albion Assembly Rooms came, fast-moving clouds curled and whisked their way across the sky. It looked like it might storm, but so far, there was no rain. Just a warm, moist wind and a warning rumble of distant thunder every now and then.

As the ladies' carriage rolled once more into the gloomy elegance of Moonlight Square, Felicity could not deny that she was disappointed by Jason's callous response to her friendly letter. He did not seem to appreciate the courage it had taken her to send it in the first place.

But she still held out hope he might come tonight, no matter what he said.

As her coachman drove past Netherford House to join the queue of carriages waiting to let off passengers in front of the Grand Albion, she leaned to gaze out the carriage window at his dark corner mansion.

Silvered by the moonglow before the dramatic clouds could plunge his grand house into shadow once again, she saw the lightless windows and thought it looked like no one was home.

She had only seen him from a distance of late, but the Duke of Scandal did not seem to be doing too well these days. Indeed, he looked more alone than ever when their paths crossed in Society, even when surrounded by his rakehell friends. But it was his own fault, his own choice.

A lady had her limits. The friendly letter was more than he'd deserved, in truth, for the way he had walked out on her. The coward.

Still, Felicity was nervous down to the very pit of her stomach. *This might be it,* she thought grimly. She could feel him slipping through her fingers, drifting ever further away. Tonight might be her final chance to win him. If he would just *talk* to her, stop shutting her out…

One dance was all she needed and she could fix this, she was sure. At least she was allowed to dance now that she was finally out of mourning.

Dressed in her glorious new gown, this was the very best she could make herself look, and if it wasn't enough…

She swallowed hard at the thought. Of course, it took more than beauty to win a man's love, but if she could at least turn Jason's head tonight, then maybe he would talk to her, and if he would talk to her, then all hope was not yet lost.

That was, if he even came in the first place. If he didn't—if, knowing how important this was to her, he didn't show up—then she had made up her mind that their little dalliance was well and truly over. She would shut him out of her heart forever, just as he had done so easily to her. If he didn't come tonight, his absence would make it painfully obvious even to a stubborn woman like her that he *really* didn't care. That he didn't want to try, and therefore, was not worthy of her love. In which case, he could go to the devil.

While her carriage waited in the slow-moving line, Felicity watched the wind rippling through the treetops of the park at the center of Moonlight Square. They swayed as though beckoning her to come explore the night-clad garden.

She studied the place, wishing she and Jason could have strolled along the winding walks, hand in hand, or sat together in the pearl-white garden folly that she could just make out above a tuft of blowing bushes.

It's a lot of trouble to go to, remodeling this place, when I doubt you'll live here very long, he had said, predicting she'd be married and living somewhere else by the end of the Season.

Why not here with you? she wondered, glancing back at his massive house. *I know we could be happy together.*

His servants, at least, were in favor of her plan. Behind their master's back—and for his own good—his fiercely loyal staff had joined in her matchmaking effort.

They hated seeing him miserable and despaired of him ever settling down. So his adorable butler, Woodcombe, his darling old cook, Hannah, and a few others had become her trusty spies within His Grace's household, providing her with discreet intelligence on his schedule so she could appear everywhere he went and foil his efforts to forget that she existed this time.

Lucky for her, the bachelor duke's staff clearly wanted him wedded and settled down, and filling the house with children for them to spoil. Mostly, they trusted her because she was Major Carvel's sister, and they were well aware that Peter had been Jason's best mate since boyhood.

So, no, it wasn't by magic or chance or destiny that she had known when to show up where. It was all part of her relentless plan to plague the "monster" into loving her.

Indeed, she had made a bit of a game of it. She knew the old saying *Out of sight, out of mind.* She did not intend to let him do that to her again.

Jason was hers. He just didn't know it yet.

At last, their turn came to get out of the carriage and go up to the ball. Mrs. Brown swiveled her portly body toward Felicity with a surprising sparkle in her eyes.

"How do I look?" she asked eagerly.

"Gorgeous," Felicity assured her. "Gerald will be stunned."

The older woman beamed. Praise heaven, it did not seem to matter to her beefy cousin that Mrs. Brown was nearly twenty years his senior. The older woman had inherited a sizable chunk of Aunt Kirby's fortune, and unlike Felicity, *she* was willing to accept his suit.

In her early fifties, the long-widowed Anastasia Brown had given up on men ages ago. But Cousin Gerald's attentions, however unscrupulously motivated, had brought new life into her recently, and quite seemed to have turned back the clock. Mrs. Brown had been much more lively and easygoing, and literally looked ten years younger than she had just a fortnight ago.

Felicity was tickled by the change. Well, romantic pursuits did seem to have that effect on people. Aunt Kirby would have laughed merrily for hours over this.

Of course, Mrs. Brown was not blind to Gerald's dubious motives, but these did not prevent her from enjoying the long-forgotten pleasures of male attention.

And bully for her, Felicity thought. According to her dandyish cousin Charles, Gerald had quickly taken to his older woman.

Charles had privately confided to Felicity that Gerald had no success at all with ladies of his own age.

"It's those demmed ruddy jowls," the fashionable viscount had said with a disapproving frown.

"I don't think it's ruddy jowls that are his problem, coz," Felicity had answered. "More the fact that he's obnoxious."

But it seemed that Mrs. Brown had been a chaperone long enough to have learned how to snap a younger person into line, and she had put these skills to good use on Felicity's rude cousin. Gerald had begun showing signs, almost, of gallantry.

As the ladies stepped out of the carriage, the evening breeze ruffled the peacock feather in Mrs. Brown's hair and lifted the gauzy pink overskirt of Felicity's fantastic ball gown a bit, baring her ankles. She pushed it back down with a small cry and hurried across the pavement in her dainty dancing slippers, dashing up the front steps of the massive, hotel-like building.

As she stepped into the marble-floored entrance hall alongside her chaperone, she braced herself to learn whether or not Jason had come. The hall was bright and crowded and noisy, with countless conversations in progress at various levels of volume. The slow-moving queue from outside now continued on foot, inching up the grand staircase toward the fabled Assembly Rooms.

She wondered if her lovable red-haired friend Trinny would be in attendance. Her family always came, but Felicity hadn't seen the Earl of Beresford's firstborn daughter since the last time she'd attended one of these coveted events, and that had been before Aunt Kirby had passed away.

As far as Felicity knew, Trinny was still on her honeymoon in Scotland with Lord Roland, after the two had so romantically eloped. After all her disappointments in love, Trinny had captured the man of her dreams—one of the rakes from Jason's own set—and Felicity couldn't wait to hear how her friend liked married life.

She glanced around and did not see the newlyweds in the crowd, but couldn't help admiring the elegant interior of the Grand Albion as she waited in the line on the staircase. Twin colonnades of gray-veined marble flanked the huge entrance hall. Behind them, stately oak paneling went partway up the walls; above it the walls were painted dark green and adorned with masterful oil paintings in gilded frames. Brass sconces added light to the bright glow of the chandeliers overhead.

Then she spotted a quiet side corridor leading toward the back of the building. At the end of the hallway, between two potted palms, she glimpsed shining wooden double doors.

Ah, she thought. *The famous gentlemen's club at the Grand Albion.*

She knew Jason was a member because he had often taken her brother along to play cards or dine with him there. Certain rowdy things went on sometimes behind those well-polished doors. Or so she had heard.

As she continued inching up the wide, red-carpeted staircase beside her chaperone, Mrs. Brown nodded to her many acquaintances. The older set seemed stunned to see their erstwhile dowdy friend resplendently arrayed in royal blue.

For her part, Felicity soon noticed that her own gown was having the effect the modiste had promised. Indeed, she was a little taken aback to note the open stares directed her way before she had even reached the top of the staircase.

Gentlemen gawked at her from the lobby below and leaned on the railing overhead to get a better look. Despite the attention she had been subjected to since word of her fortune had got out, the way they were looking at her now felt different.

It came as rather a shock to her system. But then, she was not in regular attendance at these famous Thursday night balls at the Grand Albion, and their kind thrived on novelty.

A little overwhelmed by all the male stares, she kept her gaze down, watching her step; old habits, like her prim and proper bearing, died hard. Carefully lifting her hem a bit, she ascended the staircase. It wouldn't do to go tumbling headlong down the stairs with all these eyes upon her.

Her heart was pounding when she and Mrs. Brown finally arrived at the landing above. While Mrs. Brown handed their voucher to the majordomo, Felicity noticed one fellow nearby pointing discreetly at her and asking his comrade, "Who is that stunning creature?"

It was flattering, but only one man mattered.

Would he come?

Her heart was in her throat at the prospect of learning the answer to that as the majordomo beckoned them toward the doorway.

A silent chant ran through her mind. *Please be here. Please don't let me down. Please don't break my heart, not again, or I swear I'm done with you. It's your last chance, Jason...your last chance...*

Then the majordomo announced them. "Mrs. Anastasia Brown and Miss Felicity Carvel!"

They stepped into the vast ballroom. The brilliance of the many chandeliers and the warmth from the crowd washed over her, for it was already thronged. On tenterhooks, she scanned the glittering company. With her brittle smile pasted in place, she felt her heart slowly sinking as she searched for that one beloved face…

All London seemed to be admiring her gown in that moment, but she despaired with a sense of utter defeat. The ballroom may as well have been deserted. To her, it was as empty as the deep black pit of a dormant volcano on the far edge of the world.

He's not here.

She put her head down to hide the tears that sprang into her eyes.

"Come along, dear," murmured Mrs. Brown, well aware of Felicity's true quest here tonight.

She had not told her chaperone the full extent of what had happened between her and Jason in the parlor, but given that the whole staff knew they had spent the better part of an hour together in there with the door closed, Felicity had been forced to give some account of herself.

She had admitted only to kissing him.

Though Mrs. Brown still did not approve of the duke, the mere report of a kiss had led her scandalized chaperone to conclude that Felicity must win him.

It was the only decent outcome.

Nevertheless, Felicity had forbidden Mrs. Brown from meddling by lecturing Jason or trying to force him to comply.

"You don't understand," she had told the older woman. "I love him, I know him, and if I try to pressure him, he'll never trust me, even if he does bend to my wishes. He has to come to this decision on his own, don't you understand?" she had asked through her tears. "Because of his rank, Jason has been hounded all his life by people with ulterior motives. If we pressure him, he might assume I only risked my reputation on purpose to trick him and snare myself a duke. That I took advantage of him, just like so many others would if he let his guard down. I won't have it!"

She felt sick to her stomach now, though, for she saw it didn't matter anymore. Perhaps she should have worn a little rouge on her cheeks, for as she proceeded into the ballroom, she could feel the blood draining from her face.

He had written in his letter that he wasn't coming. *I guess he meant it.* Felicity's steps faltered. The fire in her heart that had burned for him for so long became a pile of ashes in her chest as she realized the man she loved would never love her.

"Now, now, didn't you tell me he doesn't usually come out until later in the evening?" Mrs. Brown asked under her breath.

"Yes, but he knew this time was different," Felicity whispered in a strangled tone.

Just then, from behind her, the majordomo announced a name that stopped her in her tracks. "His Grace, the Duke of Netherford!"

Felicity nearly sobbed aloud.

She caught her breath and feigned a little sneeze to explain away the tears that suddenly welled too thickly in her eyes.

"Bless you," several smiling gentlemen around her offered.

Rather mortified and not daring to turn around to see Jason, she grabbed the handkerchief out of her reticule and dabbed at her eyes, her hand shaking, fool that she was. "Oh this springtime pollen, everything is blooming…"

It was all she could do not to break down crying like a true watering pot. Good Lord, she'd had no idea she had become this fragile over the past two weeks.

But then, she wondered, how could she feel otherwise? She'd been heartlessly rebuffed again and again by the only man she had ever loved. The man who did everything he could to convince them both that he wanted nothing to do with her.

Yet here he was.

I knew it. She sniffled as she managed to get hold of herself again. *I knew he'd come. He may not love me yet, but someday, he will. He has to.*

Mrs. Brown gave her arm a discreet squeeze of encouragement. Felicity glanced at her in gratitude. With that, they proceeded into the ballroom to greet the mighty patronesses of the subscription ball.

Since the terrifying ladies had been admirers of her great-aunt and were friends with Mrs. Brown, their brief review was not as painful for Felicity as it was for most other young ladies. As she went to make her curtsy to them, she still refused to look behind her, but she was dying to see Jason's face, read his reaction to her gown, and tell him with a glance how happy she was that he was there.

Yet, strangely, at the same time, she felt a pulse of anger toward him for putting her through all this. Why did he pretend not to care about her when it was so obviously a lie? Did the fool think he was being noble?

Whatever the answers were, she struggled to get her wild swings of emotion under control, knowing she must be ready for battle when they came face to face once more.

Her decision on one point was absolutely firm, however. *I've been chasing after that rogue since I was eight years old. Tonight, for once, let him come to* me.

Resolutely turning her attention to her other admirers, she waited to see if and how Jason would approach, and how long it might take him to do so.

As it turned out, he sauntered toward her through the crowd as soon as she had extricated herself from a reluctant conversation with Cousin Gerald's friend Lord Tuttle, who was known to all as a thunderous bore.

Her heart leaped when she spotted Jason heading her way, tall and striking amid the crowd. His formal black tailcoat made his shoulders look a mile wide. He wore a snowy-white cravat and a pale silk waistcoat with small, elegant silver pinstripes.

As his gaze locked on hers with his usual stormy intensity, she tried to steady herself, unsure how this long-awaited moment might go.

Surrounded by scores of other well-heeled guests in their finery, Felicity observed the proper etiquette and curtsied to him politely. "Your Grace."

"Miss Carvel." He bowed, following suit.

Then they stared at each other in guarded silence.

"You came," she said at length, acknowledging at least that.

"Hmm. Curiosity got the better of me. I had to see this gown."

She smiled ruefully and smoothed her skirts, glancing down at herself, then gazed back up at him. "And?"

He shrugged, looking her over. "If there is a word better than *splendid*, I can't think of it right now. I seem to have lost my tongue."

She was impressed with the pretty compliment. But the mention of his tongue made her shudder with blissful remembrance...

"You look delicious," he murmured, holding her stare.

The memory of their passionate encounter on her parlor couch glowed in his dark eyes. She tucked her chin to hide her blush, pleased. Sometimes he acted so distant, she wondered if he had forgotten that day, as though the memory of her had faded into the sea of women whose favors he'd enjoyed.

Well, his days of loose living would soon come to an end if she had anything to do with it.

She gave him a hard stare. "We need to talk."

His gaze fell. "I suppose."

She reined in a quick surge of exasperation with him. "You *do* know that you owe me an apology?"

His gaze swung guardedly to hers, but he gave no reply.

A duke had his pride.

"Jason."

"Would you settle for a dance?"

Her lips twisted with wry patience in spite of herself. She let out a sigh, shook her head, and shrugged. "Why not. But you'll have to wait. I've only got one opening left on my dance billet."

"I'll take it."

"It's the last dance of the night."

She could almost hear his mental groan, but to her amusement, he suppressed it. "Let me see that."

"What, you don't believe me?" she exclaimed as he pulled her dance billet out of her hand.

"Just checking..."

Half amused and half indignant—a familiar combination when it came to him—she folded her arms across her chest and waited.

For a moment, she secretly admired his patrician profile while he studied the little printed card that listed the night's dances and the names of those to whom she had promised each one.

"Right." He gave it back to her. "I'll see you then, Miss Carvel."

She arched a brow in suspicion; he gave her a wink and sauntered away. *He's actually going to behave?*

But she should've known better.

He was Naughty Netherford, after all.

Just a few songs into the ball, the gentleman with whom she was to stand up for the fifth dance did not appear. Looking around worriedly, she moved out of the way of the couples parading toward the dance floor.

"Miss Carvel!" When the fellow hastened over to her, he looked upset.

Probably due to the large red wine stain spilled down the front of his clothes.

"Oh, Miss Carvel, I'm so sorry," the unfortunate young gentleman stammered. "I fear I've had a bit of an accident! I tripped, and I— Well, I must cry off. So embarrassing. I have to go home and change at once. My apologies."

As he dashed off, mortified by the mishap, Felicity found the Duke of Netherford standing right behind him, hands folded behind his back, a polite smile on his lips, and a sparkle of deviltry in his eyes.

"Jason," she said softly, "what did you do?"

"Sorry, I don't know what you're talking about. I am here to rescue you, my darling, from the dreaded fate of being left a wallflower. I believe a spot just opened up on your dance card?"

"Unbelievable," she said under her breath, but she refused to let him see her laugh.

He held out a white-gloved hand and waited, his other arm gracefully tucked behind his back.

"You're not a monster, you are the spawn of the devil. But so be it." She slapped her gloved hand down rather cheerfully atop his.

His fingers closed around hers. Watching her with a gleam in his eyes, he led her to the dance floor.

Felicity's pulse quickened as she reached up to rest her hand on his shoulder. "Now I know why you wanted to see the list. You didn't think I was lying."

"No. I wanted the waltz."

"You would," she replied.

"What I don't understand is why you would promise such valuable real estate on your dance billet to that jackanapes." He slid his hand around her waist and tugged her just a wee bit closer.

"Only because he's been whining to me about it since that garden party last week."

"Ha. You see?" Jason murmured. "Admit it, you're glad. I rescued you."

"I admit nothing!" she averred, trembling a little at the way he cupped her right hand gently in his left. She swallowed hard. "At least you are resourceful, I'll give you that."

He smiled, scanning the ballroom during the introductory bars of music before the dance started. Then he glanced down at her, and she looked up at him, and it was as though, instantly, all the days of loneliness and suffering and fear fell away.

One moment in his arms brought the bond between them flooding back. If this was not meant to be, then nothing was. Being with this man felt like home. Even their bodies fit together perfectly.

And, loath as she was to admit it, dancing with him was something of a lifelong dream come true.

When they were youngsters, she had often been conscripted to help him and her brother practice their lessons with the dancing master. Jason had complied only because he'd had no choice. He had grumbled his way through it and stepped on her feet repeatedly, sometimes on purpose, for which she usually kicked him in the shins, while her brother had looked on, laughing uproariously at their battles.

But he had mastered the thing by now, and so had she. Except for one dance together on the night of her debut, this was the first time he had stood up with her when they were adults.

It was blissful. Even Jason seemed a little amazed. Neither of them spoke. He finally broke the silence. "You dance beautifully, Miss Carvel."

"I like the waltz," she said, feeling slightly awkward with the intensity of whatever this was between them.

"You would," he whispered, his naughty humor never failing to put her at ease. "Well, I'm here. So what did you want to talk about?"

"Us."

"Hmm." To his credit, he didn't even blanch. "You've been turning up lately everywhere I go," he remarked in a studiedly casual tone.

"You came to my church!" she retorted.

He frowned at her briefly. "There's no law against it."

"No, but imagine my surprise." She studied his chiseled face in amusement. "Did your prayer get answered, Jason? It must've been a big one for you to venture into that place. I should hope you were repenting for your wicked ways."

"You like my wicked ways," he said very softly as he held her close. His fingers dug into her waist, a wordless reminder of the passionate incident that had taken place between them on her couch.

Felicity swallowed hard.

He was quiet for a moment. "I could've been cruel to you that day, you know."

The cocky arch of his brow informed her he was referring to how she had all but begged him to make her come. She looked away with a blush, then did her best to deflect her embarrassment with a haughty demeanor.

"Well," she said, "you've been cruel ever since."

"I have *not* been cruel!"

"Cold, then. Very cold."

He clamped his jaw shut for a moment with a growl and avoided her gaze. "I'm sorry if I hurt you. I don't know why I…why I… Oh, never mind!" he bit off, with the same frustration stamped on his face that she had seen so many times, the same inability to get out of his own way and just let go.

She held on to his hand with great tenderness, staring at him. "It would work between us if you could just believe."

"You really think it's that simple?" he muttered, cynic that he was.

"It would be, if you'd trust me. I'd never hurt you, Jason. But I won't wait forever."

He looked down at her sharply.

"You're my first choice, but you're not my only choice. Do remember that."

He had furrowed his brow, and now he glared at the crowd around them in ducal annoyance. "Miss Carvel, surely you know by now that I don't get jealous."

"Well, I do. And I don't like sharing you with a harem of other women. It's not good for you, anyway. So I'm calling your bluff, Jason."

"Meaning?" He glanced down at her with suspicion.

Felicity braced herself to utter the most audacious sentence that had ever come out of her mouth. "You are in love with me," she informed him, "and for some mystifying reason, I'm in love with you, too. So I suggest you take an honest look in the mirror and decide if it's me you want or if you'd rather keep on being the Duke of Scandal. Because you can't have both."

There. Her heart pounded with such brash vigor in her bosom that she wondered if he could feel it as he held her.

"I see." His demeanor had stiffened.

His Grace looked a bit like he wanted to flee right now. He avoided her gaze, minding the steps of the dance with great care, as though he suddenly feared they might both go sprawling.

"So, you know my very heart, then?" he asked at last through gritted teeth. "My private emotions?"

"They're pretty transparent, Jason."

He eyed her warily. "I don't like being given ultimatums."

"And I don't like being treated as though I'm worthless. It hurts me, you know."

The confession seemed to rein in his temper abruptly. "Th-that wasn't my intention."

"I realize that. But there comes a point, my darling man, when good intentions aren't good enough. I need—no, I *deserve* more."

He was silent for a moment, as though unable to argue that point, but wanting to say *something* for his pride's sake. "I see. So is this the part where you get your way again by threatening to tell your brother about us?"

She lost patience as the dance ended. "My brother has no part in this! This is between you and me." Fed up with him, she released him as though touching him had burned her, and started to walk away.

"Felicity," he said.

Despite her better judgment, she paused and looked over her shoulder at him.

His face was stark. He took a deep breath. "I *have* missed you. Terribly."

Her heart leaped, but she shot back, "Good," and started to leave him again.

"Felicity," he repeated, more insistently this time, as she spotted Mrs. Brown beckoning to her.

"What?" she exclaimed, glancing back at him again.

He gazed at her with a slightly chastened expression. "Shall I call on you in a day or two? Tomorrow, perhaps?"

"That is entirely up to you, Your Grace."

"But will you be at home?" he demanded, realizing he had behaved badly enough, it seemed, to warrant being turned away at the door like her other suitors when she didn't feel like seeing them.

After what he had put her through, Felicity could not help relishing this one moment of uncertainty she had struck in his arrogant heart, overcoming his gargantuan selfishness and even his ducal pride.

"We'll see," she said with a noncommittal shrug, then returned to her chaperone.

As she strode across the ballroom, her magnificent gown floating out behind her, Felicity's step was light, her heart lifting with the first intimations of her inevitable victory.

By God, she'd bring the rogue to heel within a fortnight.

CHAPTER 11

Temper, Temper

What a debacle. Hours later, after the ball had ended, Jason wandered down to his club on the first floor of the Grand Albion to have a stronger drink and brood.

Irritating woman. Wasn't it enough that he had simply shown up? He did not appreciate Felicity trying to back him into a corner. Of course, he did not like hearing, either, that he had hurt her.

He let out a grim sigh and sat in a wing chair in the shadows, ignoring his club mates playing billiards nearby.

Oh, he knew what she wanted. She had made it very clear. Had warned him in no uncertain terms that her offer to give him the love he craved so much would soon expire.

You are in love with me, and for some mystifying reason, I'm in love with you, too. To her, it was that simple. But she had not blundered her way through the number of disastrous affairs that he had over the years, hurting others, hurting himself. In his experience, love meant pain.

Felicity was still relatively unscathed, and he dreaded trying to love her and botching the thing. What if he hurt her? Disappointed her? Failed in the relationship, as he'd failed so many times?

He took another swig from his glass and stared into space.

To be sure, this particular dance between them had been going on for a long time now. He supposed he couldn't blame her for tiring of it. A woman wanted certain things out of life.

So she had demanded a decision from him tonight, one Jason had thought he had already made. But she had persisted just that little bit longer, hanging on to him in subtle ways, just as she'd always done, refusing to let him fully walk away.

And now that it came down to it, he had to face the truth. That he could not bear the thought of losing her. Losing what she alone gave him.

Still, he was not resolved to it at all.

Yes, he had already opened Pandora's box when he had pleasured her that sweet afternoon in the parlor, but if he moved forward with this, how would he explain the change of circumstances to her brother when Pete got back to Town?

And what on earth would he say to Felicity about his children?

Would she even still want him if she knew?

He let out another low sigh, looked at his again-empty glass, and wondered why the liquor wasn't helping.

"Netherford, ol' boy, fancy a game of speculation? Ten guinea ante tonight," Lord Sidney called with his usual sunny grin.

Jason shook his head. While several other rakehells in his set sat down to play, he remained by himself in the corner, pondering his tangled existence, and feeling damned if he did and damned if he didn't.

He wasn't really listening to the other men around the room, but he half-heard some ask if their friend, Gable, Viscount Roland, was ever coming back from Scotland with the bride he'd snatched away in their elopement last month. This roused irreverent laughter from the rakes, who clinked glasses and made toasts: "Better him than us."

A new round of players took over the billiard table. Some fellows ordered food from the kitchens while others joined the card game taking shape at the long, narrow table. A small knot of men were smoking by the open French doors to the terrace. They did not step outside, however, for the storm that had been threatening all night had finally broken.

Rain lashed at the club's windows. Sidney and the other card players counted to three in unison and then carried the table farther away from the open doors so they might enjoy the night air without having to worry about their cards blowing away.

As they set it down again and carried the chairs over to their new location, a snippet of conversation from another region of the club drew Jason's ear.

The tipsy dandies lounging around on the leather club chairs and settees in front of the fireplace were bantering over the club's infamous betting book, which lay open on the low table in the middle.

Jason glanced over, saw who it was, and arched a brow in sardonic suspicion. *Oh Lord, they're here again.*

A rival set of rakehells to his own—Lord Alec Knight and his ridiculous friends, Lords Rushford, Fortescue, and Draxinger. They held memberships at the Grand Albion, but usually ruled the roost over at White's, at least now that Beau Brummell had fallen from grace.

"Egads, that girl's got a body on her, what? I can't believe I never even noticed her before," the blond-haired youngest of the innumerable Knight brothers slurred.

"Sweet heaven, yes, and those charms were on full display tonight, I daresay." Draxinger hiccupped.

"Aye, I couldn't stop staring at her bosom," Rushford, the heir to a marquessate, declared, blunt as usual. "Well, she's fair game, now that she's out of mourning."

At that, Jason's full attention suddenly homed in on the men.

He lifted his head and swiveled around in his chair to stare at them in disbelief. *They can't be talking about…*

"Did you get to dance with her?" Lord Alec asked his mates.

"Twice!" Draxinger boasted.

"I'd like to do some dancing with that lass myself…between the sheets," said Rushford.

Raucous laughter broke out among the scoundrels, and Jason stared murderously at them from the shadows.

Lord Alec laughed and loosened his cravat. "Well, you must admit she makes an irresistible little package—that face, that body, and a fortune to boot. I'm telling you, boys, Miss Carvel's all mine. You'll see. I'm not keen on marriage, God knows, but a younger son's got to do what he must."

"Well, don't count your winnings just yet, m'friend," Rushford warned, flashing a wolfish grin. "I rather fancy her myself. And when the rest of you fail in our wager, you're all going to owe me a lot of money."

Jason shot up out of his chair.

Wager?

"Personally, I don't give a fig about the money," Fortescue declared, slurring with drink. "I just want to give her a good rogerin'. So whichever of you ends up marryin' the chit, I hereby warn you in advance that I intend to cuckold you…eventually."

"You wish!" Lord Alec scoffed, and gave his mate an easy punch in the arm.

Pulse pounding, Jason somehow checked his outrage as he strolled over to the miscreants clustered around the betting book.

"Ho, Netherford," Lord Alec greeted him. "Now here's a duke I can stand, unlike that stiff-necked, top-lofty prig, my dear brother. Care to join our wager concerning this lovely little morsel, Miss Carvel?"

"You got to dance with her tonight, didn't you?" Draxinger pursued, then waved a finger at him. "Yes, I saw you with her...lookin' quite cozy, at that."

Jason didn't answer.

Fortescue squinted at him, then turned to Rushford. "What's wrong with 'im?"

"Aw, you're not going to take our little game wrong on account of her brother, are you?" Rushford goaded him, then told his comrades, "Those two are friends."

"Ah, not Netherford! His Grace has never lacked a sense of humor," Draxinger defended him. "He's one of us, my lads! A rake of the first order, remember? Besides, Major Carvel's on the other side of the world from what I hear. What he don't know won't hurt 'im, what-hey, Netherford?"

Jason glanced at the intoxicated dandy with daggers in his eyes, but still said not a word. Instead, he leaned down and studied the betting book. There, the open page revealed a list of entries from men who had laid wagers on which of them would succeed with Felicity.

The writing blurred as rage flooded into Jason's veins.

Under normal circumstances, cynic that he was, this sort of idle game might've whetted his competitive streak. It was possible he'd have joined in the jolly foxhunt after some new belle who was currently all the rage.

But not this time.

Violence welled up in his breast. His club mates were oblivious, laughing about which of them would bed her first.

Deflower *his* Felicity.

And then Jason simply went berserk.

Without warning, he reached for the bastard to his right—Fortescue—who was in the middle of uttering another ill-advised boast. "Don't worry, boys, I'll tell you all about it once I get her on her bac—"

He didn't get to finish the sentence, for suddenly, he was flying headfirst through the air, soaring toward the card game, arms flapping.

The drunken wastrel went crashing onto the table, knocking cards and ivory chips about in all directions. His flailing feet and arms knocked several men's drinks onto them, and the whole club exploded into chaos.

Fortescue's mates jumped to their feet, shouting at this crazed attack on their friend. Rushford's fist flew at Jason. He blocked it, slamming his own into the blackguard's face in a fury. Draxinger dove aside, so Jason lunged at Lord Alec—who might actually have a chance with her, given his irritating good looks.

But too bad. None of them could have her. None of them had better even think about it. Jason unleashed his wrath on them all for discussing their fantasies of doing things to Felicity that no one else on earth was allowed to do but him.

Ever.

Surely you know by now I don't get jealous, darling. He could have laughed with barbarity as he recalled his own futile claim to her earlier this evening. Why, he hadn't even realized himself that he felt quite so strongly about these matters until he had already launched into battle.

Rushford came back and tried to grab him from behind, and Jason dropped him with an elbow to the face. All the suffering and frustration of the past two weeks came bursting out in an unpremeditated explosion.

He did not care how many bastards he had to fight. He was outraged and needed to hit someone.

The lads piled on him. Four, five, six of his fellow club mates joined the fray, many of them peers. On this, at least, Whigs and Tories united, working as one to bring the "monster" down and put an end to his sudden, baffling rampage.

Jason was heedless of the blows raining on him from all directions, though he could hear Sidney yelling in the background at the others to get the hell off him. Despite at least four men who had barreled him onto the floor, variously sitting on him and pummeling him, one with a forearm locked around his neck—Jason believed it belonged to Lord Alec—he nevertheless crawled his way over to the betting book, grabbed it, and then struggled on hands and knees over to the fireplace, tearing out pages as he went.

"Nooooo!" several clubmen yelled when they realized his intention—his mate Sidney included.

But they were too late. He pitched the sacred thing into the flames with a savage roar.

Seeing this, even the chaps who had found the brawl amusing up to that point grew enraged, for the club's betting book was an object of reverence among the members, not to mention a source of income for many.

His Grace of Netherford did not give one iota of a damn.

Rivenwood arrived just then, saw what was afoot, and jumped into the fray, pulling the bleeders off him.

His fellow duke yanked Jason to his feet. "What the hell is going on here?" he demanded.

"Netherford's gone frothing mad!" Rushford shouted, wiping a trickle of blood off the corner of his mouth.

"He's possessed!" Draxinger opined.

"Or possibly in love," Lord Alec grumbled from a safer distance, rubbing his bruised jaw.

"Sod off!" Jason retorted, turning to Rivenwood and pointing at the whole loathsome pack of wolves. "They insulted the honor of a fine young lady in my hearing. You will not speak of her that way ever again!" he bellowed at them, and when Alec dared to smile as if this were amusing, Jason lunged at the blackguard.

Rivenwood jumped between them. "Have you taken leave of your senses, man?"

"I'm warning you," Jason snarled past him at them all, his chest heaving. Rivenwood held him back. "I'll bury you if I ever hear any of you speak of Felicity Carvel like that again!"

He did not care if he had to undertake a milling match against the entire male population of London on his own, and the whole damned British Army, too.

Such bandying about of her name had made him feel like he'd swallowed a tiger, and it was clawing from inside him to get out and tear them all apart.

Meanwhile, Sidney and the rest of his friends and neighbors from Moonlight Square gaped at Jason in utter astonishment. They exchanged several glances, looked around at the clubroom he had half destroyed, and despite a few of the men being even more bloodied and bruised than he—perhaps they were too drunk to care—they finally started laughing.

"What?" he nearly howled at them in rage.

"Well, well! Can it be?"

"Has somebody *finally* overthrown the great seducer?"

"Aye, she's conquered him," someone in the back said.

"Netherford wants Miss Carvel for himself!"

Even Sidney stifled a short bark of laughter.

"I'm warning you," Jason panted with a glare full of wrath.

"Yes, I think you've made your point, Your Grace," someone huffed.

"All in favor of blackballing Netherford from this club, say aye," one of the older gents announced, scowling at Jason for his utter breach of decorum.

"Now I'm sure that's not necessary," Rivenwood hastened to protest before they could start the vote.

But Jason ranted on, ignoring his only certain ally in the room. "Blackball *me*? I'm not the one speaking filth about an innocent young woman—making sport of her virtue! How dare you discuss this lady in such a fashion? You're not worthy of her, none of you! You're dirt beneath her feet, and if you ever even *look* at her again, I'll put a hole in every last one o' you bastards!"

"God, man, you've got it bad," Sidney said, shaking his head at him in shock.

"Must be he's already bedding her," one of the cardplayers said sagely.

"No!" Jason uttered, aghast that this rumor should start going around.

"With her brother away, who's to stop him?" someone in the back murmured.

"Ah, damn. Netherford hardly needs the Kirby fortune," one said with a jealous frown.

"So, how was she, Netherford?" Fortescue baited him. "Did she cry when you plucked her little cherry?"

He lurched toward the feckless fool, but Rivenwood held him back again.

"Easy! That will do, Your Grace," Rivenwood said through gritted teeth, shoving him firmly toward the door. The pale-haired duke held the rest of them at bay while steering Jason toward the exit with a hand planted on his shoulder. "Let it be, you lot. You know Netherford is a longtime family friend of the Carvels. He's known the girl since she was a child and obviously regards her as a member of his own household. So I suggest you mind your tongues. I daresay you're lucky Major Carvel isn't here. Otherwise, he'd probably kill the lot of you."

"And I'd second him!" Jason barked as Rivenwood pushed him out the door with an exasperated "Enough!"

Outside, it was raining hard. Jason's clothes were instantly soaked, his hair plastered to his head. Actually, though, he welcomed the downpour. The cold dousing helped to calm his fury and clear his mind.

Rivenwood stayed under the eaves, sensible chap, and left him alone for a moment. "You all right?" he called at length over the drumming of the rain on the pavement.

Jason grunted and paced a bit, then turned to him. "Thanks."

The mysterious, platinum-haired duke shook his head. "I hope you were planning on marrying that girl. Because if not, you *do* realize you've just destroyed her reputation?"

Jason went motionless. "I'm not the one that made that filthy wager!"

"Oh, it wasn't your intention to make every man in that room believe you've already staked a claim on her?"

"But I..." He faltered.

"A mere *friend* to a lady doesn't react like quite that much of a lunatic, Netherford. At least that's what the world is going to think. Then there's your own unique reputation to consider. Your past history?"

Jason leaned his forehead against the nearby lamppost and groaned. *Bloody hell,* he thought as a shred of sanity started to return. Enough, at least, for it to sink in, what he had just done.

His club mates' wager over Felicity had been bad enough, but at least they had been discreet. *His* sudden attack of insanity had been anything but.

Rivenwood was right. It seemed the Duke of Scandal had struck again. By morning, this tale was going to be all over London. And the *ton* would draw its own conclusions, based on his past behavior.

They would surely conclude he was already engaging in a dalliance with the ravishing Miss Carvel.

And, let's be honest. They'd be right.

God. Despite his best efforts to stay away from her over the past few years, so that everything would be proper and correct between them, his outburst in there had just encircled Felicity in scandal.

And there was only one way to fix it.

He was still slightly in shock as Rivenwood shook his head at him. "I'll see what I can do." With that, the elegant, enigmatic duke went back inside to try to smooth things over on his behalf.

Dazed, Jason turned to stare into Moonlight Square, the rain running down his face, dripping off his nose, and moistening his lips like Felicity's sweet kisses.

I have to warn her. I've got to tell her what I've done.

She was *not* going to be happy about this.

Or maybe she would, on second thought. But whether she was or wasn't, now they had no choice.

Careful what you wish for, sweeting.

Already soaked to the skin, he did not bother avoiding puddles but clomped right through them. Shoes squishing, he marched into the dark streets…

Off to go and get himself a wife.

CHAPTER 12

Scandal's Darling

Though the ball had ended and the servants had gone to bed,
Felicity was still wide-awake after all the excitement. She
could not possibly have fallen asleep in her joy over the
progress she had made with Jason tonight. The driving rain beating on
the windowpanes and the rumbles of thunder moving over the city only
added to her restlessness, so she crept through the house and went out
to sit on the covered side porch.

Curling up in a cushioned wicker chair, she drew her legs up to her
chest, crossed her arms atop her bent knees, and tucked the white linen
of her long night rail around her. She was enjoying watching the rain
from her cozy spot beneath the shelter of the porch roof. She rested her
chin on her crossed arms and savored her memories of dancing with
Jason at the ball. She chuckled as she recalled his rascally ploy for stealing
the waltz from her expected partner.

I knew all hope wasn't lost.

As the spring rain pounded upon the open portion of the terrace,
watered the garden, and blew through the trees, she smiled also to know
that she wasn't the only woman who had triumphed tonight.

Mrs. Brown had gone to an after-theater party at a friend's house
with Cousin Gerald. It had taken all of Felicity's self-control not to laugh
outright when, upon stepping out of the Grand Albion to wait for their
carriage to take them home, her chaperone had nervously turned to her
and, in hushed tones, asked *her* permission to go out, looking rather
scandalized at herself.

Felicity had encouraged her to go and have fun. Lord knew the woman had every right to become a merry widow after so many years of being a sad one. So, the newly fashionable Mrs. Brown had gone dashing off with her younger man, while Felicity had ridden home in Lady Kirby's town coach by herself.

It was now nearly two in the morning and Mrs. Brown still had not come home. Felicity suspected she would not see her until tomorrow morning. *My, my.* What she and portly Cousin Gerald might be doing right now, Felicity did not want to know. She shuddered at the thought.

Just then, she spotted the lone figure of a man walking down the street. *At this hour?* she thought, bemused. *In the middle of a rainstorm? Hmm. Must be drunk.*

But the man didn't move like a drunkard. In fact, as her stare homed in on the tall, solitary figure, she detected something familiar about the way he walked, tromping through the puddles like a master of the earth.

Whoever he was, she hoped he didn't see her sitting outside in her night rail. She had not expected to encounter anyone at this hour. She believed she was pretty well out of view in the shelter of the porch, as long as he didn't look her way. She squinted in his direction, wondering if she ought to go inside.

Fortunately, he seemed too well dressed to be a robber. Even from this distance, his black and white formal evening clothes were easily discernible, though these were surely ruined by the rain.

When he passed by one of the streetlamps lining her genteel Mayfair lane, she saw that his cravat hung undone, his midnight hair was soaked through and dripping—

She gasped with recognition and shot to her feet.

Jason!

He vaulted over the waist-high fence around her garden and landed with a *squish*.

Dread gripped her. *Something must be wrong.* Good God! Was there news of her brother? Had Peter's ship sunk?

As he began to march across the garden toward the terrace and the porch, Felicity walked over to the edge of the shelter, her heart pounding.

"Jason? What are you doing here?" she called in a shaky voice as loudly as she dared. "What's happened?"

He stopped, as though she had startled him out of his own dark musings.

"Oh," he said, pausing awkwardly. "You're awake. Good."

"Yes, I-I couldn't sleep after the ball. My brain wouldn't be quiet."

Shaking her head, she brushed off the small talk. "Jason, why are you walking the streets of London in the rain at this hour? What's wrong?"

He let out a wet sigh, blowing raindrops off his lips as he drifted over to the edge of the slightly elevated terrace; standing in the grass, he was still tall enough to rest his elbows on the wide stone balustrade around it.

Felicity remained beneath the shelter of the porch and folded her arms across her chest. "Jason, please, you're scaring me. You're acting a little mad."

He gazed at her for a long moment in misery from across the distance between them.

"I can't take it anymore," he finally said in a low tone. "I have to be with you."

Her eyes widened and her heart lurched with astonishment.

"I love you," he said with an air of defeat, barely audible beneath a rumble of thunder and the drumming of the rain on the flagstones. He shook his head, holding her shocked stare. "I do. You were right all along. I can't fight it anymore. I've tried the best I can. Your brother's just going to have to shoot me if he doesn't like it. Because there's never been anybody else for me but you. Not really. It might have looked otherwise on the outside, but the truth—"

She didn't let him finish, rushing across the wet flagstones to him in a few swift strides, heedless of the rain instantly wetting her head and shoulders, and the small puddles splashing under her bare feet.

Standing on the terrace above him, she planted her hands on his broad shoulders and leaned down across the balustrade, kissing him square on his warm, wet lips.

He tilted his head back and cupped her nape, accepting her kiss with fiery need. "Oh God, Felicity," he whispered after a moment as the rain coursed down his face. "I want you so bad." He gripped her shoulder and looked up into her eyes. "I cannot live without you anymore. I won't. You win…just like you always knew you would. You *have* to marry me. I need you."

She stared at him in tender amazement.

With an air of desperation, Jason kissed the hand she had pressed to his face. "*Please* don't choose right now to punish me for being an idiot, even though I deserve it—"

"I don't want to punish you at all. I love you, too, Jason. You know I always have."

He closed his eyes, shivering a little. "You have no idea how much I needed to hear that tonight. Could you say it again?"

"I love you," she repeated, leaning closer to breathe the words twice more in his ear.

Then she pulled back a little and studied him, mystified. "Am I dreaming, or did you just ask me to marry you?"

"It was more of an order, actually," he admitted.

A fond smile flashed across her face. "Of course it was."

"Well? Would you please answer the bloody question?"

"Hmm…an order?"

"Felicity!"

Laughing, she put her arms around him. "Of course I'll marry you, you big dunderhead. It's all I've ever wanted. Don't you know that by now?"

He gazed lovingly at her, smiling at her taunts. "I suppose I do."

She humphed. "It took you long enough."

"Forgive me," he whispered.

"Of course I forgive you, my darling." She took his face between her hands and kissed him gently again, stunned, indeed, overwhelmed with emotion to think he would truly be hers, at long last.

"Are you all right?" he murmured, caressing her arms, when he felt her tremble.

She nodded, blinking away faint tears of joy. "You know, I *would* say I'm glad you've finally seen reason, but I'm not entirely sure the phrase fits, considering we are standing in the rain. Um, what are we doing out here? Besides getting wet, of course."

He sighed. "It's a long story."

"Well, come into the house, you silly man. You're soaked to the skin. We should probably get you out of those wet clothes." She gave him a naughty little smile and ran her fingers through his dripping-wet hair.

He moaned as she leaned down from her higher position on the terrace, playfully drinking the rain off his cheeks. She kissed him all over his face.

"Why must you tease me, Felicity? I've wanted you for so long. This is just torment," he breathed as she clung to him.

"Come inside," she whispered, nuzzling his face with her nose, "and I'll give you what you want."

He pulled back a little and stared at her, looking slightly frantic at her invitation. "We should stay out here, sweet. If we start, I don't know if I'll be able to hold bac—"

"Hush." Daring him with a defiant stare to try to stop her, she climbed up onto the stone railing, then over it, and into his arms.

Jason clutched her to him, kissing her with wild passion as she wrapped her legs around his waist, her arms around his neck, now as drenched with rain as he was. He pressed her back against the stone ledge of the terrace while his tongue swirled in her mouth. His body throbbed against hers, and the chilly rain turned to steam where it touched their fevered skin.

"Please let it be tonight," she whispered between kisses. *Then you can't change your mind about this.*

"Are you sure that's what you want? Are you ready for me, Felicity?" he ground out, pinning her against the stone wall.

She clutched him harder, thrilled to her core by his sensuous growl. She stared into his eyes. "I've been ready for you for a very long time, my love."

He kissed her again in savage hunger, pausing only to watch where he was going as he carried her up the stone steps and back into the shelter of the porch. There he set her down on her feet, his stare devouring her as it moved down over her body.

"So beautiful," he whispered hoarsely. She followed his gaze as he let it travel slowly over her, taking in the sight of her rain-dampened night rail clinging to her body, her erect nipples visibly darker through the semitransparent cloth. She groaned when he touched them, and then he bent his head to lick a water droplet running down her chest.

She was shaking with desire when she took his hand a moment later, looked at him without a word, and led him into the house. Both caught up in their intense awareness of each other, Jason shut the door quietly behind them and locked it, while she went and retrieved the small, punched-copper lantern she had left burning on the pier table as a nightlight.

She picked it up to let its dim glow show the way and turned to him, lifting a finger to her lips—and then to his—to signal for silence.

We mustn't wake the servants, she told him with her gaze. He captured her finger in his mouth, seducing her where they stood with one of his devilish stares. Unable to resist, she stepped back into his arms and began kissing him once more.

Fearing they'd never make it to her bed but succumb to their passion right here in the hallway, she ended the kiss, shaking her head at him in blushing exasperation.

Come on! she mouthed at him. The blasted stairwell was not where she intended to lose her virginity.

He feigned a chastened look of obedience, his dark hair falling across his brow. She looked at him and wanted to kiss him all over his wonderful body, but she bit her lip and found her patience with a sigh. Then she led him by the hand as they tiptoed upstairs to her bedchamber.

He left wet footprints and small puddles as they went, evidence of their misbehavior, but she was past caring. It was her house, her life, her body, to give to whom she willed.

Besides, he was to be her husband.

Still reeling from his proposal, she fetched a couple of towels from the closet on the way, already fantasizing about how he'd look naked.

When they arrived at her chamber, Jason locked the door behind him while she set the little lantern on the chest of drawers. She paused to make sure the curtains were firmly drawn across the windows, and when she turned around to face him, she found him still leaning with his back against the door.

He gazed at her, looking just a wee bit overwhelmed by what was finally happening between them.

Felicity did not intend to give him the chance to go all virtuous on her again, as he had tried to do that lovely afternoon in the parlor. She brought the towel over to him and lifted a corner of it to his face, blotting away some of the rain. She wasted no time in drawing his untied cravat off his neck and parting the top of his shirt to touch his muscled chest.

"I love your body," she murmured.

"Likewise, my lady." But he caught her hand and stopped her caresses. "There's something I have to tell you first, though."

"Oh, Jason, I really don't feel like talking." She pressed herself against him, running her hand down his side. "Why don't we get out of these wet clothes, hmm?"

"No—Felicity, there's something you need to know first. If I don't tell you now, you'll be angry at me later," he said softly, leaning his head back against the door.

She furrowed her brow and looked askance at him. "Very well. What is it?"

He took the towel from her and wiped his hair. The expression on his face alerted her that he was not really keen to impart whatever it was he had to tell her.

"I, er, I made a mistake, Felicity. Well, it's just…I'm pretty sure I caused a scandal tonight after the ball," he said. "Concerning us."

Her eyebrows rose. She took a small step back. "Oh?"

"But maybe it *wasn't* really a mistake," he amended. "Because it seems to have brought so much into crystal-clear focus for me. Things…I didn't really see before. Wouldn't let myself see. Like the fact that I've been in love with you for as long as I can remember, and that's the truth."

She quaked at his darling confession but folded her arms across her chest, searching his face. "What happened, Jason?"

He sighed. "Well, for starters, I got thrown out of my club. After the ball, I mean."

"For what?"

"Punching a few people. Burning the wager book."

She arched a brow and searched his face, baffled and slightly amused. "Is that why you were walking in the rain? You were angry at your friends?"

"No, no. Not really. I just needed to think. And I needed to see you." He hesitated. "You're not going to like hearing this, I must warn you."

"All right," she said cautiously, and waited.

"There were a few chaps speaking about you at the club in a manner I didn't appreciate. Admirers of yours, of course, but they were being rather too lewd for my liking. And, well, let's just say all London knows exactly how I feel about you now. Nearly before I did," he added. "Honestly, I don't know where it all came from. I just…I heard their crude remarks about you and it seems I went berserk."

"Oh, Jason, what did you do?" she chided fondly.

"Got into a milling match. Thrashed a few chaps. Got thrashed a bit myself. And like I said, I tossed the club's betting book into the fireplace. I think I'm blackballed for that, but I'm not entirely sure. Didn't wait around to find out."

"You did all that just because of me?" she asked, ridiculously flattered. "Defending my honor?"

He scowled. "You're missing the point, love. They made a wager over you—who would win you!"

"Me?" she echoed in surprise.

"Yes, you, and I wasn't going to countenance that! I don't know what came over me. I suppose…everything I've been trying not to feel was just suddenly *there*. And it all came barreling out in the most…disgraceful fashion," he said with a wince. "The point is, in hindsight, my reaction may have been worse than the wager itself. That's why I had to see you tonight. I had to warn you, Felicity. By morning, the whole *ton* will be gossiping about us, and—me being me—some will probably speculate that we've already...you know."

"Made love?" she whispered in anticipation.

He nodded, and she could see in his eyes that he wanted it as much as she did. Perhaps even more.

But then a worrisome thought managed to pierce through her haze of desire. "So, we *have* to marry, then? Oh, Jason..." She suddenly closed her eyes. "Please tell me that's not the only reason you proposed." She flicked her eyes open in distress. "To shield my reputation? Out of duty? Respect for my brother?"

"*No!*" he whispered fiercely. He leaned closer and stared hard into her eyes. "Felicity, I'm in love with you. What happened at the club merely forced me to face it. This has nothing to do with your brother; it's about us. I'm here because you and I belong together. I know that as well as you do, and I'm done hiding from it."

Relief flowed through her as she held his gaze. How could she be angry at him when he looked at her like that? When he spoke so frankly from the heart?

"I have to thank you for your patience with me," he continued in a softer tone as he reached for her hand and drew her to him. "It seems some of us males are just too thick or too stubborn to admit how we really feel until it slams us in the face. Literally."

"Poor thing," she murmured with a tender smile, lifting her hand to his brow. "Now that you mention it, your left eye does look a little swollen, I think."

"Kiss it for me," he mumbled with a playful little sulk. He leaned down to let her brush a very light kiss to his brow, where he had apparently been pummeled.

She shook her head wryly. "I can't believe you got into a brawl over me. A duke!"

"Dukes get angry, too," he grumbled.

"You *promise* you didn't propose tonight just because you feel obligated?"

"Felicity." He slid his arms around her waist and gazed into her eyes. "I'm here because I love you and I'll wither up and die if you don't marry me." He lowered his head. "I am sorry I caused a scandal, though."

She caressed his chest. "Ah, don't worry, I knew what I was getting into with *you*, sir. But, really, if they're going to accuse us anyway, don't you think we might as well be guilty of the crime?"

"Oh, I agree," he said, running a hand down her back. "But there is the small matter of your reputation. That is, won't you be ruined?"

"Hmm, it seems fitting for a girl set to marry the Duke of Scandal." She chuckled when he grimaced at the nickname. "Darling, first of all, you're standing in my bedchamber. I'd say I've been teetering on ruin since that day in the parlor, and I regret it not a whit." She bit her lip and smiled at the memory.

As did he.

She walked her fingers down his chest and continued. "Secondly, girls who are engaged to dukes don't *get* ruined, you see. It's socially impossible."

"It is?"

"Indeed. We're far too important," she teased. "As long as your little heir doesn't arrive too far in advance of the usual nine months—as best I understand it, mind you—dukes and their future duchesses are fairly well immune to such rules."

"Is that so?" He lowered his head.

She searched his face, noticing the deeper angst that briefly seemed to flit behind his dark eyes. "Jason, what is it?"

"I'm afraid there's something *else* I have to tell you."

She shook her head. "No. No more talking. Take your clothes off, now."

"I beg your pardon?" he asked abruptly.

"You heard me. As your future wife, I want you out of those wet clothes before you catch your death."

He narrowed his eyes. "You are a saucy thing, you know that?"

"That's why you love me," she said sweetly. "Besides, you need a firm hand."

"Hmm. I'm beginning to think you know me too well."

"But not yet in the biblical sense, which I'm very keen to do. Strip, Duke."

"Yes, ma'am." A roguish smile spread across his lips as he apparently decided that, whatever else was troubling him, it could wait. They had more pressing matters to attend to. "But, darling, you're wet, too," he chided, plucking at her night rail.

When his touch grazed her nipple, both their flirtatious smiles faded.

All that was left was the raw need so long denied. He took hold of her elbow and pulled her up against his big, hard body.

She stepped into his arms as his lips swooped down onto hers. His tongue plunged into her open mouth; his hands captured her face, caressed her neck. She grasped the lapels of his ruined black tailcoat and pushed it almost roughly off his shoulders, suddenly trembling with the craving to feel his bare skin against hers.

Likewise inspired, Jason slipped his hand inside the vee-shaped neckline of her night rail. A pained sound of lust escaped him as he cupped her bare breast in his warm, large hand. Her chest heaved as he fondled her. Kissing him endlessly, Felicity fumbled with the buttons on his waistcoat. Heady moans escaped her as she worked, and before long, she had stripped it off him.

At once, he pulled his damp shirt off over his head. She bit her lip, staring with unabashed pleasure at the muscles rippling down his abdomen. Swept up in her yearning, she indulged herself with kissing his sculpted chest and his quivering stomach while her hand wandered lower.

It was not the first time she had caressed his hardness through his clothing, but tonight, still leaning against her bedroom door, Jason unfastened the placard of his trousers as he went on kissing her, untied his drawers, and gently guided her hand to touch him with no more barrier between them.

She groaned, pausing in kissing him, though his lips still covered hers. She let her fingers run slowly down the towering length of his thick, rigid manhood to its furred root. He dropped his head back against the door with a whispered groan as she wrapped her hand around his shaft and explored in fascination.

All this is supposed to fit inside me? It did not seem possible. And her touch only made him larger, harder, yet clearly gave him profound pleasure. She remembered what he had done to her that day in the parlor and mused on what might happen if she did something similar to him.

Intrigued to find out, she kissed her way down below his navel, going slowly to her knees.

He watched her in the dim candlelight, riveted, encouraging her with a coaxing stroke of his thumb across her swollen lips, parting them.

She obliged him, taking his member into her mouth, as much as she could fit. She had to open wide, but even then, could manage only a few inches of its smooth head. The rest she gripped with her hand. He sank back against the door, uttering an expletive of outrageous bliss as she licked the warm, damp hint of rain off him slowly.

His hands alighted on her head, and he smoothed her hair back from her face, watching her repay the favor with a look of complete intoxication.

"Oh, Felicity, a lady doesn't do those sorts of things," he chided breathlessly after a few minutes.

She eased it from her mouth with a naughty little nibble on the tip. "I won't tell if you won't."

He gripped her shoulder. "Come here," he growled. He lifted her almost roughly to her feet to claim the mouth that had pleasured him.

She thrilled to his demand as he tore her night rail off her.

"Get in the bed," he ordered. He kicked off his shoes and quickly shed the rest of his clothes while she obeyed.

As she lay down, his blazing stare devoured her waiting, naked body. He wrenched the covers back and slid her under them for warmth. Then he climbed into bed with her, looming above her on all fours.

She arched her back beneath him, trembling as she waited for him to ravish her. She braced herself for the pain that she'd heard could be a part of this, the first time. But perhaps he had read a certain degree of anxiety in her eyes, for he checked his raging passion, and succumbed to a doting half-smile.

"Don't be nervous. I'll take good care of you, I promise."

"I know," she murmured.

Then he proceeded to kiss his way up and down her body, paying particular attention to her breasts and her belly and the juncture of her thighs, until she writhed with need, clutching the covers and biting back moans that might've been loud enough to wake the servants.

"Do you want me now?" he teased at her ear.

"Oh God, Jason, *yes*."

She dug her fingers into his back, undulating with impatience. Leaning on his elbows, he kissed her with deep, drugging slowness; she felt him guide his manhood to her teeming core. He began pressing into her, filling her with his splendid incursion.

Felicity paid acute attention to every scintilla of sensation, mesmerized. Her legs wrapped around him with a will of their own.

He laced his fingers through hers, catching her small cry on his tongue as he split the barrier of her maidenhead with a sudden, decisive thrust of his hips.

His whisper was ragged. "Now you're mine forever." He cradled her to him in stillness while she absorbed the pain.

In truth, it was very slight, given her crazed desire for him and all her anticipation of this finally happening between them.

"Are you all right, sweeting?" he breathed.

"I think so. Yes." Her heart thundered against his hot, bare chest.

"We can stop if you—"

"No. I love you, Jason." She looked up into his eyes. "I'm so glad we're doing this."

"Me too. I only wish I would've waited for you instead of…the way I've been."

The regret in his gaze made her caress his head and hush him. "I understand, sweeting. You wanted to feel as though somebody loved you, I know. And now you have that."

He kissed her forehead. "Such an angel you are. Thank you for not giving up on me, Felicity. Do you know how happy you make me? Everything had begun to seem so meaningless, but you make me glad to be alive."

"Oh, Jason."

His whispered love words were the sweetest distraction, delighting her away from all the discomfort of how he'd made her bleed.

At length, she kissed his shoulder. Though he had waited patiently, she could feel him throbbing inside her and knew he needed more.

So did she.

She lifted her hips cautiously, signaling to him that she was ready for him to continue her ravishment. He moaned at the reprieve and kissed her in a storm of tender passion. He looked into her eyes as he braced himself on his hands above her.

His dark-eyed gaze was as tempestuous as the night outside as he resumed their candlelit dance with agonizing slowness. Felicity was enraptured; they both savored every pulse-pounding second of their fated joining.

In a growing state of ecstasy, she draped her arms around his broad shoulders as he quickened the pace, panting, his own desire taking hold.

She read the fierce hunger in his stare, his desire to make her his, at last, in every way imaginable. She could feel it in every feverish stroke of his body, so deep and satisfying.

"Mmm." She closed her eyes, wanting nothing more than to belong to him. *I am going to make you so happy, my darling man.*

Then all thought dissolved away as the wind gusted and the rain dripped off the roof's edge, and Jason made love to her in the darkness, coaxing her body toward release. Desperate for him, she encircled him with her arms and legs, her mouth open to his, her heart beating in time with his.

They were one.

"Come for me, Felicity," he ground out, and with his next smooth thrust, she could do naught but obey.

She gasped and clung to him as he brought her to a shattering climax, then he followed her over the edge with a ragged cry of surrender. Convulsions of wild pleasure racked them both. Nearly sobbing with release, Felicity finally subsided into stillness, and Jason collapsed on top of her, a warm, heavy, delicious weight.

"*Ahh,*" she sighed at last, kissing his shoulder in sweaty bliss. She could still feel his heart pounding against her.

He smiled down at her for a moment, then kissed her nose and wrapped her in a decidedly possessive embrace. She cuddled against him, unable to wipe the smile of complete satisfaction off her face. This moment was everything she had ever longed for, and as he held her, drifting on a sea of enchantment, she knew that from this night forward, they would always be together.

And her life would never be the same.

CHAPTER 13

Paterfamilias

*E*xperienced as he was in matters of scandal, Jason knew the most important thing was to get out ahead of the gossip. Or if possible, drown it out with an even bigger piece of news.

So the next morning, well before dawn, he immediately went about taking care of the situation, dragging himself away from his future bride's bed with many kisses and promises to see her later in the day.

Then he sneaked out of her house before the servants awoke to start the morning fires.

Borrowing her carriage, he went straight to the newspaper offices on Fleet Street and managed by the slimmest margin to rush their betrothal announcement into the afternoon edition of the newspaper. The morning edition would have been preferable, but it was already on its way out the door.

When Jason got home, he sent a note to the biggest gossips he knew telling them the happy news, and as soon as he had washed up and dressed for the day, he rushed out of the house again, this time for the jewelers, where he got his beautiful fiancée the most obnoxiously large diamond ring he could acquire on such short notice. She might not be able to lift her hand, but he doubted she would mind.

By midday, the *ton* was in an uproar with the news, and Jason had his whole staff seated around the long dining table, frantically writing out invitations to their engagement party, to be held at Netherford House in a fortnight.

Now the story of how he had burned the club's betting book and punched several members in the face for their ungentlemanly wager all combined to create an even greater sensation in the eyes of Society.

Naughty Netherford, they said, had fallen madly in love.

And this time, for once, the gossips were right.

"Aha, no wonder you got so angry with us!" one of his club mates said. A few of those involved in the previous night's antics showed up at his house to tell him he was no longer blackballed, thanks to today's logical explanation of matters, as well as Rivenwood's diplomacy.

The daylight also helped to cast a damning glare on the dishonorable behavior of those who made a contest out of bedding the young lady in the first place, now that their wager was exposed. Some of the rakehells at least had the decency to look a little sheepish, and so Jason was vindicated, for once.

"Why didn't you say anything, ol' boy?" a few of them exclaimed.

"Well, because it was none of your demmed business, and besides, she hadn't given me her answer yet," he lied in a reasonable tone, smiling from ear to ear to know he had finally caught his quarry. Once he had crossed the Rubicon of *allowing* himself to chase her, the rest had been easy; the decision itself had been the hard part. But it still remained to be seen how her brother would take the news when he returned to Town.

"Are we to understand that the chit made even a duke wait?" Sidney drawled.

"Oh yes," Jason averred, although in truth, they had done everything *but* wait last night. No matter. He carefully veiled his now-carnal knowledge of his future duchess.

In reality, it was Felicity who had waited so patiently for him, but he gave the men a long-suffering nod, knowing this would make her look good when word of it traveled back to the ladies of the *ton*.

"Well!" some Society ladies said during morning calls all across the West End. "Miss Carvel will certainly have her work cut out for her with that one."

A few girls cried, their hopes dashed, Jason later learned, but surely they had known deep down they'd never catch him.

The important thing was that everybody wanted to be invited to the grand engagement party, which, of course, colored their reactions, as Jason had known it would. The desire for an invitation helped tamp down the urge to start indecorous rumors. Many fashionable folk had wondered for years what the inside of the duke's massive corner mansion looked like, but as a bachelor, he had not been in the habit of throwing open his doors and entertaining polite Society. Single men were not expected to do much of that until they had a lady of the house to act as hostess.

Of course, Netherford House had now and then been filled with drunken rakehells and a small army of the demimonde's most desired courtesans.

But those days were over. A new era had dawned in the life of Netherford House *and* its master.

In the future, he would have a wife to be his hostess, and Jason savored the thought of his soon-to-be duchess. Making love to her had been a dream beyond compare.

Unfortunately, he still had to have a very serious conversation with her. One that couldn't wait much longer. He would tell her about his children when she came over later that afternoon to start planning their engagement party.

But when she and Mrs. Brown arrived, his staff—who strangely adored her already—had prepared a cake and bought a bottle of champagne with their own money. They gathered around and offered her a toast, gushing about how they couldn't wait to have her as the lady of the house.

Bemused, Jason folded his arms across his chest and looked on as she thanked them for their kindness and, with an almost conspiratorial wink, insisted they all have a splash of the champagne with her.

Well, she won them over forever with that, he mused, warmed to the cockles of his heart as he watched the vision of his future household unfolding right before his eyes. A deep sense of belonging settled over him, and indeed, a true feeling of home for the first time in his life. She had changed the atmosphere. There was no doubt Felicity utterly belonged there, with all of them, and he belonged with her.

Of course, he supposed it was somewhat out of order for a future duchess to have a drink with her staff, but he already knew this would be no ordinary household, not with him as head of the family.

Ordinary bored him, anyway.

But thoughts of households and families returned his mind to the serious news he had to tell her. Jason was nervous. Happily, her brief, tiny party with the servants had put her in very good spirits.

At length, Woodcombe ordered everybody back to work. Jason asked Mrs. Brown if they might be spared a few minutes alone and, behind Felicity's back, showed her the ring box.

"Ah, of course," Mrs. Brown said, then repaired to the garden to sit in the shade, at Woodcombe's suggestion.

Jason took Felicity's hand and led her up to the drawing room, his heart already pounding over how she was going to take his confession. He hoped to God she didn't cry, then he shut the drawing room door.

Once they were alone, he took her hand, leaned down, and kissed her cheek. "How are you feeling today?" he whispered meaningfully.

She blushed. "Oh…a little sore, but I've never been happier in my whole life."

"Me neither." He smiled and gestured toward the sofa. "Shall we sit?"

She nodded, and they did.

"Now close your eyes," he said.

"Why?" she asked.

"Just do it," he said, and smiling, she obeyed.

He took out the little velvet box in which the ring sat. "Open them."

When she lifted her lashes, she drew in a sharp breath. Her hand flew to her mouth, and she met his gaze, wide-eyed.

"I know the matter is already settled, but I thought I'd better make it official." He paused. "Will you do me the honor, Miss Carvel, of being my wife?"

She looked breathlessly at him and then at the diamond. Leaning close, she pressed a tremulous kiss to his lips. "Yes, a thousand times, forever," she whispered.

When she ended the kiss, tears glistened in her eyes, but she peeled off her gloves at his gentle urging and let him slide the ring onto her finger.

The band was a little loose, but that could be fixed.

"It's perfect, Jason." She stared at it glittering on her finger, then looked at him adoringly. "*You're* perfect."

"Oh, far from it."

"Well, you make *me* perfectly happy." She took his face between her hands and kissed him with a fervent tenderness that stole his breath away.

Eyes closed, Jason quivered at the bliss of her mouth on his. He never wanted this moment to end.

Especially when the next one was sure to be so much more difficult.

Deep down, he knew it was very wrong of him to have made love to her and to have ensured that he had the ring on her finger before sharing the information he was about to reveal. But he needed her too much. He couldn't take the chance of her backing out on him, abandoning him. She simply *had* to be his wife. Besides, he had *tried* to tell her on multiple occasions before, but something always kept them from the conversation.

"Darling," Jason whispered, "there's something I have to tell you."

"So serious," she murmured in surprise. Obviously feeling very fond of him at the moment, she snuggled close to his side, cupping his hand between her own.

He hesitated. She seemed so happy. Should he wait? But if he waited, someone else might tell her about the children before he could, and that would be even more of a disaster.

"Did your club take you back? It seems like Society is happy for us, doesn't it? I'm so excited! Where do you want to get married? Where shall we go on our honeymoon? We're going to have so much fun togeth—"

"Felicity, please listen."

Her face fell and her brow furrowed. "What's wrong?"

"I'm trying to tell you something very important. And…you're probably not going to like it."

"Oh." She tilted her head and stared at him for a second. "There *was* something else you wanted to tell me last night, as I recall. But we got…distracted."

She grinned, but his smile was more guarded. She hadn't wanted to hear it last night, and he had not insisted on making her listen when, perhaps, looking at it now in the bright light of day, he should have.

"Very well." Her posture straightened. She withdrew her hands and folded them in her lap, obediently waiting.

Jason's heart pounded. He was terrified of her reaction, but the moment of truth had come.

"Felicity—" He gulped, fell silent, wavered, then decided to just get it over with, and the words tumbled out all in a rush. "I'm a father. I have two children. By former mistresses. My son, Simon, he's four years old, and my daughter, Annabelle, she just turned two."

Her jaw dropped.

"I'm sorry I never told you till now. I was embarrassed, and it didn't seem proper to speak of one's…one's by-blows with a lady, anyway. And frankly, you and I haven't been that close for the past few years. Your brother knows," he added haltingly.

Felicity gaped at him, speechless.

"The children live with their mothers north of Town," he added. "I go and see them once a week. That…is what I wanted to tell you."

"Oh…" she forced out slowly at last, sounding a bit as though the wind had been knocked out of her. "I…see."

She nodded as the information gradually sank in, but then fell silent, her downcast gaze fixed on her hands, her fingers tensely knotted and her face pale.

"They're…very sweet," he offered, on tenterhooks, "though I'm not my son's favorite person."

He stopped himself from rambling out of nervousness.

She just looked at him.

"Please—say something." His heartbeat slammed in the quiet. He held perfectly still, holding his breath. Waiting to hear his fate.

She started to speak, but nothing came out. She cleared her throat and tried again. "So…when do I get to meet them?"

Jason blinked in astonishment. "W-we could go right now, if you wish."

Felicity shot to her feet and stood a little unsteadily. "Yes. Let's," she said, walking toward the drawing room door with jerky strides.

He stood up uneasily, rather baffled. *No yelling? No tears?*

Not even any discussion of this monumental revelation?

"Felicity, I'm sorry."

She stopped halfway across the room but did not turn to him.

He stared at the graceful line of her back. "Are you…not angry?"

Though she did not turn to him, he saw her spine straighten, saw her square her delicate shoulders and lift her chin. "Jason, I love you," she said firmly to the wall. "What happened in your life before we…fell in love…well, it's not my place to judge you. I know you've had many women. Everyone knows that. I never thought about it, but it only makes sense that children would be the natural result."

She turned around and gazed at him from across the room, her eyes looking slightly glassy with shock. "I'm not happy about it, of course. But these children are a part of you," she said resolutely, "so I know I'll love them, too."

He stared at her, incredulous.

He breathed her name and started toward her in amazement. Awash with stunned gratitude, he meant to take her in his arms, but she stepped away before he reached her, stiffening.

Despite her answer, he could see the hurt in her sea-green eyes. It stabbed him through the heart, even though he deserved it.

He dropped his gaze. *Of course.*

"Thank you," he forced out in a low tone.

She granted him a slight nod, seeming every inch a duchess, then marched on to the door, obviously determined to take it in her stride as best she could. "Take me to them."

He followed her, not knowing what to say. But he hoped to God the tots were in good humor.

Maybe they could charm her. Because it was clear that the future Duchess of Netherford was not happy with him at all.

# # #

Felicity was reeling, though determined to be as supportive and understanding as she could manage. She could barely even remember what excuse she had given Mrs. Brown about why they had to dash off.

Wedding business. A meeting with the priest. Of all the lies to have told! It was the only thing she could think of at the moment. She'd reveal the truth later.

She kept telling herself that she had known what she was getting into from the start with Naughty Netherford, a legend among rakehells. It *was* only logical, given his previous mode of life, that unplanned pregnancies would have occurred. It was hardly uncommon among men of their class, though it was never discussed in polite society.

But as she sat in the carriage, stunned and staring into space, she could hardly absorb the reality of it. How like him to make her head spin this way!

Her deflowering last night, their engagement today. It had barely sunk in that she was about to become his duchess when he sprang this news on her. Could he not let her just be happy for one day?

Sometimes she thought the man was the very devil.

Why had she never heard about these children until now? Even her brother could easily have told her. He had long known of her interest in anything having to do with Jason. But such was the two chums' loyalty to each other.

Well, she thought, her jaw tightening, these little by-blows of the lusty Duke of Scandal were, no doubt, part of the reason why her brother had wanted to keep them apart.

Oh, but it was awful to think of Jason hiding these two innocent youngsters away like they were a source of shame.

On the other hand, now that she understood what sex truly was, she felt herself getting angrier and angrier about his liaisons as the carriage rolled along.

What he had done with her last night, he had done God only knew how many times in the past with other women. That was the only way the children could have resulted, obviously! The bloody stork hadn't brought them.

Maybe they weren't really his, she wondered in dismay. A vain hope, no doubt. She shook her head at herself, ignoring her fiancé's guilty, anxious gaze, which had been fixed on her for a while now.

She could feel irrationality building in her and tried to contain it. It was unlike her.

Of course, she was perfectly content to meet the tots, but facing their mothers was another story. She already hated them on some instinctual level with a jealous rage. They were sure to be very beautiful. The best bedmates money could buy...

She clenched her jaw tighter. Despite the fact that Felicity knew she was the one Jason loved, the one he'd marry, it made her ill to realize that because of the children, these past concubines of his would have to be tolerated, lurking around the outskirts of their future family for the rest of their married lives.

For that, she was furious at him. For his foolish lack of foresight. For his selfishness. For his overlong period of spoiled immaturity, sowing his wild oats.

She could only hope that Peter would have addressed these faults with him, since he was the only one Jason ever listened to. Not that her brother was much better, if she was honest. After all, Naughty Netherford hadn't always gone to those brothels alone, to be sure. She wasn't the most worldly woman, but she wasn't blind, either. Suffice to say she had noticed that a soldier liked to spend his leave with the ladies, too.

No wonder the two blackguards got along so well...

Feeling ever colder toward her too-handsome, too-experienced, too-seductive fiancé, she said not a word all the way to Islington, the neat, tidy, out-of-the-way neighborhood north of Town where gentlemen of means apparently kept their mistresses. Out of sight, out of mind. How could these women stand to be treated this way?

Meanwhile, Jason kept looking at her nervously. It was bad of her, but angry as she was, she rather enjoyed his mounting worry. She still did not even want to look at him.

How could you do this? Have you no respect for yourself?

And, worst of all, after all the women he'd bedded, did last night with her really even mean anything to him?

A pang wrenched her heart with that thought, though she knew she was going too far. Jason loved her. He did…in his own hapless way, one step forward and two steps back. The bed sport was his forte, not dealing in affairs of the heart. She was well aware of that. And she would help him get better at confronting emotional matters…just as soon as she got over her own fury.

At last, she allowed herself to look over at him. He was gazing hopefully at her, his chocolate-brown eyes full of vulnerability—for once. He did not speak, but the distraught look on his face hinted that, inside, he was desperately willing her to make good on her magnanimous words back at his house. Her brow puckered in resentment of her own noble answer back there. She knew she had said the right and proper thing in the moment—the thing a true duchess ought to say—but she wasn't feeling quite so generous just now.

Mere moments after hearing his secret, perhaps she had been too much in shock even to *know* what she felt. She still wasn't sure.

Did he think he could kiss her and give her a diamond and everything would instantly be all better between them?

She just shook her head at him and looked away, refusing to be melted by his obvious distress.

What am I going to do with you?

Was it even safe to soften toward him when he clearly knew so well how to play her? She was well aware he had waited until he got what he'd wanted before breaking the news to her about his children.

She clenched her jaw and stared out the window until the carriage stopped in front of a quaint, roomy cottage.

"Whom are we meeting first?" she asked crisply.

"Simon. Annabelle will still be down for her nap."

She managed a nod, pained to realize the man she loved had this whole other side of his life that she had known nothing about. She felt bereft.

"And who is the mother, please?" she asked as they got out of the coach. "So I might brace myself."

"Er, her name is Chloe Moore."

Her eyes widened as she turned to him. "The actress?"

Oh hell, flashed through his dark eyes. "You know who she is?"

She nodded and turned away, feeling ill. "Everybody knows who she is, Jason. Your son must be a very handsome boy."

Her heart pounding, her stomach in knots, Felicity was momentarily mesmerized by the terrible whispers of self-doubt in her head. *I can't compete with that. I'm just an ordinary woman. She's a star of the stage. Famous, talented, gorgeous—albeit a walking scandal. Oh, what a perfect couple those two must have been...*

Jason grasped her chin gently and lifted her face to meet his gaze. "There is nothing between us, Felicity, except the boy. It was nearly five years ago, and we were bored of each other within a month. She wanted my money; I was only looking for a bit of fun. That's *all* it was ever meant to be. We had both moved on when she found out she was with child. The timing told her it was mine. Not that there's any doubt, once you see him."

She winced. He lowered his hand to his side, searching her face in dismay.

"I'm so sorry," he said softly. "I'm sorry for who I've been in life. Please—it's different now. You know that, don't you? I've changed, truly. Everything is different now that I'm with you. You're the one I love. The only one I've ever loved. You must believe me..."

She blinked away the threat of tears and nodded but wondered if she looked as ill and ashen-faced as she felt.

He opened the wooden front gate for her. She stepped through, then waited for him to pass her. Stoically, she followed him up the flower-lined pathway to the arched front door, her knees shaking beneath her.

Everything in her wanted to run. *I can't do this. What do I say to this woman? What possible topic of conversation could we have? "Pleased to meet you, Miss Moore. So...isn't he good in bed?"*

Jason knocked before entering, but when they stepped into the neat little cottage, Felicity could have collapsed with relief when the maid revealed that the actress was not at home.

Unfortunately, they also learned that everybody in the house was sick to the point of retching.

Including Simon's nurse, Jane.

The haggard-faced woman dragged herself out to greet her employer while Felicity stared into the parlor at the small, dark-haired boy curled up on the sofa in his nightshirt. He had a blanket embroidered with sailboats tucked around him and a stuffed toy dog in his arms.

Standing in the foyer, Felicity had gone motionless. She couldn't take her eyes off the child.

The intense emotion of the past twenty-four hours nearly overcame her as she stared in wonder, suddenly choked up at the sight of Jason's firstborn.

Oh my God, she thought. *He's beautiful.*

And her eyes welled up with tears. He was like a little miniature Jason sitting there, hugging his little cloth dog.

Meanwhile, behind her, the nurse was making apologies. "Oh, Your Grace, I'm so relieved to see you, but you can't have got my note yet. I just sent it moments ago."

"No. What is it?" he inquired.

"Well, I hated to bother you, but you said to write whenever we needed help, and I'm afraid, well, I've asked my niece, Polly, to come in and help look after him. She's willing, but she can't get here till tonight. She's a housemaid for the Ellsmeres," she explained with a glance at Felicity.

"Polly's a good girl," Jason said with a nod. "She's helped you here before."

"Yes, sir. You see, poor little Master Simon came down with the fever yesterday afternoon. Nothing too serious, you needn't worry," she assured him. "Just some sort of stomach virus that's been going around. The children down the street had it last week and they're fine now. Unfortunately, I seem to have caught it, too. The fever hit me this morning."

Indeed, Nurse Jane looked like she could hardly stand.

"You must let us help. You should be in bed," Felicity said abruptly, blinking away her tears and only just managing to tear her gaze from Simon, who'd been staring back at her with a Jason-like look of suspicion.

"This is Miss Carvel," Jason told the nurse. "The reason we actually came is that I wanted her to meet the lad, as she is to be my wife."

The governess exclaimed over this news with amazement, but then Jason hurriedly asked, "Where *is* Chloe?"

She seemed hesitant to answer in front of Felicity, who managed a taut smile.

"It's all right," Felicity said.

"Er, Miss Moore is still in Brighton with Lord Hayworth, Your Grace. They were…going sailing on his yacht, I believe."

"Have you written to her yet?" he asked.

The woman nodded wearily. "But if she's out on the boat somewhere, I don't know when she'll get the message."

Jason's face darkened. "Typical."

"Jason, why don't you introduce me to the child?" Felicity asked, nodding toward the tot on the couch. "Once Simon's comfortable, Nurse Jane can go to bed."

"Oh, miss," she protested.

"Not at all. You must rest and get better," Felicity told her. "We can look after the boy until your niece arrives."

"It'll be all day."

"We'll manage," she assured her. "His Grace is the child's father, after all. 'Tis his duty."

Felicity gave him a sharp look askance, and Jason nodded to the nurse, as though he dared not argue with his future wife's decree.

"Come," he said, then stepped into the parlor. "Hullo, Simon. I hear you're feeling poorly."

The small boy nodded as he twisted the floppy ear of his toy dog.

"I've been giving him a little burnt toast and peppermint tea to soothe his stomach," Nurse Jane informed them. "He's been in bed all morning. He just woke up."

Felicity was already taking off her pelisse. "Well, we'll keep him entertained."

"Miss Carvel, you are welcome to have my driver take you back to Town," Jason said, taking off his coat. "I'll stay. I don't want you catching whatever these two have."

"Nonsense," she replied with a frosty glance at the child's errant father. What did a barely ex-rakehell duke know about taking care of a sick child, even his own? She, on the other hand, had spent the past several years taking care of a frail old lady. It couldn't be that different.

"I don't have any other plans today. I can stay. Off with you, now, Nurse Jane," she said in a kindly tone.

Before the governess took her advice, she stopped to show Felicity where a few things were in the kitchen and such before gratefully accepting the suggestion.

Familiar enough after these instructions, Felicity returned to the parlor. She noticed Simon straightened up and hugged his dog tighter as his father sat down on the couch beside him.

Jason reached over and laid his hand across the boy's forehead, checking for fever. "How are you feeling, son?"

Simon shrugged, warily eyeing Felicity as she approached.

"Simon, I brought this lady here today to meet you. This is Miss Felicity. She's Uncle Pete's sister."

"Uncle Pete?" He brightened up at the mention of her brother. "Is he back from the jungle?"

"Not yet. But soon. Don't you think so, Felicity?" he asked, trying to include her in the conversation.

"Oh, I'm sure he'll be back any day now. It's nice to meet you, Simon." She offered him a smile. "I'm sorry you're sick."

He just looked at her, not sure what to make of all this, then turned to his sire.

"Can I have ice cream?" he asked rather slyly.

Felicity pressed her lips together to conceal her amusement at this unexpected ploy. "He's your son, all right."

Jason smiled ruefully at her, then at the boy. "Not till Nurse Jane says so, you little schemer."

"That's a nice dog," Felicity offered, smoothing her skirts as she sat down on the ottoman beside the couch. "What's his name?"

"He doesn't have one."

"No name?" she asked in surprise.

"He's just pretend!" the little patient said in a prickly tone. "Mama says I can't have a real doggy. When is she coming home?" he asked in a whiny tone, poor thing.

Felicity winced at the question, a pointed reminder of the love-starved childhood that had certainly played a role in shaping the man Jason had become.

Having grown up on the next estate, she well remembered Jason's daily five-o'clock ritual that had often foiled their playtime. That was when he had to rush home and make himself presentable to be marched in front of one or both of his parents for approximately ten minutes a day—at least on those occasions when they were in residence at Netherford Hall rather than in Town.

They would treat their son to an interview of a few stilted questions, keeping him at arm's length, of course, as they did not believe in indecorous shows of affection. They'd merely make sure their heir was still alive and then send him back to his caretakers. Felicity supposed the rogue had drawn the conclusion from all this that people had to be paid to love and care for him. That was all he'd ever known.

No wonder he'd taken to frequenting brothels as soon as the boy had become a man, she thought sadly.

But now he was causing history to repeat itself with his own son. She looked from one to the other. *I'm not going to let you do that to him.* In all fairness, though, she supposed Jason needed someone to *show* him how to love, and who better than his future wife?

Her mission clear, somehow Felicity kept her mouth shut about the absence of the boy's mother. What mattered right now was Simon.

The awkward distance between father and son was obvious, though she could tell Jason yearned to break through the boy's standoffish attitude toward him. It was written all over his face—confusion and uncertainty, with equal parts affection.

She could see he wanted to be a good papa, he just wasn't sure how. It made her heart ache.

As for little Simon, he looked decidedly intimidated by his sire—not because he saw Jason as a threat, but he looked somewhat in awe of the big man, and eyed him as though he were something of a stranger.

Well, today, perhaps some good could come out of the boy's illness. This would at least give the two a chance to get to know each other better. She resolved to do all she could to help the process along.

"Your mother will be back as soon as she gets Nurse Jane's letter," Jason was saying, smoothing the boy's tousled hair back from his forehead. "But don't worry, we'll take care of you till Polly gets here to help. You like Polly."

"She's funny," he conceded.

Felicity tried again to engage the tot. "How old are you, Simon?"

He clearly didn't feel like talking—at least not to her—but he held up four fingers.

"My goodness! Four years old. Do you want something to drink?"

He was still reluctant, but their attention gradually drew him out. He giggled when Jason took his toy from him and pretended to make the dog bite him.

Unfortunately, Simon wasn't entirely out of the woods yet. Later in the day, he started looking a little queasy and then suddenly leaned over and puked on the floor, even splashing some onto Jason's fine leather shoes.

Felicity got a washcloth and wiped the child's face but stopped herself from volunteering to clean up the vomit. "You're his father. This is what parents *do*," she told the duke, handing him a bucket and some rags.

He stared at her in astonishment, but all things considered—well aware that he was still on shaky ground with her—he wisely pressed his lips shut and cleaned it up without complaint.

She opened a window to let some fresh air in to rid the room of the smell, but, feeling better, Simon giggled at the sight of his towering, scary, important father cleaning up his vomit. The little rascal began experimenting with rhymes involving *duke* and *puke*.

"He really is you all over again," Felicity remarked with a chuckle at the boy's cheeky sense of humor.

"I'm not sure that's a compliment," Jason said wryly, giving his smaller copy a playful scowl. "No more puking. It's disgusting."

"It's funny!" Simon insisted, giggling like mad.

"Humph." Jason left to get rid of the nasty bucket and wash his hands.

By nightfall, however, a change had come over His Grace.

Simon was well enough by then to nibble another piece of toast and have more tea. Felicity made Jason get the snack ready for the boy himself while she went to check on Nurse Jane. She took her time about it, too, deliberately leaving her rich, powerful fiancé to muddle his way through snack time and the various tasks involved in getting his son ready for bed.

After sauntering back down the upstairs hallway from checking on Nurse Jane, Felicity glanced in the doorway of Simon's bedchamber, watching the Duke of Scandal doing his best to clean his boy up a bit for bed.

Jason looked up just then, blowing out a sigh of weary exhalation, and when he saw her there, he tried to conscript her. But she shook her head stubbornly and simply reminded him of the basic tasks that needed doing.

"Don't forget to make him brush his teeth."

"Yes, ma'am." Jason looked at his wee shadow. "You heard the lady."

She could not help spying on their progress, however, tickled as she watched Jason helping the tot change his little nightshirt. He combed Simon's tousled hair before the mirror, oversaw the brushing of his tiny white teeth, turned down his son's bed for him, and lit his night-light.

When Felicity returned again from getting tea and toast for Nurse Jane, she found Jason seated in the rocking chair in his son's room, looking slightly exhausted with the child on his lap.

Sleeves rolled up, cravat loosened, he was reading the boy a story. She had never heard his deep, rich voice sound so soft before.

Simon, meanwhile, was toying with the buttons on his father's waistcoat as he read to him, his head resting on Jason's broad chest like it was the best place in the world to be.

Felicity knew from experience that it was.

Loath to intrude on their sweet moment together, she almost continued past, but Jason caught her eye.

"Felicity, stay," he called. "You must wait and hear the ending of this riveting tale."

"Papa, they *find* the lost kitty," Simon said flatly. "Nurse reads me this book every night. It's my favorite one."

"Well, you didn't have to ruin the ending for me, pup," he teased gently, giving him a chiding little hug. Simon giggled and kicked his feet in contentment. Then Jason glanced lovingly at her over his son's head. "Stay, you. I mean it," he said, while his dark eyes sent her a heartfelt thank-you.

She returned his smile tenderly, leaning in the doorway. There was no way to stay angry with such a man.

She might have been furious when they had arrived, but seeing him like this, she could not help falling in love with him even more deeply. She was also ridiculously proud of him right now. He'd had it in him all along.

Just as she had always known.

"I'll stay," she whispered, her own sentiments equally transparent in her eyes.

All is forgiven, she told him with her gaze.

Folding her arms across her chest, she remained in the doorway and listened to him read the rest of the silly rhyming book about a mischievous cat getting stuck in a tree.

By the time the story ended, Simon was fast asleep, so Jason rose, laid his little son in his bed, and gently tucked him in.

CHAPTER 14

Making Up Properly

They did not leave until Polly arrived to take over, but riding back to Town in Jason's carriage, they were both utterly worn out. It was astonishing how one small, sick child could outlast two healthy adults.

"Of course, Chloe won't return until he's better," Jason grumbled.

"You're going to have to deal with that, you know. Her neglect. It's not right of her to leave him so often. Rein her in, Jason. If you don't, I will—once I'm your duchess."

He glanced at her in surprise.

"Simon is too precious to be put through this," she added.

He nodded, though he was at his wit's end with his former mistress. "She says it's unfair. That I have no right to try to 'control her life.'"

"I don't care if it's fair or not," Felicity said with a stern frown. "The boy needs his mother. If she doesn't want to be there for him, then bring him home with us. I would never willingly take a child away from its mother, but if Miss Moore refuses to behave like a parent…blame it on me. I'm perfectly willing to play the villainess in this situation, as long as Simon's needs are met. The same for Annabelle. Don't forget, the law does favor the father. You would be perfectly well within your rights to alter the arrangements as you see fit."

"Yes, but wouldn't you be worried about…?"

"About what?"

"How it would look? Wouldn't you mind? I mean, not many wives would put up with that. Surely the presence of my natural children in our house would only remind you constantly of how I…was."

She glanced at him in fond reproach. "Surely you know me better than that by now. What matters are the children, not what Society thinks of anything. You're a duke, anyway. You can fairly well do as you please. Haven't you always?" she teased. "Anyway, the *ton's* opinion hardly bothered you when you were causing scandals."

"Yes, but this is different. I only had myself to worry about. If I am to become properly respectable—"

"You? Properly respectable? Perish the thought." She chuckled with affection.

"I could!" he defended with a wry frown.

"You have a very black-and-white way of looking at things, don't you?"

"Good or bad, it all seems pretty clear to me," he admitted. "I just didn't *mind* being bad when it was only my own reputation I had to worry about."

"Hmm. No wonder you've felt so torn about what to do in life," she murmured, caressing him to assure him it was not an accusation, merely an observation. "I think I see now. But darling, life's not that simple. Sometimes things are more gray. Personally I don't care if Simon and Annabelle are illegitimate. I just want what's best for them."

"As do I. I don't really know what that might be, though. What do I know about children? Other than how to make them?"

"Well, it would be best for them to stay with their mothers, I presume, but only if these women can be made to care for them properly. All that aside, I truly do want the children to visit us at least once a week, preferably together. They need to know their father, and each other. They need to have some sense of belonging in a family. I won't try to be their mother, it's not my place, but they can look on me, oh, as a doting auntie who has their best interests at heart. What is it?"

He was studying her in the darkness. "You see?" he murmured. "This is why I love you."

He leaned near and kissed her on the temple.

"I love you, too, Jason." She let him pull her near. With his arm around her, she leaned her head on his brawny shoulder and whispered, "Whatever you do, don't hide these little darlings away like you're ashamed of them…because they'll know. And it will hurt them terribly as they grow up and understand more. They'll never forgive you. You know how it feels to be ignored by your parents," she reminded him.

He nodded.

"So let's bring them into our lives, bring them out into the open. They belong to you, so let's love them," she whispered.

Holding on to her hand, he was silent for a moment. "I was never ashamed of my children," he said quietly. "I hope they never, ever think that. I was only ashamed of myself."

Felicity gazed at him. It was quite an admission from the Duke of Scandal.

"Well, you need to let that go, my love. Shame serves no purpose. It will only hurt you. You've changed, as you said. I know you meant it. You've had a new start, with me, and it will be all right. But no more babies from now on," she whispered, only half in jest, "unless they're from me."

"I am so looking forward to that." He pulled her closer and kissed her on the head.

"I think you're a good father," Felicity said after a moment.

"Really?" he asked hopefully.

She nodded, moved by the warmth in his voice. "You did very well back there tonight. You see? All you needed was a little practice. And fewer servants doing everything for you, to force you into doing what you could have done all along."

"How now, are you saying I'm spoiled, Miss Carvel?" He tilted his head with an indignant little smile.

She grinned. "Maybe a little. But where would you leave it?"

"Humph. We'll see what you have to say about it once I've spoiled *you*."

"You're welcome to try." Laughing, she tilted her head back and kissed his lips softly.

He looked into her eyes as their kiss ended. "Come home with me tonight," he breathed. "We have some making up to do, as I recall."

"Mmm, tempting."

"We worked hard. We should relax... Take a bath after that little miscreant puked on me." He laughed softly, then added, "Did you know my house has hot running water? I'm not sure the Prince Regent even has that at Carlton House."

"See? Spoiled."

He looked at her. "Very well, you may have a point. Nevertheless. Makes you feel like a Caesar sliding into that thing. Nice, sunken, tiled bath. Classical mosaics... You could spend the night," he whispered, giving her a caress on her thigh through her skirts. "We can do this quite discreetly, if you're game."

"What about Mrs. Brown?"

"She's not invited," he said wickedly, in her ear. "Ah, she won't miss you. Spend the night with me, my darling. I promise, I'll make it worth your while."

Felicity shivered with desire at his silken invitation. "What about your neighbors? Society? It's too risky."

"Don't worry, I can get you in and out of my house without being seen. I have a *system*."

"Jason!"

"From the old days," he hastily amended. "The staff will know you're there, but they're already in love with you, and nothing I do shocks them anymore."

"I'll bet." She sighed with pleasure as he nuzzled her earlobe.

"Come, my duchess. As I told you, it is my goal in life to spoil you from here on out. I'll give you a nice hot bath, and then I'll put *you* to bed."

She quivered in spite of herself, well aware what that meant. He was just too naughty and so irresistible. "I suppose...I could come over for a little while..."

"Attagirl." He pulled her onto his lap with a devilish smile.

She relaxed into his arms and laid her head on his shoulder. "We're going to be very happy together, aren't we, Jason?" she asked after a moment.

"Darling, I already am," he confided softly. "Happier than I've ever been, thanks to you."

"Me too," she whispered, giving him a tender smile. Then she kissed him once more, her blood already heating in anticipation of the night ahead.

# # #

With her warm body jostling gently on his lap in time with the rocking motion of his carriage, Jason was already aroused and salivating at the prospect of getting her into his bed. He needed to confirm in the most primal way that he hadn't lost her.

When the vehicle rolled into the coach house and halted amid the familiar scent of horses and hay, he jumped out while his servants saw to the team.

Turning to hand Felicity down from the carriage, he saw the glow in her eyes that told him she, too, was already excited. His pulse quickened with eagerness. His fingers closed around her delicate wrist, then he led her over to the slim, wrought iron spiral staircase that he'd long since had installed in the corner.

Up the steps he hurried her, circling to the top, where the shadows darkened. Then he spirited her into the enclosed, elevated walkway that discreetly connected his home and the coach house. The little covered footbridge with white gingerbread trim along the roof was quite picturesque from the outside. On the inside, their footfalls clomped over the wooden planks of the floor.

"I can't believe you had this built to accommodate your trysts," she remarked.

"You can't?" he asked dryly.

She paused midway through the passage, glancing out one of the narrow windows, through which the moonlight shone. "Nice view of the garden."

"No dawdling. Come." Unlocking the door at the end of the passageway, he escorted her into the second story of his house. The rarely used chamber on the receiving end of the passage had once been a garden-facing sitting room with a balcony, so the doors and some of the structural supports had already been in place when he had been wickedly inspired.

But in truth, the passage had been a great convenience for a dedicated rakehell. It stopped nosy neighbors and gossip columnists from spying on him and his various female guests.

Of course, it was unlikely that anyone believed his excuse that he'd only had it built to keep him dry when he had to go out in inclement weather. His Grace wouldn't want to catch a cold, now, would he? Thankfully, his blood was already quite hot as he whisked his bride-to-be into his house, unseen by prying eyes.

With her deflowering out of the way, he couldn't wait for their second time together. He knew when a woman wanted him, and the desire radiating from her thrilled him to his core. Perhaps she needed to affirm their bond, as well, after it had been tested by the day's events.

The awareness between them was intense as he tried to act natural in front of the night footman, who took their coats and offered him a lighted candelabra.

"We do not wish to be disturbed," Jason said pointedly, taking it from him.

"Yes, Your Grace." The footman bowed and retreated, well aware what that meant.

As Jason turned back to Felicity, he hoped it wasn't too obvious to her or the servant that he was already panting for the woman. Truly, though, the plans he had in mind for her tonight were very much a fantasy come true for him.

He laced his fingers through hers and, holding the candle branch in his other hand, led her up the marble staircase into the lofty, shadowed recesses of the third floor and down the hallway to his bedchamber.

She balked just a little at the threshold, staring wide-eyed at his huge, gilded canopy bed.

He kissed her to remind her it was safe. "Welcome," he murmured.

"To your lair?" she asked with a breathless little catch in her voice.

He tugged her close with an arm around her waist. "Our lair, soon. Make yourself at home." He stole a kiss and let her go. "I'm going to draw the bath. Don't run away," he cajoled her with a playful half-smile as he moved toward the smaller, connecting room.

She tracked him with a vixenish gaze. "I'm not going anywhere."

"Good." He stepped into the bathing room, placed the stopper in the drain, and turned on the hot water tap over the elegant, sunken tub. The whole setup had cost him a fortune, from the cistern on the rooftop to the coal furnace heating the water.

But this was one luxury that had proved absolutely worth it. It had soothed his muscles divinely on many occasions after a particularly hard session at the fencing or boxing studios where he trained.

When he returned to his bedchamber, Felicity was wandering around, shyly looking at everything. The rich gold draperies hanging from his canopy bed. The pillows piled against the headboard, with its painted medallion bearing his ducal crest. She gazed at the rug and the white hearth piece. Loath to rush her—indeed, savoring their time together—Jason let her get accustomed to her surroundings and went over to light another few candles.

Felicity glanced at herself as she wandered past the large cheval glass, then paused by his dressing table and took a sniff from the bottle of his cologne, smiling at him. "It smells like you. I love that smell."

From there, she continued along to the closed French doors leading to the balcony off his bedchamber and pulled the curtains shut. "It's a very nice room. Quite luxurious…just as I'd expect."

He folded his arms across his chest, entertained by her interest. "I'm glad you're pleased."

Drifting past him, she peered into the bathing room, scanned the mosaics, the tropical plants in urns, the woven rug on the floor, and the basket of plush towels waiting for them. He watched her saunter over to the bathing tub itself and glance into it.

"It's terribly convenient, isn't it?" she remarked.

"It is," he replied, his heart pounding with anticipation.

"It's starting to get deep," she said as she came back into the bedroom.

"Then we should get undressed," he said, trying to sound nonchalant.

"I have buttons," she warned, turning around and pointing at her back.

"Indeed you do." He crossed to her at once, his fingers already tingling for the task. He did not point it out, but he was something of an expert at getting women out of their clothing.

Felicity lifted the wispy, golden curls at her nape while he unfastened the buttons there. His fingers continued speedily down her mid-back and into the supple arch of her lower back. She sighed with pleasure when he slipped his hands into her parted gown and touched her hips through her chemise.

"How did I let you talk me into this?" she purred.

"Trust me, you'll love it," he bent to whisper in her ear. "May I unlace your stays, milady?"

She nodded. "Please."

Working quickly and efficiently, he untied the bow and plucked away the ribbon lacing, then trailed his finger down her spine just for fun, and roused a shiver from her before loosening the firm satin panels corseting her slim waist.

She stood limp, letting him do as he pleased, her gown hanging partway off her body. He kissed her on the shoulder as he drew the sleeves off her. As she stepped out of the pool of fabric, he had half a mind to ravish her there and then, but she took the gown away from him and went and laid it neatly over the back of a nearby chair.

The way she smoothed out the wrinkles so carefully did strange things to his heart.

"You are adorable," he informed her in tender amusement.

She arched a brow at him and returned to him clad in little more than her chemise. He sat her down on a damask chair to rid her of her stockings. He enjoyed the task very much, going down on one knee before her and untying the little ribbons that held the silk stockings to her garters.

Felicity watched him work with fire in her eyes. He ran his hands down each lovely leg as he stripped her stockings from her. Then he rose, leaving her there, and held her gaze as he undressed for her.

He did not mind her watching him at all. He wasn't vain, but women usually found much to like about his body.

When they were both naked, he drew her to him and kissed her. He was enraptured with the silken warmth of her pressed against him. Kissing her again and again, caressing her neck and hair and her beautiful face, he suddenly remembered to check the bath water.

"Oh, bloody hell! One moment!" She laughed as he made a naked dash back into the bathing room and turned off the tap just in time.

Felicity minced after him with dainty steps, laughing. "Did we cause a flood?"

"Nearly! You distracted me," he scolded with an intimate smile. Then he nodded at the water. "Well, get in."

She shook her head. "You first."

He did so without hesitation, lifting the stopper to let a little of the water drain out, lest it overflow. But rather than joining him, Felicity suddenly seemed struck shy. She spun away, as though the sight of her future husband stark nude in front of her was too much for the demure little lady. "I think we could use another candle in here."

Jason grinned and tilted his head to watch her retreat as he settled into the tub. The sight of her curvy bare bottom as she hurried off to fetch the candelabra charmed him.

But then she returned, and with one mouthwatering look at her, he shook his head and sighed. "God, woman," he uttered in admiration, particularly entranced by the plump contours of her breasts.

Growing bolder, she put her hand on her hip and let him look, lifting her chin a bit. "You like what you see, Duke?"

"The word *perfection* comes to mind. Sanfratello's marble goddess is nothing compared to you, my darling."

"Why, thank you, sir." With a coy motion of her shoulder, she set the candelabra on a small pedestal and approached cautiously. Jason put his hand out and steadied her so she wouldn't slip as she joined him in the water.

"Oh, this does feel good," she admitted, getting comfortable. "You were right. I do feel like an empress."

"See? I told you."

Once she had settled in, she flashed a flirtatious smile at him and came closer. "Now, then. Does my dirty boy need a bath?"

He laughed at her naughty approach, then quickly groaned with pleasure as she touched him. Things progressed quickly from there. The water sloshed, the steam rose, bringing out curly tendrils in her golden tresses. Rosy with heat and desire, she looked like an angel, utterly irresistible. He didn't even try but, instead, gathered her to him and plied her silken body with fine lavender soap, running his hands all over her.

She did the same to him with great care, smoothing away the tension of the day as they went slipping and sliding against each other. He claimed her luscious mouth in a fiery kiss as his lust mounted, his hard, needy cock throbbing against her thigh.

She plunged her hand beneath the waterline and grasped it, stroking him, her palm slick with soap. Unable to bear her teasing anymore, Jason pulled her onto his lap and slowly entered her. On her knees across his thighs, she braced her hands on his wet shoulders.

He hoped this position wasn't too much for her, considering she was still a neophyte. It was only their second time, though he had done all these things with her many times before in his mind…

The reality exceeded even his wildest dreams. The bathing tub was just a little narrow for them as she rode him, though. She could not spread her lovely legs very wide, but bit by bit, she lowered herself onto his massive erection, taking as much of him as she could. He groaned, intoxicated by her tightness. Then he lay back against the edge of the tub while she rode him, feeling like a veritable king.

She stroked his chest and bent to kiss him. He could feel her trembling. But as good as it was, she was too new at this to take him in all the way in this position. He sat up and wrapped his arms around her sleek, naked waist. "I want you in my bed."

Her chest heaving, she nodded eagerly.

They barely bothered drying off as they returned to his chamber, and dampened his sheets with their bodies as they slid into his bed.

Then the sweet, satin warmth of her curves yielded to his weight; he moved atop her damp pink body, nudging her legs open nice and wide for him at last. But, hungry for the taste of her, he could not resist pleasuring her for a while, licking her deeply to make sure she was fully ready for him. When she gripped his shoulders, dragging him up again in frantic desperation, he smiled wickedly and complied.

He loved her like this best of all—uninhibited, wild with passion. All signs of the prim-and-proper miss that she should never have become long gone. "I want you," she ground out.

"I noticed," he teased in a whisper.

"Just take me, you scoundrel!" she begged him with a laugh. Running her hands down his sides and then holding him by the waist, she sought his member and she groaned as he pressed into her again, obliging fellow that he was.

"Oh God, yes, Jason." Panting, she closed her eyes in relief, lips parted, pleasure etched all over her lovely face with his every thrust.

He took her almost roughly. "You're all mine, Felicity," he whispered as she bucked beneath him.

"Always," she wrenched out breathlessly. *"Jason!"*

"I love you," he uttered as he brought her to a crazed climax. She said it back to him in almost incoherent gasps as she came, suddenly bursting into tears of exquisite release.

He was so astonished that he nearly lost his rhythm, but he got it right back, yet his heart was melting even as he reached his own thunderous climax. He was buried to the hilt in her now, but God help him, it was she who had so pierced and penetrated to the very soul of him.

Novice that she was, she did not understand why she was crying, but he did. As his heaving shudders of bliss started to ease, he lowered himself to his elbows atop her and cradled her in his arms, kissing the salt tears off her cheeks. "Shh, it's all right, sweeting."

"Oh, Jason. It's just that I've loved you so much for so long," she sobbed out, hugging him. "I still can't believe this is all really happening."

He closed his eyes as his heart clenched, and kissed her forehead. "I know, darling. I feel the same for you. I love you so much it hurts."

"But it's wonderful, too," she said with a sniffle.

You're wonderful, he thought. "Never leave me," he breathed.

She shook her head, apparently having lost her voice. He withdrew from her body, then rolled wearily onto his back and held her in his arms, her head resting on his chest.

Her tears had stilled, and they both were calm now. He petted her hair as they lay together, deeply moved by her vulnerability, her innocence. He had never felt closer to any living being than to her in that moment. He loved her patience, her kindness, her clarity, her humor, her unpretentious simplicity...

As he cuddled her in his embrace, he paused to tuck a lock of hair behind her ear.

"I will love you all my life," he whispered, then he sealed his vow with a soft kiss on her forehead, and watched her until they both drifted off to dreamland.

CHAPTER 15

Mt. Netherford

They had not meant to fall asleep, but given the vigor of their continued activities throughout the night, Felicity supposed it was understandable. She dozed with her head resting on Jason's chest, her fingers gliding over the smooth, muscled contours of his chiseled abdomen. She savored the luxurious sense of contentment in his warm, strong arms.

Thoroughly ravished, she felt so safe with him now. She could not bring herself to leave. She had stayed all night, and it was risky, of course, to tarry any longer. By all rights, she shouldn't even have been there at all. But his arms around her made her feel as though nothing bad could ever happen to her—to either of them, as long as they were together.

Besides, he did have his *system* for spiriting certain guests in and out of Netherford House unseen, the rogue.

When a longcase clock in the hallway began to toll the hour, she listened intently and counted seven muffled bongs.

Good. His servants would be up now and well about their day, so she probably couldn't avoid them, but they already knew she was there, anyway. As for his neighbors, she had no doubt that she could hie off home before the fashionable denizens of Moonlight Square even stirred.

Lulled by the slow, peaceful rhythm of Jason's breathing, Felicity smiled at the rakish nature of her own thoughts, planning her stealthy escape after last night's secret tryst.

Perhaps it was inevitable that after all the time she'd been spending lately with the Duke of Scandal that she should start showing signs of scandalousness herself.

"Jason? Are you awake?" she whispered, lifting her head to gaze at him.

"No," he mumbled, eyes closed.

She smiled and shifted positions, rolling back to brace herself on her elbow. "I could tickle you awake."

"I don't advise it."

She started to drag a featherlight touch down his stomach, but he flicked his eyes open and grasped her hand.

"How now, naughty miss?" he scolded with a throaty chuckle as she let out a mock shriek and tried halfheartedly to fight her way free. "You'd better be careful or you're going to wake up more of me than you bargained for, love."

She feigned a pout as he rolled on top of her. "See? I knew you were awake."

His gaze softened with great tenderness, his dark hair tousled, his eyes full of devotion. He stared down at her before lowering his lips to hers for a lingering kiss. "Good morning, beautiful," he whispered.

A small sigh escaped her. She could not help but glow at such a sweet greeting from the man she adored. She wrapped her arms around his lean waist. "I missed you."

"I'm starving," he said.

"I'll bet. You worked up quite an appetite last night." She bit her lip on a smile full of mischief.

"So did you!" he retorted in a scratchy voice. Then he lifted himself off her and swung his legs over the edge of the bed, pausing to sit there for a moment, stretching his neck and shoulders. "Come on. Let's go get some food."

He stood, and Felicity sat up, holding the sheet to her chest. "Go where?"

"Downstairs. Morning room." Gloriously nude, her soon-to-be husband shuffled across his chamber to the bathing room for his morning ablutions.

Distracted by the lovely sight of him, it took a moment for his answer to sink in, then she gasped. "Jason, I can't go down there!"

"Why not, darling?"

She whimpered with embarrassment and pulled the sheet up over her nose, hiding all but her eyeballs. He laughed.

"It's all right. We're all adults here."

"Can't you just have them bring the food up here for us?"

"Do you know how big this house is? Nobody likes cold eggs, love. Here. You can wear this down to breakfast." He grabbed a dark blue satin dressing gown off a peg on the wall and tossed it to her.

"You want me to wear this in front of the servants?" she asked dubiously, examining it.

"Don't worry, sweeting, nobody's going to care. It's not like they don't know what we've been doing in here. Besides, I can't face all those buttons of yours until I've had my tea. Contrary to appearances, I am not actually awake yet." With that, he ducked into the bathing room and shut the door behind him.

Felicity pursed her lips, weighing the matter with uncertainty. At length, she concluded that the staff had seen much more shocking things than this, and knew better than to gossip about the future lady of the house.

Besides, she'd be leaving soon, anyway.

When Jason returned, she was out of bed and had donned his dressing gown. The only thing she had on underneath it was her chemise.

"You're sure none of your neighbors can see into the morning room?" she asked, tying the cloth belt around her waist and taking care not to step on the hem, for it was quite long on her.

"Stop worrying," he reassured her as she passed him, taking her turn in the bathing room.

"I don't know why I let you talk me into these things."

"Because you're such a good, obedient, little— Ow!" he cried with a laugh as she reached up and grasped his ear for that rascally remark, pulling him down to her like a naughty schoolboy.

"Obedient, am I? Say it again, please, Duke," she taunted sweetly.

"Darling, you are as biddable as a tropical typhoon."

"Humph. That's better." She freed the rogue to let him put on at least a few items of clothing. He pulled on a pair of loose linen Cossack trousers and, shirtless, donned a burgundy-colored banyan, which he left hanging untied.

She eyed his bare chest in possessive pleasure. He really was much too good-looking for any woman's peace of mind.

When he was ready to go down to breakfast, he took her hand between his own and whisked her out of his chamber, leading her stealthily to the backstairs. After all, the servants might know she was there, but she did not really wish to face them if she didn't have to. From there, they sneaked down to the first floor and dashed across the central corridor to the very pleasant morning room at the back of the house.

The morning room had pale yellow walls with arched windows, through which the clear morning sunshine streamed. Beyond those windows lay a charming view of the sculpted garden and the quaint elevated walkway crossing above it.

Since the morning room sat right next to the kitchen, the food would indeed arrive hot when it was brought to them. They sat down at a round table with cottage-style chairs. A selection of morning newspapers had already been procured and lay waiting on the sideboard, but Jason showed no interest in them, and Felicity was glad. She loved having his undivided attention.

When his old cook, Hannah, came in personally to ask what she could make for them, Felicity was suddenly seized with embarrassment about her brazen choice to spend the night with Jason, flouting all propriety. Oh, of course, the lower orders did that sort of thing all the time, she supposed, in their private lives. But granddaughters of marquesses were supposed to hold themselves to higher standards of behavior, even when they *could* get away with being slightly wicked.

On the other hand, Aunt Kirby would've been as pleased as punch that she had finally done something truly scandalous.

In any case, Felicity dropped her gaze and resorted to murmuring demurely that she'd be glad to eat whatever was put in front of her.

The plump old cook couldn't have been kinder; indeed, Hannah was the soul of discretion. She clearly doted on her handsome young master and seemed eager to spoil them both.

Before long, Hannah carried in the large tray by herself. When still no other servants entered, Felicity realized the cook was going out of her way to spare her modesty—or what was left of it.

Deeply appreciative of the considerate gesture, though surely it was too much for one servant to do all by herself, she thanked the woman profusely.

Hannah set the teapot and covered dishes down before them. "It's no trouble a'tall, milady," she murmured, glancing from Felicity to Jason and back again, as though she could barely contain her exaltation over their pending match. "Is there anything else I can get for ye?"

"Thank you, we have everything we need, Hannah," Jason told her with a smile, and Hannah left them alone to eat.

"She's wonderful," Felicity whispered after the cook had gone.

He nodded. "Hannah's topnotch. She's always taken good care of me, and I warn you now, her cooking is addictive. So, what've we got here?" He lifted the lids on the various dishes and started to serve them while Felicity poured the tea.

It wasn't easy, considering her hands had only just stopped trembling after having to face a near-stranger who knew full well that she had just spent the night in the Duke of Scandal's bed.

Jason must have noticed she was just a wee bit rattled, for he struck up an idle conversation, probably to distract her. "So what have you got planned for today?"

"Oh...I'm not sure. You?"

They chatted about nothing in particular while he finished heaping their plates with eggs and toast, sausage and beans.

Felicity removed the lid from the dainty sugar bowl but paused with the tiny silver sugar tongs in midair. "How do you take your tea, anyway? This is essential information for a lady to know about her future husband."

"Maybe I should make you guess," he said with a grin.

"You *are* in an especially roguish mood this morning, aren't you?"

"Feeling my oats," he admitted with a wink. "But that's your fault."

"Do you want sugar or not?" she insisted with an arch look in return. "Tell me quickly, or I'll put whatever I want in and make you drink it anyway."

"As long as you sweeten it with a kiss." He leaned across the table and stole one.

But even as their smiling lips met, a sound from the direction of the entrance hall broke into their warm, playful bonding and stopped them both cold.

The front door creaked open and promptly banged shut.

"Anybody home?" a deep, strong, cheerful, and all-too-familiar voice called. "Ho, Netherford! I'm back!"

Jason and Felicity jolted apart with a gasp and stared at each other in shock for a heartbeat.

Woodcombe ran past the morning room doorway to the entrance hall as fast as his old legs could carry him. "Major Carvel! H-how very fine to see you, sir! His Grace will be so—surprised."

"Will he? Good!" Peter said in a jovial tone, audibly clapping the old butler on the shoulder, which might have sent him flying across the entrance hall. "I just stepped off the ship half an hour ago. We docked in the Thames and I came straight here. Next stop, Great-Aunt Kirby's.

Must let my sister know I'm still alive."

"Er, yes, sir," they heard Woodcombe say.

Felicity sat motionless. With her stare locked on her lover, she found just enough of her voice to choke out a terrified "Oh my God."

"It's all right," Jason forced out in a low tone, but the color had drained from his face. He rose to his feet and took a few steps toward the open doorway, then stopped in the middle of the room, as though debating with himself.

"Go shut the door!" she whispered. "He'll kill you if he finds us!"

"I don't want to lie to him!" Jason whispered back, looking distraught, while out in the entrance hall just a few yards down the central corridor, the thump of a heavy pack landing on the marble floor informed them that her brother was fully prepared to make himself at home in his best mate's house.

"Well, don't just stand there, Woodcombe," Peter ordered Jason's butler. "Go and wake the blackguard! I don't care how many whores he's with. If he can drag himself away from them, I daresay the esteemed patron of our expedition will be pleased to hear he's now got a mountain named after him. Get up, you lazy sod!" Peter hollered cheerfully up the grand staircase, unaware. "Damn me, I'm starved. Something smells delicious! What's Hannah got cooking this morning?"

"Er, Major!"

The familiar pounding of her brother's boot heels striking the floor, coming ever closer, made Felicity consider hiding under the table. But thankfully, as Peter headed for the kitchen, a bevy of servants ran past the doorway of the morning room to intercept their friendly intruder and try to turn him in a different direction.

At least three footmen and a few maids gathered, and by the sound of it, they arrayed themselves in a defensive line across the corridor, barring Peter from going any farther.

She could hear them trying to act like they were merely happy to see him.

"M-Major Carvel! You're back!"

"We're so glad you're safe."

"Your trip must've been very exciting, sir."

"D-did you make any new discoveries?"

"Did you get to see wild elephants?"

Despite their valiant efforts to distract the returning adventurer, Jason and Felicity were still stuck in the room, unless they fancied jumping out the window. There was nowhere to run, no place to hide, and when Jason glanced grimly at Felicity, she realized he did not intend to try.

"This is stupid," he said in a taut voice. "I'm not going to lie to my best friend."

"But he *won't* be your best friend anymore if he finds the two of us like this!"

It was too late, though. Peter had already smelled a rat in the servants' odd behavior.

"What's going on, you lot?" he asked suspiciously.

"Please don't do this," Felicity begged Jason in a helpless whisper, but the duke stood strong and called firmly to his servants, "It's all right! Let him in."

"Netherford?" Peter called cheerfully, sounding all the more confused. "What, he's already awake—at this hour? Astounding."

"Morning room!" Jason yelled back.

The servants must have parted to let her brother pass. Felicity braced herself, standing behind the breakfast table, wearing naught but her chemise, her shiny new engagement ring, and Jason's dressing gown. This she drew tighter around herself, as if it would help to shield her from her brother's certain wrath.

She knew how bad this looked, and stood there mentally cursing herself. What if finding them this way knocked Peter back to how poorly he'd been doing before? It would be all their fault.

Out in the hallway, she could hear him brush past the well-meaning servants with a good-natured scoff.

Jason lifted his chin and squared his shoulders, then suddenly, there he was, her beloved big brother. The tall, rugged adventurer, suntanned and scruffy-jawed, with eyes matching the blue-green of her own.

He stepped into the doorway of the morning room wearing the same brown leather coat in which she had last seen him, except now it was worn and weather-beaten.

"Jason, your servants are acting damned strange…" he started, but his words trailed off as he spotted Felicity standing there. His bronzed face turned white.

She swallowed hard, trying to hide her dread. "Peter," she greeted him with a nod. "Welcome home, brother."

"What the—" He grabbed hold of the lintel and took a step back as though he had been punched in the stomach. For a second, he stared at her incredulously. "What are you doing here?" The words had barely escaped him when he realized the obvious answer to his own question. "Oh my God."

"Peter—" she started.

"You!" Looking sickened by the realization, he turned murderously to Jason, his eyes narrowed to slashes. "What have you done to my little sister?"

# # #

It was actually pretty clear, though, Jason thought. Especially considering that the well-ravished beauty was wrapped in his dressing gown, her golden hair flowing loose around her shoulders, her face still glowing from their long night of love play.

Jason stood acutely aware of his own state of undress. He had pulled his trousers back on, thank God, but not his shirt. Instead he wore his banyan open down his chest and was too proud even to close it.

The time had come to own up.

To all of it.

Pete's stunned gaze took in the scene before him, traveling over the two of them standing guiltily together with their eggs getting cold on the table between them.

"How could you?" he uttered as his stare returned to Jason in furious accusation. "You son of a bitch."

"Easy," Jason started, but the military man newly returned from the wild was used to solving problems the simplest way. He reached for his pistol and pointed it at him.

"Peter, no!" Felicity cried, rushing over to stand in front of her brother's gun, her arms lifted. "It's not Jason's fault!"

"Oh yes, it is. Get behind me, you little hussy," he said through gritted teeth. "I'm taking you out of here."

"You think I need rescue? Peter, by all that's holy, put the gun away! Have you taken leave of your senses? He's your best friend—and we're in love!"

At last, her brother looked dazedly at his hand, as though barely aware of having drawn the weapon. The breath left his flared nostrils in seething fury, but he lowered the pistol to his side.

When he looked at Jason again, it was with daggers in his eyes. "I told you to stay away from my sister. Is this why you sent me away? So that as soon as I set sail, she'd be left unprotected and you could have your way with her?"

"If you really thought you'd left her unprotected, you should not have set sail," Jason countered in a steely tone. "I protected her while you were gone, actually."

"Gentlemen, please!" Felicity tried, but Pete shook his head with a low, bitter laugh.

"You villain."

"Oh, come! Is that what you really think of me?" Jason burst out, his face reddening, his stomach in knots.

"It's hard not to! Look at the two of you! I'm not blind!" Pete bellowed. "It's more than obvious what you've been doing here! What, she actually spent the night with you? How long has this been going on? While I was away at the war, too?"

"Peter! Oh, for heaven's sake. We are to be married! Look!" Felicity marched forward, lifting her hand to show him the gigantic engagement ring that had not yet been on her finger for twenty-four hours. "You see? I am going to be the next Duchess of Netherford. Isn't that wonderful news?" she demanded, forcing him to focus on her words.

Pete stared at the ring, then furrowed his brow, apparently unconvinced. But he holstered his pistol. "Why? Are you pregnant?"

"Peter!" she cried.

"She's not!" Jason bit out, though he knew he deserved that one.

Pete glared at his sister. "Why are you sleeping with him if you aren't married yet? Our mother raised you better than that! I suppose this is our aunt's influence on you." He shook his head in withering disapproval. "Oh, Felicity. I always knew you had a weakness for this one, but after I warned you so many times how he treats women, how could you let him seduce you—"

"Actually," she cut him off, "I'd say it was pretty well mutual, Peter. We seduced each other. And I will not apologize for that. I love him. I always have." She took a step closer, striving to calm her brother's fury. "Peter, try to understand. Jason and I are to be married. I'd hope you could be happy for us."

He eyed her in stunned, brooding disapproval. "Happy?"

"Jason was there for me when I needed him. You were on the other side of the world, as usual." She glanced over her shoulder at Jason, as though seeking reassurance.

When he nodded gently at her, she faced her brother again and continued. "You don't know how close we've become in these past weeks."

"Oh, I'll bet." Pete glowered past his sister at Jason, but for his part, all he could do was stand there, woodenly, feeling awful and numb, and thinking himself the worst, lowest bounder in the world.

Pete clearly agreed with that assessment. "So naive," he said coldly to his sister. "You don't know him like I do, Felicity." His scowl swung back to Jason. "But I want to hear what this cur has to say for himself."

The major took another menacing step into the room. "How long have you been scheming this little game of yours, Jase?"

"I didn't scheme anything. And it isn't a game! You weren't here, you don't know. And you obviously aren't listening," Jason mumbled.

Felicity maneuvered to keep herself between them, apparently worried that violence might yet break out. "Peter, I understand you're only being protective, and I love you for it, but he's good to me. I know he earned his nickname as the Duke of Scandal in the past, but it's different between us. He's changed."

He scoffed at her. "Do you know how many other silly females have believed that before you?"

"It *is* different," Jason vowed, starting to get a little offended. "It's true. Everybody grows up sometime, Carvel. Maybe it takes a woman to force it on the likes of us."

"Don't compare *me* to the way that you've behaved! I haven't peopled the world with bastards."

"Peter!" Felicity smacked her brother lightly on the arm for calling the children that, but Jason merely shook his head.

"At least I'm not always running away," he murmured to his friend with a knowing look.

Pete had no answer to that accusation, it seemed; he merely folded his arms across his chest and pinned Jason in a withering stare.

"Look," Jason said in a resolute tone, "I know she'll always be your baby sister, but Felicity is not a little girl anymore."

"Not a virgin anymore, either," Pete muttered in disgust.

"She's a grown woman—and damn it, I adore her, as you well know!" Jason exploded. "I'm marrying her, so shoot me if you have to. She'd be worth it." He swallowed hard and did his best to check his anger. "Just don't ask me to live without her. Because I can't. I won't. She's everything to me."

Felicity gazed at him with tenderness shining in her eyes at his blunt confession. The love pouring out of her steadied him, even though he feared he was even now losing his best friend.

But if that was the sacrifice he had to make, the last remnant of his overlong boyhood, then so be it.

She truly was worth it.

Pete scrutinized the glance that passed between them. Jason looked at him again, ready to face whatever consequences came, pay whatever price.

Still, he didn't want to hurt Pete. God knew the poor bastard had been through a lot. "Carvel, there's no man alive I respect more than you," Jason said. "I've known you all my life. I would never betray you. I stayed away from her for as long as I could. I know exactly why you feel this way—no one knows the sordid details of my past better than you do. But people can change."

He paused, and swallowed hard. "Felicity loves me. None of those other women ever did, and I...I need her, you see. The two of us belong together, and I won't apologize for that. Only for my timing. So hate me if you must. Call me out and shoot me if it makes you feel better. I'll delope before I'd ever pull the trigger at you. But know this. Nothing you can do or say will ever change my love for her. I'd die for her without a qualm."

"Well, don't do that," Felicity mumbled with a frown, glancing anxiously from him to Pete.

Pete stared at him, brow furrowed in skeptical confusion. He was well aware that Jason had never uttered such heartfelt sentiments about any woman—indeed, any topic—before in his entire life, cynic that he had always been.

"Well, well." Pete glanced at Felicity, then back at him, suspiciously. "So while I was out taming the wilderness, it looks like little sis was back in Town taming the rogue from hell. Is that it?"

Jason lifted his chin. "Yes," he said firmly, more than willing to swallow his pride for once and just admit it. "Felicity changed everything. You know how special she is, Pete. She brings out the best in me." He glanced at her. "She makes me want to be a better man."

"Well, you couldn't be worse," Pete muttered, but Jason and Felicity both ignored his sardonic quip, staring at each other.

"Sweeting," she whispered, and came over to stand beside Jason, taking his hand.

Jason clung to it, staring at her with his heart in his eyes and emotions welling inside him that he could never have put words to. She was so precious to him. His life before this love had flowered between them seemed like nothing but a dark, restless dream. He had been asleep, indeed, until that morning she'd come banging on his door. She had woken him up in more ways than one, and he had never felt more alive.

She turned to her brother. "Peter, please. We both love you so much, but you have to understand. We need to be together. We'd like to have your blessing."

Pete directed his answer to Jason. "Are you telling me she knows about your children?"

"I do," she answered for him, nodding. "We spent all of yesterday taking care of Simon, who's very keen to see you, by the way. I understand you are his godfather."

Pete's angry expression softened just a little at the mention of the four-year-old who idolized him.

"Peter, don't you see?" Felicity pleaded softly. "We could all be…a family now. Jason's never had that. Not like you and I did, though even ours ended too soon. Brother, please, don't choose bitterness. You've been gone so long, and I've been so worried about you. So much has happened. I want to tell you all of it—"

"Er, some things I *don't* want to know, trust me," he interrupted, rolling his eyes and lifting a hand to stop her from revealing certain details that, of course, she'd had no intention of sharing.

Like the first time they had made love on that wonderful stormy night…

Lord, was that just two nights ago? Jason thought, amazed. He already felt as though their love had existed forever.

But Felicity had faltered at her elder brother's reproach. Guilt flickered across her lovely face. "Peter, I know we should've waited, um, for marriage—but I didn't want to! You know I've always been in love with him."

"Aye. I know," Pete finally admitted, starting to relent. He looked at Jason. "I'm your oldest friend, you idiot. You think I didn't notice that my sister's infatuation with you was hardly one-sided?"

Felicity glanced up at Jason in surprise. "It wasn't?"

"Why do you think I took such pains to stay away from you?" he muttered.

"I just didn't want you to *hurt* her!" Pete exclaimed. "I didn't want you playing with her heart. She's my sister. And she's not like the women you are used to."

"I know that, Pete. You must believe me," Jason said sincerely. "I want no part of that mad life anymore. It was killing me, and I know full well it's wrong. All I want from now on is Felicity, and for you to accept this as best you can. I promise you, I'll treat her like a queen."

"He already does," she said. "You should've heard how he defended my honor when you were away."

"Oh, really?" Pete gave her a skeptical frown and leaned down to prop his elbow on a nearby wooden chairback.

Felicity nodded. "He fought all the men in his club for my sake."

"You're jesting. The Grand Albion?"

"Yes, because those rogues made a wager over me."

"What?"

"It's all taken care of," Jason assured him before Pete was inspired to vent his wrath elsewhere.

The major looked displeased and confused, arching a brow at this additional news, but he was clearly considering matters, and perhaps realizing there was nothing he could do to stop this. "Well, I suppose the chit could do worse than snare herself a duke. Even one who's a bloody scapegrace of a bounder."

Jason sighed and lowered his head, but with his gaze downcast, he missed the faintest hint of sardonic humor that had begun to gleam in his friend's eyes.

"Well, damn me," the adventurer drawled at last. "Looks like somebody finally brought the Duke of Scandal to heel. I'm proud of you, sis."

Jason lifted his head abruptly, hearing the humor in Pete's voice.

Her brother wasn't scowling anymore.

"You're not…angry?" Jason asked hopefully.

Pete snorted, then directed his answer to Felicity. "I've been waiting for years for this blackguard to get his head on straight so I could give him leave to chase you. But looking at the two of you now, well, I suppose the two of you deserve each other — a headstrong little vixen and Naughty Netherford. That's just bloody perfect, ain't it?"

"We think so." Felicity grinned at her brother and hugged Jason's arm, but then shot a mock scowl at Pete. "Don't call him that anymore. He's a good boy now."

Pete scoffed, and even Jason feared that was taking things a bit too far.

"I'll believe it when I see it," Pete replied. Then he let out a jaundiced sigh. "Very well, if you two are fixed on this daft plan, I can hardly stop you. Who am I to stand in the way of true love? But I'm warning you, man—"

"I *know*," Jason interrupted.

"As for you." Pete turned to his sister. "It's on your own head now. If your good boy breaks your heart, don't come cryin' to me."

"Hold on—if *I* get hurt?" she shot back. "You think me marrying Jason is risky? This from a man who just spent six months in the jungle? With the tigers and the snakes and the malaria?"

"Don't forget the headhunters," Jason reminded her, then quirked a smile at his friend. "Well, she does have a point."

"You *do* remember, brother, how I begged you not to go? But did you listen to me? Of course not. Maybe Aunt Kirby was right all along, and it's just not in our blood to play it safe. Trekking off with the tigers was what you needed to do. And Jason was the one who made it possible for you, don't forget."

"Not that his generosity entitled him to my sister's virtue," Pete replied with yet another disapproving smirk.

"Not that that's any of your business!" Felicity cried with a scarlet blush. "Anyway, it's not like you can talk, brother. I mean, you're not married, and I rather doubt *you're* a virgin."

Pete's jaw dropped at her frank observation, while Jason grinned. "That's none of your affair! Such talk!" The major snorted with a sheepish blush. "I daresay this blackguard's been a bad influence on you."

"Maybe. But he makes me deliriously happy, Peter, and I love him." She slipped her arms around Jason's waist.

He rested his arm across her shoulders in turn. "Pete, I'm marrying your sister, end of story," he informed him, giving up on diplomacy. "I'd be grateful if you could accept it, but if not, too damned bad. I can't do without her. I won't give her up. Don't ask me to apologize for loving her. I don't regret a thing. Felicity is like no other woman in this world—and frankly, you're not the only one who was dying inside."

Everyone fell silent.

Jason and Felicity exchanged a heartfelt look while Pete pondered his confession.

"Well," her brother muttered at last, "I guess there's only one thing left to say."

They both looked at him anxiously.

"Congratulations," he grumbled.

Felicity let out a soft cry of gratitude and released Jason, rushing forward to hug her brother.

Pete returned her embrace awkwardly after a moment, then took a deep breath and met Jason's gaze over her shoulder, sending him a nod of begrudging assent to the match.

Felicity kissed him on the cheek. "Welcome home, brother. Your friends and family missed you. But, Lud, you smell!"

"Well, pardon me, little miss duchess! I was on a ship for the past two months, if you don't mind."

Jason smiled ruefully. "Do you want some breakfast?"

Pete eyed him warily for a minute. "I could eat. I *have* missed Hannah's cooking," he admitted.

"Yes! Come, sit down and eat with us," Felicity said. "I have so much to tell you. Sad news about Great-Aunt Kirby, I'm afraid. That's how this all started…"

Behind him, Felicity launched into telling him all that had happened and cajoled her brother into taking the chair across from her at the table.

Jason went to the doorway and beckoned to Woodcombe, who was waiting anxiously in the corridor.

He rejoined the Carvels with his worried old butler just a few steps behind. He gestured at Pete. "Tell Woodcombe what you'd like Hannah to make you for breakfast. Then we want to hear all about your discoveries. And those elephants."

"Oh, yes, did you see any out there in the wilds?" Felicity seconded, since all of them were rather desperate for a change of subject.

As Pete glanced over to tell Woodcombe what he wanted Hannah to make for him, Jason sent his bride-to-be a private look of relief.

She reached over discreetly and gave his hand a reassuring squeeze. Slowly exhaling, Jason sat down beside her, turned his palm upward under the table, and linked his fingers through hers, out of sight.

Funny how one touch from her made everything better. But, 'sblood, that could have turned into a tragedy just now, he was well aware. Pete seemed better than before he'd gone away, but it was hard to tell for sure, given the rude homecoming he had just received.

Having told Woodcombe his breakfast order, Pete accepted a cup of tea from Felicity but still studied Jason with a certain degree of wariness, as though weighing whether the changes in him were real.

Jason returned his stare openly with nothing left to hide, not even the slight twinge of envy that while his friend got to go traipsing round the world having adventures, duty and fatherhood kept him here.

As for the matter of their pending marriage, though, Jason's stoic gaze told Pete the one simple fact: He and Felicity were going to be together, come what may.

And on that point, he was as immovable as the great stone mountain that her brother had named after him.

EPILOGUE

As It Should Be

The stars twinkled over Moonlight Square, but Netherford House was lit up brilliantly on the night of their engagement party.

Felicity had chosen a pale green gown for the grand occasion, while Jason looked dashing in a plum-colored tailcoat. Given the sensation their match had created, they had decided on throwing a rout for the event.

This brisk-paced style of gathering would move guests in and out quickly, for there were hundreds of people who wanted to attend.

The wedding, by contrast, would be a small, private affair, and would take place at Jason's ancestral pile in the country. After playing on the castle grounds throughout her childhood, Felicity could barely believe the place was about to become her home.

Tonight, however, given the erstwhile Duke of Scandal's popularity as one of the leading rakehells in Society—*former* rakehells—it was a crush.

The noise was deafening, and everybody came. Jason and she stood in the receiving line for hours. Felicity relished greeting the *ton* by his side, having everybody know they were together now.

She also enjoyed revisiting everyone who had been involved in their finally getting together and finding out how their own affairs were progressing.

Cousin Gerald, for example. Her ruddy-cheeked, fortune-hunting cousin was finally beginning to grasp that Mrs. Brown had no intention of ever marrying him. However, the lady had bailed him out of the sponging house when his creditors had recently caught up with him. So, rather than trying to land a rich wife, plump, pushy Cousin Gerald had resigned himself to becoming the world's most unlikely kept man.

Felicity found it hilarious. Even their cousin Charles was amused, though he had been a little glum ever since he had received a troubling report on the state of his health.

The consumption he'd long lived with was growing more serious. Felicity fretted at the news, having warned him many times to leave off his dreadful tobacco habit; taking snuff would only harm his lungs. Maybe now he'd start to listen, if not to her, then to his physician, who had suggested the viscount start making plans to spend the winter months this year in a warmer climate—sunny Portugal or Malta, perhaps.

Still, Charles managed a smile despite his worry as he congratulated her and Jason on their pending nuptials. Then he sauntered off to chat with her brother.

Peter, thank goodness, had finally come to terms with the marriage of his sister to his best friend. Felicity had been confident that he would...eventually. To her relief, Jason had also reported that Peter's mental state seemed better now than before he'd gone away.

At the moment, Peter was talking with Atticus Sloan, the eccentric Scottish inventor in Jason's patronage, along with the three Italian artists. The bespectacled scientist looked fascinated, asking Peter question after question about his travels.

Peter was distracted, however, by the small boy sitting on his shoulders. Simon perched there, holding on to his godfather's head and looking around at all the people from this high vantage point, a grin splashed across his face.

His wee half sister, Annabelle, was in her father's arms as he stood next to Felicity. The children had been to Netherford House on several occasions in the preceding weeks—and had quickly learned they'd be doted on there, and not just by the kindly servants.

The duke himself was smitten with his children. All he had needed was a little encouragement. Little Simon had warmed up to his father considerably ever since the puking incident, no bribes required. There was, however, talk of getting the boy his first pony so he could start learning to ride.

Despite Simon's earlier standoffishness, Felicity recognized the child's painful hunger to have a bond with his sire. She had seen it before—in Jason as a boy. Only, *his* father had died without ever making the necessary adjustments.

In any case, while Jason's relationship with his son was drastically improving, Felicity had learned that he'd always been on amicable terms with his two-year-old daughter.

Indeed, he was the hero of Annabelle's world. Whenever anything scared her or made her feel shy, she went running straight to her papa, knowing she would be scooped up in his arms.

Presently, she sat on his hip in a gorgeous frothy dress, with her chubby arms wrapped tightly around his neck.

A few guests frowned at this seeming lack of decorum. But for them, Jason reserved the full frost of his ducal displeasure, staring down his nose at them with the same lordly disdain he had long since learned from his own sire.

They scurried away, realizing their error.

Guests moved through the mansion all evening long, until eventually, even the pack of rogues who had made the wager about Felicity arrived. She was surprised to see them; it was still early in the night for their hard-drinking, fast-living set.

To her amusement, his chastened club mates actually showed signs of real remorse as they filed in and greeted her. Clearly, the rakehells had hoped she had remained blissfully ignorant about their wager, but she had no intention of letting the golden-haired Lord Alec Knight and his friends off the hook so easily.

Instead, she made a point of teasing them about it, knowing that if she did not signal that all was forgiven, it could be awkward for years to come, seeing them in Society. So she made light of it.

After all, the love she had found with Jason made it easier to look upon the whole world with abundant goodwill.

They all looked relieved by her forgiveness, still laughing sheepishly.

"We meant it as a compliment, truly!" Lord Draxinger insisted.

"Then I think you gentlemen might need to reexamine your notion of what a compliment *is*," she said archly.

"Ah, let's be honest. Some girls would've been flattered," the tall and intimidating Lord Rushford suggested, while his friend, Lord Fortescue, merely leered at her until Jason looked at him.

Felicity shook her head at them and laughed. "You fellows are too much. I'm glad Netherford put the lot of you in your place."

"So am I," Jason drawled while the rogues scoffed at the suggestion that he had done any such thing.

"Did my mild-mannered fiancé really get into a brawl against all these gentlemen?" Felicity asked the Duke of Rivenwood in amusement as he walked in after them.

"It was at least six to one when I arrived," he answered with a half-smile.

She chuckled. "Well, thank you for getting him out of it."

Rivenwood inclined his head in an elegant nod, smiling wryly, while the rogues wandered off to investigate Lady Simone, Lord and Lady Pelletier's daughter.

"I've been meaning to ask you," Jason murmured in her ear after Rivenwood had drifted off to fetch a drink, "do you by chance know a raven-haired girl by the name of Lady Serena Parker?"

"Yes, actually, we are acquainted. Why do you ask?"

"I noticed at the Pelletiers' musicale that she couldn't stop staring at Rivenwood."

"Hmm, that's strange. I mean, of course, he is an interesting fellow, and I'm forever in his debt for getting you out of your scrape. But as I recall, Lady Serena is all but betrothed to some bookish gentleman." She furrowed her brow. "His name escapes me at the moment. Younger son of a marquess... Sorry, I can't remember his name."

"That's quite all right," Jason answered. "I just found it strange how absorbed she was in Rivenwood."

Felicity shrugged. "Everything about him seems a bit, shall we say, unique."

Suddenly a chime sounded, filling the house.

Annabelle gasped and looked at her papa in question.

"What was that?" Jason teased the baby, giving her a squeeze.

"Everybody, that's the signal that it's time for the concert to start!" Felicity told all the guests around them.

"Come on, Annie. Do you want to go and hear some pretty music?" Jason asked his daughter, carrying her with him as the party moved outside.

With as crowded as the house was, the musicians had set up their ensemble on the garden terrace.

Signore Leandro Giovanelli had finally finished his long-awaited string quartet, and had chosen this night to unveil it publicly as his gift to the happy couple.

Felicity beckoned to Peter, who brought Simon with him. Jason led the way to the few chairs that had been reserved for them in the front row.

"This had better be worth the wait," Jason murmured under his breath as they took their seats right in front of the musicians.

Peter sat, plopping Simon down on the chair between them. Annabelle remained on Jason's lap, nibbling on a cinnamon biscuit.

"A-ladies and a-gentlemen," the flamboyant Italian said, "it is-a my great honor to present this song to His Grace, the Duke of Netherford, and his soon-to-be de duchess, de beautiful Miss Carvel. From my whole ensemble and the artists, from de bottom of our hearts, we wish you the love and the happiness for all eternity." He raised his wineglass to them. *"Salute!"*

Jason and Felicity both nodded their thanks while the guests joined the toast and then applauded in anticipation, including Lord and Lady Pelletier, who exchanged an adoring glance and then gazed knowingly at the two of them.

My word, Felicity thought as Jason took her hand, *we're worse than they are.*

Then the music started, lively and graceful, and apparently too charming for two small children to resist. Simon jumped off his chair, seemingly electrified by the romping rhythm of the opening allegro. He stared up at the musicians for a second, motionless.

Seeing her big brother leap to his feet, Annabelle naturally had to follow suit, and climbed off Jason's lap to join him. She toddled over to Simon and looked at him as if to say, *What are we doing next?*

Felicity understood completely. She elbowed Peter, and he looked askance at her, well aware of her meaning. He slipped her a private smile and gave her a fond squeeze about the shoulders.

Giovanelli, meanwhile, fiercely concentrating on directing his ensemble with his back to the audience, must have wondered why everyone had started chuckling. He cast an alarmed glance over his shoulder, but then grinned when he saw the two tots dancing around in the open space between the players and the guests.

Felicity covered her mouth with her hand, but Jason burst out laughing as Simon waved his head back and forth like some silly little flower tossed by a violent wind. Annabelle, meanwhile, held out her purple dress and slowly turned around and around in a wobbly spin.

Their laughing papa clapped for them in encouragement, while

Felicity's heart simply clenched. She shook her head at the children's antics as tears of joy and affection rose in her eyes. She never would have thought that anyone could be as happy as she was now.

Thankfully, Giovanelli was too thoroughly Italian to take offense at a couple of children dancing, despite their stealing the show on his big night. The whole crowd responded to the tots' performance with muffled laughter.

Then the rogues decided to join in. Slinging their arms around one another's shoulders, they swayed merrily back and forth where they stood.

Warmth flooded the whole of Netherford House, chasing away any last shadow of the loneliness that had once lived there. Now it was filled with light and music, friendship and love.

And, to be sure, Giovanelli had outdone himself.

"The melody, it's a-beautiful," Felicity whispered in a fond imitation of the composer, and glanced at her fiancé only to find him already staring at her.

Jason had been gazing at her as though memorizing the smile on her face while she watched the children and swayed in time a little with the minuet.

He lifted her hand to his lips and gave it a light kiss.

"Beautiful, indeed," he answered in a husky, doting whisper. But the glow in his dark eyes said so much more. *Thank you*, and, *I love you very much.*

She squeezed his hand as she held his tender stare, knowing in that moment that *their* song would never end.

MOONLIGHT SQUARE, BOOK 2

Duke of Secrets

Romance is in the air at Moonlight Square ~ Regency London's most exclusive address!

Jilted by her beau over shocking family secrets of which she had no inkling—and which her parents refuse to discuss—Lady Serena Parker discovers that only one man in the *ton* can give her the answers she now desperately seeks: Azrael Chambers, the mysterious Duke of Rivenwood. Unfortunately, the rumors about *his* family are even darker than what she's learned about her own. Somehow, though, Serena summons up her courage to seek the help of the wealthy but enigmatic loner.

Though dazzled by her beauty, Azrael abhors the whole topic of the past and has good reason to keep these explosive secrets hidden. Instead of providing information, he warns the luscious, raven-haired minx not to go prying into dangerous matters best left forgotten. But when he sees her stubbornly persisting in her quest for the truth, Azrael relents for the girl's own safety—on one condition. He demands her silence, and mere promises will not suffice. Before he dares trust her with what he knows, the lady must compromise herself by her own willing actions. If she wants knowledge, then she must pay the price…in his bed. *Let the games begin.*

"*Sexy and sizzling.*" *~Mary Jo Putney*

"*Delectably entertaining, lusciously sensual… an irresistible author.*" *~Booklist*

One Moonlit Night
(Moonlight Square: A Prequel Novella)

At the ripe old age of two-and-twenty, Lady Katrina Glendon just can't seem to snare a husband. Whether her frank tongue or slightly eccentric ways bear the blame, she faces a houseful of younger sisters clamoring for her, the eldest, to marry and move aside before they all end up as spinsters. When her latest suitor defects and proposes to another girl, Trinny throws up her hands in despair of ever finding a fiancé. But sometimes destiny waits just around the corner...and love lives right across the square!

Gable Winston-McCray, the charming, understated Viscount Roland saunters through life as a wealthy, sophisticated rakehell and man-about-town. Heir to an earldom, the handsome hedonist would rather dally with bored Society wives than acquire a bride of his own, much to his father's dismay. Until, one moonlit night, fate strikes! Unsuspecting neighbors meet and become flirtatious allies. So when Gable receives his father's ultimatum to wed or go penniless, he offers Trinny a marriage of convenience. Alas, the pretty redhead cannot possibly accept such an unfeeling proposal—even if her dear "Lord Sweet Cheeks" might be the man of her dreams...

"Enchanting, intriguing, fun." ~Stephanie Laurens, #1 New York Times Bestseller

"Run, do not walk, to your nearest bookstore and snatch up everything you can find that this amazing author has ever written!" ~The Romance Readers' Connection

Age of Heroes, Book 1
Paladin's Prize

New York Times bestselling author Gaelen Foley leads readers on a magical journey to a fairytale land where good battles evil, adventure beckons the daring, and epic love awaits the true of heart.

Resolutely noble, impossibly brave, paladin Sir Thaydor Clarenbeld serves as royal champion for the kingdom of Veraidel. But when the king becomes corrupt, Thaydor speaks out—and promptly ends up banished from court, sent off as a knight errant on an endless round of quests meant to get him killed. One mission nearly does. Covered in wounds after a monstrous battle, he lies at death's door when rescue arrives in the form of the beautiful, mystic healer known as the Maid of the Mount.

The lady Wrynne du Mere gave up a luxurious life to devote herself to caring for others. When she finds the famous hero broken and bleeding, saving him will take all her skill—and a fateful dash of magic. And it will cost her dearly. For the dangerous spell will leave their souls forever entwined, and his foes, so many and so powerful, will target her, as well. Wrynne knows to survive and restore justice to the land, they must join forces. But for how long can they resist the searing temptation of desire?

"4½ Stars! The perfect blending of high fantasy and romance." ~Romance Junkies

"One of the finest adventure/romance authors does it again. Foley never sacrifices character or romance while whisking readers away on fast-paced escapades and daring missions and giving them a glorious deep-sigh read." ~Kathe Robin, RT Book Reviews

And writing as E.G. Foley

Enter a world of wonder and whimsy, adventure and peril in the series that's as much fun for grownups as it is for kids. *Now optioned for a movie!* (This book is accepted in the Advanced Reader Program in schools throughout the US. Ages 10 and up. Also available in audio.)

Book 1: THE LOST HEIR

Strange new talents…

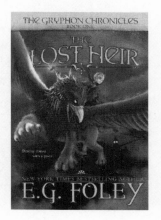

Jake is a scrappy orphaned pickpocket living by his wits on the streets of Victorian London. Lately he's started seeing ghosts and can move solid objects with his mind! He has no idea why. Next thing he knows, a Sinister Gentleman and his minions come hunting him, and Jake is plunged headlong into a mysterious world of magic and deadly peril. A world that holds the secret of who he really is: the long-lost heir of an aristocratic family with magical powers.

But with treacherous enemies closing in, it will take all of his wily street instincts and the help of his friends—both human and magical—to solve the mystery of what happened to his parents and defeat the foes who never wanted the Lost Heir of Griffon to be found…

"A wonderful novel in the same vein as Harry Potter, full of nonstop action, magical creatures, and the reality that was Queen Victoria's England." ~The Reading Café

Other books in the series:

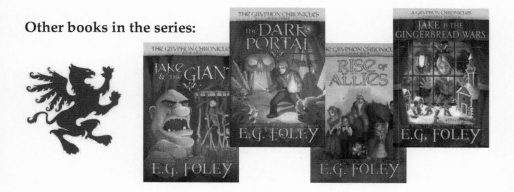

About the Author

Noted for her "complex, subtly shaded characters, richly sensual love scenes, and elegantly fluid prose" (*Booklist*), Gaelen Foley is the *New York Times*, *USA Today*, and *Publisher's Weekly* bestselling author of over twenty historical romances from Random House/Ballantine and HarperCollins. Her award-winning novels are available worldwide in seventeen languages, with millions of copies sold. Gaelen holds a BA in English Literature and lives in Pennsylvania with her husband, Eric, with whom she also co-writes family-friendly "PG-Rated" fantasy adventure novels for kids and adults under the penname E.G. Foley. (Book One in their Gryphon Chronicles series, *The Lost Heir*, has been optioned for a movie!)

Visit www.GaelenFoley.com and sign up for her mailing list if you'd like to receive an email alert when her next book is available. As a *Thank You* for signing up, you'll receive her famous *Regency Glossary*—a **free** 52-page booklet (PDF) chock full of fun little historical tidbits to enhance your Regency reading pleasure. Gaelen also holds occasional sweepstakes exclusively for subscribers, so there might be a prize in your future if you're one of her lucky winners.

Thanks for reading!

15587892R00124

Printed in Great Britain
by Amazon